*Dan kept his eyes on the trail ahead, sitting ramrod-*straight in the saddle, reins loose in his hand. It was as though he were talking to the soft breeze that carried his words to Calico, who rode slightly behind him. "I know we ain't never talked much about it—don't seem men have t' say a lot when they understand each other's well as you an' me—but I want you to know I meant what I said. These kids may be my blood kin, but you're the closest thing I got to real family. I just didn't want you to think their comin' would make a difference far as you an' me's concerned."

Calico spurred Dusty gently until they were riding side-by-side.

"Hell, Uncle Dan, ya think I'd mind whatever ya did? Ya don't owe me nothin'. It's me that owes you. You're the one saved my hide when my folks was killed, an' took me in an' looked after me all these years. Where'd I'd o' been without ya?"

For the first time, Dan turned his head to look him straight in the eye.

"You know, boy—" he began

The shot was like a whipcrack through the quiet air.

Also by Dorien Grey

THE DICK HARDESTY MYSTERY SERIES

The Ninth Man, 2001, GLB Publishers

The Butcher's Son, 2001, GLB Publishers

The Bar Watcher, 2002, GLB Publishers

The Hired Man, 2002, GLB Publishers

The Good Cop, 2002, GLB Publishers

The Bottle Ghosts, 2003, GLB Publishers.

The Dirt Peddler, 2003, GLB Publishers.

The Role Players, 2004, GLB Publishers.

The Popsicle Tree, 2005. GLB Publishers

The Paper Mirror, 2005, GLB Publishers

CALICO

BY

DORIEN GREY

ZUMAYA PUBLICATIONS AUSTIN TX

2006

This book is a work of fiction. Names, characters, places and incidents are products of the author's imagination or are used fictitiously. Any resemblance to actual persons or events is purely coincidental.

CALICO

ISBN 13: 978-1-934135-33-4
ISBN 10: 1-934135-33-X

Cover art and design by Martine Jardin

Look for us online at http://www.zumayapublications.com

Library of Congress Cataloging-in-Publication Data

Grey, Dorien.
Calico / by Dorien Grey. -- 1st Zumaya ed.
p. cm.
ISBN-13: 978-1-934135-33-4
ISBN-10: 1-934135-33-X
1. Gay men--Fiction. I. Title.
PS3557.R48165C35 2006
813'.6--dc22

2006029952

Published in the United States of America

To my readers, new and old, who have purchased tickets
for this little adventure. May you enjoy the trip!

CHAPTER 1

CALICO RAMSAY WAS TIRED, AND HUNGRY, AND READY FOR THE DAY TO END. SO, WHEN HE topped the small rise and looked down onto the cluster of ranch buildings spread out before him, yellow lights just beginning to appear in the windows, he heaved a deep sigh of relief and sat up tall, stretching his shoulders back and lifting his head to relieve the tension in his muscles.

A sudden lightning storm the night before had stampeded the cattle on the east range. Calico had spent the entire day with the hands, rounding up as many strays as they could find. Ten were still unaccounted for, so the rest of the men had camped out in the area and would find the remaining strays the next day.

He bedded his horse and entered the bunkhouse just after dark to find Sven, the cook, muttering and cursing over a burnt supper of beef and beans. Calico was too hungry and tired to care.

Dinner finished, he went over to the main house to check in with the ranch owner—the man he called Uncle Dan, who had been his unofficial guardian since Calico was twelve.

The house was dark, which told him he would find Dan in his office, a small shed-like building a few dozen feet from the main house. He found him with his feet up on the battered table that served as his desk, reading a letter.

At sixty-five, Dan Overholt was still a man to be reckoned with, though his massive frame had begun to settle around his middle. He was totally bald in the center of his head, but his sunburned scalp was surrounded by a wild shock of thick white hair—when Calico was a boy, he'd always thought it looked like mashed potatoes around a steak.

Dan looked up as Calico entered, grunted a greeting and laid the letter aside to light up a huge warped cigar.

"Get 'em all?" he asked, after blowing an enormous cloud of smoke into the room.

"All but ten, 's far as we can tell. Tim and the boys camped out up near the ridge. They'll find 'em in the morning."

Dan shifted his cigar from one corner of his mouth to the other and nodded. He motioned Calico to a chair then picked up the letter.

"You know I had a brother," he said, removing the cigar from his mouth and staring at the glowing end, as if talking to it rather than to Calico. It was a habit he had whenever he had something really serious to talk about.

"I heard ya mention him, once or twice."

"Yeah. Well, we never did get along all that good. He married a rich woman when we was barely more than kids, and she and me didn't get on no way. So, I came out West and he stayed in Chicago and got even richer, and we just sort of drifted apart." Dan took another long draw from his cigar. "By the time his wife died some years back, we'd pretty much lost track of one another." He paused to pick a bit of tobacco from his bottom lip. "Anyway, now he's dead, too."

Calico, not knowing exactly what to say, stared at his boots. After a moment, Dan continued.

"Him and his wife had two kids—both girls. I never seen either one of 'em. But they both growed up and got married; one of 'em moved out here to Colorado somewheres, and the other married a city feller and stayed in Chicago. The Chicago one, she had two kids, twins, just about the time I runned into you. Then, 'bout six years ago, she and her husband was killed in a fire, and the twins was orphaned. I never knew a thing about any of it, 'cept what this lawyer feller tells me in this here letter."

Calico was both surprised and touched by the unfamiliar tone of regret in the older man's voice. Noting his cigar had gone out, Dan re-lit it before continuing.

"They'd be about seventeen now, I reckon. Almost growed up, but by law they got to have a guardian at least till they're eighteen."

He paused again, staring at the tip of his cigar. Calico didn't think he expected him to say anything, so he remained silent.

"I get the idea there was something peculiar about that fire that killed their folks. Lawyer didn't come right out and say anything, mind, but…" Apparently suddenly aware Calico was staring at him, Dan took one last puff on the cigar and stubbed it out on a rock paperweight. "Anyways, my brother took on the raising of the kids and now he's dead. Lawyer says the kids get all the money, 'cept for a little bit to the Colorado daughter, which is fine with me, but, well, my brother, he asked that I take the kids till they're of age." He looked straight at Calico and shook his head in wonderment. "Hell, I don't know nothin' about raisin' kids."

Calico gave his adopted uncle a broad grin. "Well, if they're seventeen, they're 'bout ready to fend for themselves. Shouldn't be much raisin' involved. 'Sides, you didn't exactly do too bad with me, if I do say so myself."

For the first time since Calico had entered the office, Dan's solemn air broke, and he could see him relax.

"Yeah, but that was different—you was a boy, and a farm boy at that. If your folks hadn't o' got killed, you'd o' still turned out okay. But these two's different. Out here, by the time you're eighteen, you're on your own. But rich city kids is different. One's a boy, true, but like I say, they're city kids. What the hell do they know about ranchin'?"

"Well, I expect they could learn, don't you?"

Dan sighed, his entire huge frame rising and falling with the motion. "I expect they'll have to."

Calico sat silent for a moment, his lips pursed in thought. "Well, if ya don't want the kids, why not ship 'em off to their aunt? Least she's a woman."

Dan shrugged. "If my brother'd wanted 'em sent out to her, he'd o' sent 'em to her."

His face once again became serious, and Calico had the feeling there was something he wanted to say but couldn't—or wouldn't.

"'Sides," Dan continued, "they wouldn't be no better off with her—she lives even farther from civilization than we do. No, I'll abide by my brother's wishes. Kin is kin, and even if we never met, the young'uns is kin."

Calico had learned long before not to question the older man once his mind was made up. It was none of his affair, anyway.

He raised his hands from his lap and let them slap back against his thighs. "Well, I guess that's it, then. When they comin'?"

Dan fumbled in his vest for another cigar. "I'm supposed to go pick 'em up in Fort Collins three weeks tomorrow. They got school to finish, things to take care of back there. Lawyer's puttin' 'em on the train on the fifteenth."

"Ya want I should go fetch 'em?" Calico asked. Then, fearful that he might have offended the older man by implying he wasn't in condition to make the trip, hastened to add, "I mean, Fort Collins's a full three days' ride, an' you havin' so much to do 'round here..."

Dan stared at him for a moment, lighted match poised just short of making contact with the end of his cigar, and Calico thought he saw a flicker of amusement in the older man's eyes. He held the match until it had burned almost to his fingers then, with the precision timing born of long practice, lit the cigar and blew out the match with casual unconcern.

"Nope, boy, it's my duty, an' I'll do it. But I'll want you to run things while I'm gone."

Calico started to object. "But Caleb's your foreman. He—"

"I know who Caleb is, boy. No buts about it. You're the closest thing I got to real kin, and it's about time you started t' take over things. I ain't gonna last forever, ya know. I'll do my duty by these kids, but don't you worry—when I go, this ranch and everything on it's yours."

In the fifteen years since Dan found him in the smoking ruins of the wagon train, this was the first time they had ever spoken of such things. Both suddenly realized they were dangerously close to openly showing the deep affection they felt for one another and were appropriately embarrassed.

After a long pause, during which Dan shuffled through a stack of papers and Calico studied a fly strolling across the toe of his left boot, Dan cleared his throat and said, "You find them ten head tomorrow, hear?"

Calico rose quickly to his feet, rubbed his index finger under his nose self-consciously and backed awkwardly toward the door.

"Sure. First thing. Ah...well, guess I better hit the hay, get an early start. See ya, Uncle Dan."

Dan did not glance up, just dismissed him with a cursory wave of one large hand.

Three days later, in Grady to pick up supplies, Calico stopped in at the general store. Calvin Grubb, the store's owner, adjusted his armband and shifted his green eye-shade as he looked up from the ledger open on the countertop in front of him.

Calico had known the man for fifteen years, and had yet to see him smile.

"Howdy, Calico," Calvin said with a curt nod. It was the same greeting he'd used since Calico first stood before him, an unsure twelve-year-old at Dan's side. He remembered the meeting very well because it was the first time, and one of the very few times, in his entire life someone he met had not commented on the origin of his nickname—the fact he had one brown eye and one blue. He'd always held Calvin in special regard because of it.

"Calvin."

They shook hands, and Calico gave a nod to Evie-Mae, Calvin's oldest daughter, who came out from the back room, apparently at the sound of his voice. He'd known Evie-Mae since they were kids, and it was no secret she had set her eye on him long ago—a prospect that now, as then, made him extremely uncomfortable. He knew he was the object of the attention of many of the young women in town, but he simply wasn't interested. He much preferred the company of the ranch hands and cowboys. Women—specifically, those with a romantic interest in him—made him painfully ill at ease.

Nonetheless, he smiled, touched the brim of his hat and said "Howdy, Evie-Mae."

She gave him a smile that had more than casual greeting in it and made his toes curl inside his boots.

"Hello, Calico," she said, as though his name was soft butter and she was spreading it on a slice of fresh-baked bread.

He turned quickly to Calvin and handed him the list of supplies. Usually, it was Sven or one of the other hands who made the trip to town, but Dan had specifically requested Calico go this time, so he could send a confirming wire to the Chicago lawyer.

"I'll be by in an hour or so to pick everything up," he said, adjusting his hat on the back of his head and nodding goodbye to Evie-Mae.

He was just turning to leave when she said, "Will we be seeing you at the social Saturday night, Calico?"

"'Fraid not," he replied. "I'm headin' out Saturday morning to do some fence-fixin' an' probably won't be back till Sunday afternoon sometime." He truly did not like lying, but sometimes it was necessary, and he felt this was one of those times.

Evie-Mae was obviously disappointed. "You never come to our socials," she said, with just a hint of petulance. "Some of the girls and I were talking, and we were wondering if you're deliberately avoiding us."

Calico managed a grin. "O'course not. I'm just real busy...and not much into socializin'."

He turned to make another break for the door when Calvin stopped him.

"'Second, Calico," he called, reaching behind a counter into the special drawer reserved for incoming mail. "It 'pears your Uncle Dan's a mighty popular man all of a sudden."

Calico took the letter and looked at it as though it were some fragile living thing. Two personal letters in one week was an almost unheard-of occurrence for Dan Overholt—and Calico had never received a letter in his life. He searched the envelope for clues, but could only determine that it was written in a woman's hand.

"Thanks, Calvin," he said then slipped the letter into his shirt pocket, making double sure it was pushed all the way in so it wouldn't fall out on the way home.

By the time he reached the stagecoach office, though, he'd pretty much forgotten the letter. He gave the message to the stage line manager to go with the next stage to Fort Collins, where both the rail and telegraph lines ended.

From there, he went to the saloon to pick up an order of Dan's favorite whiskey and to have a beer. Whiskey was plentiful at the ranch, but cold beer was a luxury to be found only in town.

Tim Hibler, owner of Grady's biggest saloon, was also one of the town's most respected citizens, and was looked on as something of a genius by the drinking men of the community—which was to say all of them. Tim had built his saloon with a deep basement with double-thick stone walls. Every winter, he hired men to cut river ice to fill his basement, alternating layers of ice with layers of straw. It not only kept the saloon fairly cool well through summer, but it enabled Tim to serve cold beer even during the warm months. Calico always enjoyed dropping by to see Tim whenever he got into town.

After Calico's second beer, Tim, who had been busy in the small back room, came out to greet his customer. His big, beefy face broke into a wide, snaggle-toothed grin as he saw Calico, and he came over to grab him by the shoulders and shake him vigorously—a habit that usually thoroughly drenched any customers not familiar enough with the practice to hastily set their drinks down when they saw him coming. Calico had seen Tim enter, and had ample time to set his beer aside.

"Good to see ya, Tim," he managed after the hearty shaking.

"You, too, Calico, you, too," Tim boomed. Then his face took on an air of mock seriousness. "But I'm afraid your Uncle Dan's not gonna be so happy to see you when you arrive home empty-handed."

"What do ya mean?"

"Well, them nitwits from Fort Collins ain't got here with the shipment yet. You know I got to order Dan's in special. So I ain't got it t' give you. Can you come by again next week, or send one of the boys for it? It'll be here by then, sure."

"Well," Calico said, rubbing his chin, "I 'spect Uncle Dan's got a bottle or two stashed away somewheres to last him through. He'll live." Then he grinned. "But how's about another beer? I helped myself to two while ya was out back."

"Sure thing. Fact, I'll join you—all this hard work makes me thirsty."

He poured two beers, and Calico knew what was coming next. It was another ritual, one Tim reserved only for him.

"Here's to your blue eye, Calico..." Tim took a healthy drink "...and here's to your brown."

He drained his mug. Calico just grinned, shaking his head, then, just a little more slowly than Tim, drained his own mug.

"I'd best be gettin' back to deliver the bad news. I'll try to make it in next week, or send somebody. Ya take care now, hear?"

The two men shook hands, and Calico headed back for Calvin's store, the supplies and home.

By the time he reached the ranch, unhitched the team and unloaded the supplies, it was nearly dark. He was just ready to join the hands for supper when he remembered the letter in his shirt pocket and hurried to deliver it to Dan. He found him in the kitchen, stirring a large pot of rabbit stew. Dan motioned him to sit at the table.

"Be with you in a second, Calico. Sven got a couple of rabbits this morning out around his garden. Not enough for the whole crew, though, so I decided to make me a little stew. Be pleased to have company."

Calico removed his hat and hung it on a hook behind the door, then opened the huge, rough-wood cupboard to get dishes and set the table. Dan usually ate with the rest of the hands, but from time to time he preferred eating alone, or with Caleb, his foreman and longtime crony, or with Calico. On these occasions, he usually did the cooking himself, or had Sven prepare something special in the early afternoon before starting supper for the hands. Calico always enjoyed the chance for him and Dan to eat together, just the two of them—a pleasure enhanced by the fact that Dan was an excellent cook.

The men ate, as usual, more or less in silence, talking only briefly about ranch business or news Calico had picked up in town.

"You happen t' run into Evie-Mae while you was at Calvin's?" Dan asked with a grin.

"Yeah, I did."

"I figgered. Manage t' fight her off?"

It was Calico's turn to grin. "Well, it didn't quite come t' that," he said. "But I'd o' won."

Dan just nodded and kept grinning.

"The world ain't always easy, boy," he said, and Calico once again knew that Dan understood him better than any other human being.

As they finished dinner and Calico rose from the table to get the coffee pot for their third refill of coffee, he suddenly remembered the letter. Taking it from his shirt pocket, he laid it in front of Dan.

"This come for ya," he said, then filled both cups and returned the pot to the stove.

Dan studied it much as Calico had, then opened it and read in silence. Calico stared into his coffee cup, until he was aware of Dan's sliding the letter casually across the table toward him.

"Read it," Dan said.

Calico wiped his hand on his pants before picking up the letter. The handwriting, he noted, was large and penmanship-perfect. Definitely a woman.

> Dear Mr. Overholt,
>
> I have been informed of my father's passing by his Chicago attorney, and of his stated intention of placing my late sister's children in your custody.
>
> I think I should point out to you, Mr. Overholt (I regret my inability to call you "Uncle," but since we have never met, I feel such familiarity would not be appropriate), that the tragic death of my dear sister and her husband, following so shortly as they did after the death of my mother, had adversely affected my father's mind to the point where, near the end of his life, his decision-making capabilities were seriously impaired.
>
> I apologize, on my father's behalf, for the inconvenience and imposition his request to you may have caused. My husband and I have ample facilities for caring for my niece and nephew, and since I understand that you are unmarried, I am sure you would agree they would be far better off in a more homelike setting.
>
> I shall be happy to make all the necessary arrangements to have them sent to me, thus sparing you unnecessary inconvenience and expense.
>
> Trusting this letter finds you in good health, and thanking you in advance for your cooperation and

understanding, I remain,

Most Sincerely,

Mrs. Rebecca Durant
Cold Springs Ranch
Bow Ridge, Colorado

Calico handed it back across the table without comment. Dan took it, folded it carefully and put it in his shirt pocket behind his cigars.

"When's that stage leave for Fort Collins?" he asked.

"Tomorrow morning, 'bout noon...if it's on time, which it usually ain't."

Dan took out a cigar, bit the end off and expertly spat it into a spittoon near the stove, then lit it before speaking.

"Want you to ride into town first thing," he said, staring at the glowing red tip of cigar, "and give the stagemaster two more wires—one to the lawyer sayin' never mind what he hears from Mrs. Rebecca Durant of Bow Ridge, Colorado, he's to put those youngsters on the train to Fort Collins like scheduled. The second to Mrs. Rebecca Durant sayin' much obliged, but I'll abide by my brother's wishes. Got that?"

Calico nodded. He realized he knew almost nothing about Dan's past or his family prior to hearing of the brother's death and the existence of the twins. He was mildly curious but didn't consider it any of his business. He knew the twins' arrival could not help but affect his daily life in some way, but he was confident his relationship with Dan would not change.

He'd come across the word "Stoicism" in a dictionary once and decided that it was a word that described the fabric of his life—there would undoubtedly be changes, but what happened would happen, and he would deal with it when the time came.

They finished their coffee in silence, Dan lost in his thoughts and Calico staring intently into his coffee cup. When he looked up, he saw that Dan had nodded off.

He cleared the dishes away, stacked them on the counter then washed them in the iron dish kettle that was always kept hot on the stove. He considered waking Uncle Dan before he left but thought better of it. Instead, he closed the door loudly behind him as he went out, hoping the sound would awaken the older man and he'd go to bed.

CHAPTER TWO

Calico left for town at sunup the next morning as instructed and sent off the two wires. The following weeks passed quickly, as time always did on a busy ranch. He spent most of his time helping the hands move cattle from one section of range to another. It had been a particularly dry year, and the grass was sparse. Several of the smaller ponds had all but dried up. The ranch, luckily, was large enough to include both hills and flat prairie, and there was a small river marking the eastern boundary.

On the Tuesday before Dan's scheduled departure for Fort Collins to pick up the twins, he asked Calico to ride with him into Grady. They left early to avoid the heat of the day, which had been oppressive for the last several days. It was a bright, clear day, and they enjoyed the ride.

There had been a brief but very welcome rain the night before that, while not enough to improve the dry conditions, kept the trail dust down. It had even left a few small puddles in low-lying areas, where birds splashed loudly, and Calico noted a fox and two deer drinking. The air was still, the fresh smell brought by the rain not totally diminished; the main part of the cloudbank had moved off to the west, leaving only a few scattered remnants.

The four-hour ride passed largely in silence, and Calico used the time to consider what the long-term effect of the twins on life at the ranch might be for Dan. He had no doubt Dan would be able to handle whatever challenges they presented, but he also knew it would be just one more responsibility for a man who already had more than enough. He hoped Dan would not be too proud to turn to him if there was anything he could do to make the job easier.

As they approached the last high ridge before town, he felt the hair on the back of his neck rise, as it had on several occasions in his life when danger was imminent. He had the distinct impression they were being watched, and he thought he saw a momentary flash of movement near one of a cluster of boulders at the top of the rise. Dan was obviously occupied with his own thoughts, so Calico said nothing, but as they topped the rise he saw the dust of another rider far ahead of them, heading into town.

In town, they hitched their horses in front of Tim Hibler's saloon. Calico assumed Dan was going to join him for a beer, but he left him at the door, saying he was going over to Calvin's general store for a badly needed new saddlebag.

The saloon was, as usual, dark, cool, and smelled of stale beer and spilled whiskey. Charlie Coats and Bart Miller, two hands from the Culbertson ranch just to the west of Dan's, were at the bar, and Calico returned their nod of greeting. At the far end, near the storeroom and in the shadows, Tim stood talking to a short, dark man he didn't recognize.

Calico leaned across the bar, took a glass and poured himself a beer as Tim turned toward him

"Well, look who's here," he bellowed, striding over to greet him. He had never heard Tim speak in anything under a roar.

He put his glass aside just in time as Tim grabbed him by the shoulders and gave him a neck-snapping shake.

"You come for the stuff for your old Uncle Dan, didn't you? I seen him at the door—how come he didn't come in with you?"

Calico rolled his shoulders to get the blood circulating again, then said, "He's over t' Calvin's for a minute. Be here shortly."

"He better," Tim said jovially. "Friend of his here lookin' for him."

Calico looked around. "Yeah? Where?"

"Why, right down there at the..." Tim's voice trailed off as he looked toward the end of the bar only to find the stranger gone. He shook his head in puzzlement. "Well, I'll be! He just come in a few minutes before you, had a beer, an' when you two showed up at the door, he says, 'Ain't that Dan Overholt?' An' I says, 'Yeah, you know Dan?' An' he says, 'Yeah, we're old pals, but don't say nothin' 'cause I want to surprise him.' Then you come in, an' he ups and disappears. Must o' gone out through the storeroom." He shook his head again. "Now if that don't beat all."

Calico felt the hairs on his neck rising again. He downed his beer, tossed a coin on the bar, and said "Yeah, that's real strange. Look, Tim, I gotta get something at Calvin's, too. I'll be right back."

He hurried over to the general store, nearly running into Dan, who stood just inside the doorway talking to Calvin.

"Howdy, Calico," Calvin said.

"Howdy, Calvin." He eased past Dan into the store. "Uncle Dan, you expectin' t' meet somebody in town here t'day?"

Dan looked at him and pursed his lips. "Nope, can't say's I was. Why'd you ask?"

Calico suddenly felt a little foolish. "No reason. Just some guy over to Tim's said you an' him's old friends, an' I never seen him before. Little short guy, dark. Couldn't see him too well—you know how dark it is in Tim's."

Dan shook his head. "Don't sound like nobody I know. What'd he say his name was?"

"He didn't say. He must have walked out while Tim was rattlin' my teeth. I just thought it was a might peculiar."

"I think *Tim's* a might peculiar at times." Dan laughed. "But he serves the best whiskey this side o' St. Louis, and that's enough to excuse a man a lot of peculiarities. You go on back there an' see if you can find anything else about this stranger fella. Did you see him, Calvin?"

Calvin looked up from the box he was unpacking. "Nope. I never see nothin', stuck behind this counter all day."

Calico returned to Tim's saloon, where Dan joined him a few minutes later.

"Find out anything?" he asked, leaning against the bar next to him.

"Nothin'," Calico admitted.

"Well, if whatever he wanted was important, I reckon he'll be back," Dan said with a shrug, then hollered toward the back room, into which Tim had disappeared shortly before, "Hey, Tim, how's about two beers down here? You expect a man t' die o' thirst?"

As he spoke, he winked at Calico and reached behind the bar for two mugs, which he had filled by the time Tim came lumbering back into the room with a tub full of ice.

Tim grinned broadly when he saw Dan but, with his arms full, spared the older man his usual bone-jarring greeting. The three men spent the next half-hour drinking beer and swapping stories, but Calico kept glancing toward the front door, and he noticed that Dan did, too.

They left the saloon, attended to a few other errands then mounted for the ride back to the ranch. Calico was vaguely uneasy, but wasn't sure why.

"Hey, Uncle Dan, why don't we take the long way home?" he suggested, trying to sound casual but for some reason not wanting to take the ridge road. "The Martins got some new breedin' stock down by Deep Lake, an' I figured we could take a look at 'em, maybe try t' get that prize bull o' theirs for stud later."

Dan shook his head. "Not today, boy. I got some things need doin' back at the ranch before sundown. We c'n stop by the Martins' after I get back with the kids."

They rode up the steep trail to the crest of the ridge then started down into the next small valley. Without trying to appear obvious, Calico kept a sharp eye on every clump of trees and outcropping of rocks large enough to hide a man and horse.

"You know, Calico, what I was sayin' the other night, 'bout you and the ranch..." Dan kept his eyes on the trail ahead, sitting ramrod-straight in the saddle, reins loose in his hand. It was as though he were talking to the soft breeze that carried his words to Calico, who rode slightly behind him. "I know we ain't never talked much about it—don't seem men have t' say a lot when they understand each other's well as you an' me—but I want you to know I meant what I said. These kids may be my blood kin, but you're the closest thing I got to real family. I just didn't want you to think their comin' would make a difference far as you an' me's concerned."

Calico spurred Dusty gently until they were riding side-by-side.

"Hell, Uncle Dan, ya think I'd mind whatever ya did? Ya don't owe me nothin'. It's me that owes you. You're the one saved my hide when my folks was killed, an' took me in an' looked after me all these years. Where'd I'd o' been without ya?"

For the first time, Dan turned his head to look him straight in the eye.

"You know, boy—" he began

The shot was like a whipcrack through the quiet air. The bullet caught Dan directly between the shoulders, and he pitched forward in the saddle.

"Uncle Dan!" Calico yelled, lunging sideways to try to keep the older man from falling to the ground.

A second shot rang out, lead whistling past his right ear. He reined his horse up short and leapt off in the same motion, catching the reins of Dan's horse with one hand and easing Dan's fall to the ground with the other. He dragged him like a sack of grain behind a nearby rock as three more shots came in rapid succession, the bullets sending up little spurts of dust and dirt on either side of their temporary shelter.

Safely behind the rock, Calico tore off his hat and put it as a cushion beneath Dan's head. Dan's eyes were open but slightly unfocused.

"Uncle Dan! C'n ya hear me?" he said, forgetting the hidden gunman, forgetting everything but the wounded man and his concern for him.

Dan coughed, and a trickle of blood appeared at the corner of his mouth.

"Of course, I c'n hear you, boy," he said, lifting one hand weakly. "You don't worry 'bout me. You just concentrate on gettin' that son of a bitch that shot me!"

Calico's fear for his adopted uncle turned to rage as still another bullet chipped the top of the boulder not three feet from his head. He looked around for the horses. Dan's was down on his side, having been hit by one of the bushwhacker's shots. Dusty paced nervously about twenty feet away, head bobbing and right front hoof pawing the ground. Calico could see his rifle was in its scabbard. If only he could get to it...

He removed his neckerchief, grabbed a long stick and draped the kerchief over the end. Slowly, he raised it to the top of the rock. When there was no responding fire, he peered cautiously around the edge of the boulder, keeping his head low to the ground.

At the top of the ridge they'd just passed he saw the dust of a horse moving off—fast. With a quick look at Dan, who now lay with his eyes closed, breathing heavily, he dashed across the open space to Dusty, leaped on, grabbed the reins with his left hand and the rifle with the other and spurred Dusty to a gallop.

Despite the bright sunshine, Calico felt as if he were riding through a long, dark tunnel—all he could see was the receding cloud of dust in front of him. It was as though he were looking out through someone else's eyes, seeing nothing, feeling nothing but an all-consuming hatred for the man he was trailing.

The jolting gallop over the rough terrain gradually brought back some of his self-control, and what had been wild rage was slowly replaced by an icy determination. As he crested the ridge, he could see the other rider below, moving through a gulch that made a wide circle around the town. By riding hard straight through town he just might be able to head him off.

He reined Dusty to the left, to the smoother and straighter trail, then spurred him to go even faster. The horse responded, and the wind whipped Calico's hair across his eyes.

As he approached town, he saw several people on the main street staring at him as he approached at full speed. With his rifle hand, he waved them out of the way, and they scattered like chickens as he thundered past. He rounded the corner onto the side road leading past the last few houses and into the open territory beyond. As he did, a woman, oblivious of his approach, pushed a baby carriage across the street directly in front of him.

There was no time to stop or swerve. With Calico's urging Dusty leapt into the air, his hind legs clearing the carriage by inches. The woman fell into the street in a faint.

The last houses were behind him, and Calico saw dust rising from the gulch just a short way ahead.

"Just a little farther, boy," he said to his straining mount.

The gulch fanned out onto more or less open plain a hundred yards or so ahead of the fast-moving rider; a short distance beyond that was a large grove of trees. Calico knew that once the rider got to the grove his chances of catching him were slim—there were too many places to hide, too many directions he might take.

The rider was now less than fifty yards ahead of and below him. Calico reined Dusty up short on a slight rise and raised his rifle.

For the first time in his twenty-seven years of life, Calico Ramsay had another human being in his rifle sight. A human life. He hesitated, his finger on the trigger.

Then he saw, in his mind's eye, Dan pitching forward, a bullet between his shoulders, and he fired.

The rider toppled from his horse and bounced three times as he hit the ground, legs and arms flailing like a rag doll. Rifle re-cocked, Calico spurred his tired horse forward, down the hill toward the unmoving figure. He got close enough to see that the man was short and dark—the stranger from the saloon—and that he was dead.

Without dismounting, he turned back toward Grady...back toward Uncle Dan.

As he galloped through town again, the streets were full of people staring, pointing, gossiping. As he approached Tim Hibler's saloon, he saw Tim standing in the doorway. Without slowing, he yelled, "Uncle Dan's been shot. Up beyond Taylor's Ridge. Get Doc Enders quick!"

He saw Tim wave and start running up the street toward the doctor's house.

Dusty was exhausted but sensed his rider's urgency and gave his full effort in climbing the steep ridge. Spotting the boulder behind which they had taken refuge, Calico saw Dan's legs protruding from one side. He was out of the saddle before he had fully stopped, and at Dan's side in an instant.

The older man was still alive, but his breath came in labored rasps. Calico took his hand and felt it was very cold.

"Uncle Dan! Uncle Dan!" he said, his voice nearly breaking.

Dan opened his eyes and gave a weak grin. "We get him, son?"

Tears welled up in Calico's eyes and ran down his cheeks. He tried to speak but couldn't, so he merely nodded.

"Knew it," Dan said then began coughing, blood gushing from his mouth.

Calico propped him up, hoping to stop the bleeding and make his breathing easier. He realized he was squeezing the older man's hand, trying to force life back into him.

"Calico…" Dan's voice was weaker. "The kids…the kids…"

Another coughing fit wracked his huge frame. Blood was running down the front of his neck, staining his shirt. Calico was terrified, and sick with the knowledge there was nothing he could do.

Dan muttered something he didn't hear, and he lowered his head until his ear was only inches from Dan's lips.

"Rebecca…Rebecca…Durant…"

"I understand, Uncle Dan. It's okay. I'll see that the kids get to her."

The limp hand suddenly grasped Calico's so tightly it nearly made him wince. Dan made an effort to sit up, opened his mouth to say something and then collapsed, his final breath leaving him in a long, rattling sigh.

"Uncle Dan…" Calico whispered, lowering him gently to the ground.

And then, for the first time in fifteen years, since that day in the wreckage of the wagon train, Calico Ramsay cried.

CHAPTER 3

THE FUNERAL WAS SIMPLE, AS CALICO KNEW DAN WOULD HAVE WANTED IT. HE WAS buried by a clump of trees on a small rise overlooking the ranch, where the only sounds were the whisper of the wind, the occasional call of a hoot owl and, now and again, the lowing of grazing cattle. There were few mourners—Dan's own ranch hands, the owners of nearby spreads and their wives, Calvin, Tim, Dan's lawyer Silas Turner and a smattering of other townspeople. The death of friends and neighbors was too common an occurrence to cause too great a stir in the daily lives of most people.

Calico stood throughout the service, ramrod straight, his face impassive but his heart sick with grief. At the end he reached out and touched the rough wooden coffin Bill Riley, one of the hands and the ranch's de-facto carpenter, had built. As it was lowered into the ground, he bent over to pick up a handful of dirt and tossed it into the grave. The sound it made as it spattered on the coffin lid reminded him of rain.

Then, with the others, he turned and walked away, not looking back as Marv and Casey, Dan's oldest hands, began shoveling dirt back into the gaping hole.

As he headed toward the tree where he'd tethered Dusty, Silas Turner stopped him.

"A word with you, Calico," he said. "I know you've got…things to do, so I won't go through the formalities of calling you in for a reading of Dan's will."

Though wills were the last thing on Calico's mind at the moment, he was mildly surprised Dan had even made one.

"The ranch is yours," Silas went on. "I just wanted you to know that straight out." He patted him on the back awkwardly then turned toward his carriage.

Dan's killer, Calico had learned the evening of the ambush, had no name. He had ridden into Grady that same morning, asked directions to the ranch at the livery stable and headed off in that direction, only to return shortly before Calico and Dan appeared in town. No one had ever seen him before or knew who he was or why—other than to kill Dan Overholt—he had come. Calico had nothing other than his gut-deep instinct, reinforced by the sheriff's assessment, that the man looked to be a hired gun. That the man had not acted alone.

The killer was buried in a rocky corner of Grady's cemetery with no marker on his grave.

As for who had wanted Dan dead, no one, including Calico, had any idea. He had never known him to have an enemy in the world. There had been a bit of bad blood recently between him and a neighboring rancher known to carry a grudge over some watering rights, but Calico couldn't comprehend it could have led to murder. The sheriff had questioned the man and was satisfied he'd had nothing to do with it.

Calico had vowed he would not rest until whomever was responsible for Dan's murder was brought to justice. However, his investigation would have to wait—he had sworn an obligation to Dan, and he intended to honor it before doing anything else. The twins had to be taken to their aunt, and he was going to take them.

The train came chuffing and wheezing into the station like an asthmatic dragon, wreathed in smoke and steam. Its great black wheels slowed wearily to a crawl, bell clanging in unnecessary notification of its arrival. Calico stood on the platform, watching the grimy windows move past.

The train ground to a creaky, squealing halt, and the thick clouds of steam slowly disappeared like ghosts at dawn. He tried to search in both directions at once as the cars emptied around him—men in derbies with long straight cigars, cowboys toting saddles and saddlebags, gloved and parasolled ladies in frilly hats and bustles, ranch women looking ill-at-ease in their Sunday best, young children skipping and jumping and screaming in excitement either at the wonder of seeing the iron monster up close or in joy at being freed from its confines. People greeted one another, hugging, shaking hands, milling about. Calico wondered how in hell he was going to spot two half-grown kids in all the melee.

Then his eyes locked on to the far end of the rear car, where a gangly young man in Eastern clothes stepped down from the coach carrying two large valises, which he set down to turn and extend his hand to a well-dressed young lady. Calico knew his charges had arrived—and, he suspected, his own adventures just begun.

With a resigned sigh, he moved down the platform to greet them.

They were younger, he saw as he approached, than they had looked at a distance. It was obvious they were twins. With fair skin, wide blue eyes and curly dark-brown hair, the boy was a masculine image of his sister. The girl, Calico could tell, would develop into a beautiful woman; the boy into a handsome, strong man. The youth stood, still with a bit of adolescent awkwardness, just at the brink of manhood—his first shave wasn't far behind him, Calico was sure—yet there was something about the boy he felt drawn to. He could understand why their grandfather had been so concerned for their welfare, and why he had entrusted them to Dan's care. Without understanding why, he felt protective just looking at them.

He was also reminded he didn't even know their names—Dan, if he knew, had never mentioned them, and they did not appear in any of the correspondence Calico had seen. He felt not a little stupid.

Both twins seemed to notice him approaching in their direction at the same time, and their faces reflected a mixture of relief, slight confusion and anticipation.

"Howdy," he said as he reached them. "I'm Calico Ramsay, and I reckon you're expectin' my uncle Dan."

The young man stepped forward and extended his hand. "I'm Josh Howard, and this is my sister Sarah. It was kind of you to meet us."

His handshake was strong, and warm, and Calico was mildly puzzled not only by his reluctance to end it but by the distinct impression the reluctance was mutual. It took a conscious effort to let go, and when he did, he thought he detected just the hint of a smile on the boy's face.

Then, quickly, Josh looked past him and searched the now-thinning crowd. "Isn't Mr. Overholt here?"

Calico shook his head. "I'm afraid not, son. It's a long story, and I'll tell you all about it on the way."

He moved to pick up the grips, but the lanky young man got to them first.

"I can take these," he said, though the bags were obviously heavier than he could carry for long.

Calico took a step forward. "Tell you what, Josh, let's both take one, okay?"

Josh grinned. "Okay."

Again he sensed something important in the way the boy studied him.

"Now, let's get away from here before the smoke outright kills us."

As they left the station and walked across the busy street to a large hotel, Calico explained that Dan had died suddenly—he didn't feel it necessary to go into the details of how—and that it was his last request that Calico see to it they got to their aunt Rebecca. He'd sent a wire to her shortly after the funeral, notifying her of his intentions.

Though the twins were obviously confused and uncertain of their future, they said nothing.

He had rented two adjoining rooms at the hotel.

"When I saw the train was goin' t' be six hours late, I figured we better stay overnight here in Fort Collins an' get an early start come morning,"

He had never been in a city as large as Fort Collins, or stayed in a hotel before. The three-story structure was bigger by far than anything Grady had to offer, but then, Fort Collins was a big city—nearly 4,000 people, all crammed together in one place.

The twins, however, seemed unimpressed by its size. He could hardly imagine a city being as large as he'd heard Chicago was.

They stopped at the desk for the keys and climbed the stairs to the third floor. It was as high in a building as he had ever been, except perhaps for the loft in the main barn. Their rooms were at the far end of the hall, and when he opened the door to the first one it occurred to him he had something of a problem on his hands.

Each room had a large double bed, and he was suddenly aware of the possible awkwardness of the sleeping arrangements. The twins were beyond the age of sleeping together.

"Sarah, you take this room here, an' Josh, you c'n have the other," he said casually, as if he'd had it planned that way all along.

"What about you, Mr. Ramsay?" Sarah asked. "Where's your room?"

It struck him he couldn't remember ever being called "Mr. Ramsay" before. It made him feel like an old man.

He smiled.

"I'd feel more comfortable if you'd call me Calico."

Sarah returned the smile and repeated her question. "So, where is your room... Calico?"

"Well, I..." Calico began, wishing he had a quick answer for her.

"Calico can sleep with me," Josh said, sensing the dilemma. "The bed's plenty big enough. Right, Calico?"

Surprised and strangely pleased by the offer, he hesitated only a moment.

"I guess so. Or I can just camp out on the floor. We'll work it out."

Josh had laid Sarah's suitcase on her bed, and as she opened it, Calico was surprised to see how many clothes she had managed to pack inside it—fancy dresses and shoes far better than most local women's Sunday best. They seemed totally out of place in the world she had just entered. He was almost relieved to think the twins would be going to stay with their aunt—he couldn't imagine that kind of clothing being worn on Uncle Dan's ranch. When he noticed her lifting out a stack of white things he recognized as undergarments, he turned quickly and went into the other room.

The twins put their belongings away, neatly hanging up their clothes and putting various items in dresser drawers while he stood awkwardly in the doorway connecting the two rooms. All he had with him was a change of shirt, a couple pair of socks and another pair of pants in his saddlebag stored at the nearby livery stable. He'd go get them after supper.

They washed up and went down to the hotel dining room for the evening meal. The sun was going down, and the gaslights were being lit as they entered. The room was fairly crowded—a strange mixture of city folks, ranchers, cattle buyers and whatnot.

They took a table near the door to the lobby, Calico sitting with his back to the room, the twins across from him. As he studied the menu, he became aware of their stares, and glanced up at them. Sarah blushed and looked away, but Josh's eyes remained fixed on his own.

"Somethin' wrong?"

Josh broke his gaze and shot an embarrassed look at his sister.

"No. Why?"

"Nothin'. I just figured there might be somethin' wrong, you starin' at me like that."

"I'm sorry. It's just that..."

"Just what?" Calico asked, knowing full well what was coming.

"It's your eyes," Josh admitted boldly. "We've never seen anyone with one blue eye and one brown before."

Calico forced himself not to smile. "Well, you have now," he said, turning his attention back to the menu.

"How...how'd you get them?" Josh asked, his question followed immediately by a pained yelp. "What'd you kick me for?" he growled at his sister, who sat innocently studying her menu.

Calico released his grin and set his menu on the table. "I was born with 'em, o' course. There's a name for it, but I forget what it's called. Not many of us around, as you can tell."

"My brother didn't mean to be rude, Mister...Calico," Sarah said, ignoring Josh's glare.

He shrugged. "Heck, that's okay. It used to bother me when I was younger—bein' different does bother a person, I reckon. But it saved my life once."

Josh was suddenly all eyes and ears, leaning forward excitedly. "It did? How?"

Calico leaned back in his chair. "Well, my folks was farmers, and we lived in Iowa most of my life. Wasn't like Chicago, where you kids is from...you could ride for a day an' hardly see another livin' soul. But it began fillin' up, an' my pa decided to move us out West. He sold everythin', bought a prairie schooner an' a yoke o' oxen, an' we joined a wagon train outta St. Joe."

At this point in his tale, the waitress came for their order, and Josh obviously could barely wait until she was gone.

"Then what happened?" he asked eagerly.

Calico rubbed his index finger under his nose and sighed as he relived the sights and sounds of that journey.

"The train was near three weeks late gettin' started, due to a spell o' sickness and what-all, an' the wagonmaster knew the first winter storms'd be startin' before the train got to Laramie, so they decided to break the train up into two sections. My folks an' me went with the first section. There were rumors of a couple of renegade bands of Indians that'd gone off the reservation causin' trouble for settlers along the route we'd be takin', but nobody thought much 'bout it."

He grew silent a moment, caught up in the memory of that time, which now seemed so long ago. The twins sat in rapt attention, as if not daring to say a word. Finally, he pulled himself out of his reverie and picked up his narrative.

"Well, we shoulda. Halfway through Indian Territory, the train was attacked. We was caught in a small valley, with the Indians all around—we didn't stand a chance. They was up above, shootin' down at us. My ma was killed first, then my pa. Then I got grazed on the forehead by an arrow or a bullet or somethin'. The next thing I knowed, somebody was pullin' at my hair an' I opened up my eyes an' found myself starin' at the biggest, meanest-lookin' Indian I ever did see, with his knife raised, just ready to take my scalp.

"Then he seen my eyes, an' he dropped my head like it was on fire an' let out a big yelp. Some of the other braves come runnin' over an' they all took a good look at me an' started jabberin' 'mongst themselves an' lookin' at me an' pointin', an' then they just moved off. I musta passed out again, 'cause the next thing I remember was Uncle Dan—your granddaddy's brother—washin' my forehead with a wet cloth."

He sighed. "An' him an' me was together ever since, until...well, like I told ya on the way over here, until he died. That was only five days ago—not enough time for anybody to let ya know before ya got on the train. So I'm goin' to make sure you two get to your aunt Rebecca out there in Bow Ridge. She wanted ya to come be with her all along, an' I know ya'll have a good home with her."

"We didn't want to come, you know," Josh volunteered. "At least, Sarah didn't. We'll be eighteen in less than two weeks, and then we can do as we please. But until then, our lawyer says we have to have a legal guardian."

"Well, Uncle Dan woulda been a good one," Calico said. "I'm real sorry ya won't ever get t' know him like I did."

There were a few minutes of silence, and then Sarah asked, "Do you miss your parents, Mister...Calico?"

He nodded. "'Course I do. Young as I was, I remember 'em real clear." He reached into his vest pocket and pulled out a large, round railroad watch. "This here's all I got to remember them by that I can touch. It was my pa's." He carefully replaced the watch into his pocket. "But Uncle Dan, he came t' be just like folks to me. So you two 'n' me got a lot in common. We're all orphans. It ain't easy, but ya learn to accept things life throws ya, an' ya deal with it."

He found it difficult, on studying the twins' faces, to read their expressions. Confusion? Sadness? Disappointment? But he was very aware that Josh kept watching him, and whenever their eyes met, Josh seemed to have just the ghost of a smile.

He was also, surreptitiously, concentrating most of his attention on the young man, and he recognized in that fact an attraction he had felt often in the past but never allowed himself to fully explore.

He had always preferred the company of men and felt ill at ease around females his own age. Part of it was just a natural result of ranch living, but he knew it was more than that. The ranch hands sometimes teased him about his shyness around women, but respected him too much to ever push him on it. A man who fit in on all other levels was allowed his idiosyncracies when it came to his private life.

Still, it hadn't been easy, recognizing and acknowledging certain things within himself without being able to act on them.

Now, here, far from the ranch and the constraints of his normal day-to-day world, and in the company of a handsome young stranger, Calico was all at once examining more closely some of these suppressed feelings. He did not fool himself into thinking they could lead to anything, but just the thoughts alone brought an odd sense of relief and freedom.

His efforts to determine just what Josh might be thinking were interrupted by the arrival of the waitress with their food. They ate in relative silence, Calico frequently aware of Josh's eyes on him; and despite his conscious efforts to avoid making his own interest obvious, he caught himself looking at the young man more often than he intended.

Toward the end of the meal, he noticed Sarah glancing over his shoulder frequently, as if she saw something odd across the room. At the same time, he felt the hair on his neck begin to rise. He didn't turn around, but she saw him watching her.

"Do you have any friends in Fort Collins, Mister…Calico?" she asked.

"Not as I know of." The familiar feeling of impending danger grew inside him. "Why'd ya ask?"

"Well, those two men over there in the far corner have been staring at us ever since we came in. I thought maybe they were someone you knew."

Calico turned around slowly in his chair. The room was still fairly crowded, but he spotted the pair Sarah was talking about almost immediately. Two men—big, rough-looking cowhand types—sat at a table by the far wall, studiously avoiding looking at him.

"The one in the maroon vest an' the one in the brown hat," he said, not needing to put the statement in the form of a question.

"Yes. Do you know them?"

"Never seen 'em before."

He turned back around. He didn't know them, but he had the definite impression they knew him, and that it was time to leave the dining room.

He gave an exaggerated stretch and yawn for the benefit of the twins, then said, "Well, I guess it's 'bout time we turned in. Got to get a real early start in the morning."

The three rose together; Calico paid the bill and ushered the twins out of the room ahead of him. At the doorway, he looked back into the room, just in time to catch a hostile glare from one of the men at the table. He had no idea what the glare meant, but he sensed it did not bode well.

When they got to their rooms, he made sure both doors to the hallway were locked and left the connecting door slightly ajar. Josh undressed and donned a beige nightshirt he took from a bureau drawer; Calico, who had never worn a nightshirt in his life and usually slept in the raw, was a little embarrassed.

Josh crawled under the covers as Calico made a project of turning down the gaslights.

He realized then he'd not returned to the livery stable for his bedroll, and thought about making one from a blanket at the foot of the bed, except, he now saw, there was no extra blanket. It was summer, after all.

"Aren't you coming to bed?" Josh asked, his voice already misted with the fatigue of the long day.

"Yeah. Just be a minute." He sat on the edge of the mattress to remove his boots. Josh moved over to the far side to give him plenty of room then lay still, and in a moment he could tell from his breathing the youth was asleep.

He stared at the handsome young face, aware once again of feelings not unfamiliar but long repressed—feelings both warm and confusing. He knew his heart was beating faster than normal, and he had the urge to reach across the short distance between them and touch the young man's cheek. He shook his head vigorously, as if to force it back inside.

He waited a few minutes more then, still fully clothed, stretched out on top of the blankets. In another moment he, too, was asleep.

He awakened to the smell of smoke. Muffled sounds of movement came from the next room—Sarah's room.

He shot upright, leaped from the bed and raced to the door between the two rooms, the door he had left ajar and which was now both closed and locked. The smell of smoke was stronger, and through the crack at the bottom of the door, he could see the faint flicker of fire.

"Josh!" he yelled. "Get up!" He heard the young man stirring groggily, making little disturbed-sleep noises. "Get up!" he yelled again as he ran to the door to the hallway. The key dangled by its tip from the lock. He tried to put it back in and turn it, but it wouldn't work—something was blocking it from the other side.

Josh was now out of bed, the smell of the smoke growing stronger, small wisps beginning to curl under the door. He ran over and, finding it locked, began to pound on the thick wood.

"Sarah! Sarah! Wake up! There's a fire! Sarah, wake up!"

There was no answer.

The door opened inward into Sarah's room, the hinges, therefore, on her side. Realizing that not even his 180-pound frame would be likely to be able to batter it open, he grabbed his rifle and, using the butt as a battering ram, smashed through the thankfully thin panel just above and to the left of the lock. The wood splintered, and reaching through the hole he found and turned the key.

He caught a glimpse of two bulky forms on either side of the room, firebrands in their hands One, having just applied his torch to the edge of the quilt on the bed, was turning toward the heavy-curtained window while the other lit a framed picture on the wall near the doorway to the hall. In the center of the bed lay the unmoving form of an unconscious Sarah.

Calico flung himself at the intruder nearest the door, smashing his fist into the man's jaw. The man grunted and raised his firebrand to strike him on the head, but Calico's other fist caught him in the pit of the stomach. The man doubled forward, and Calico caught him again on the chin with a low-swung right, sending him toppling backward into the wall.

"Calico, look out!" Josh called, and he turned just in time to see the other man rushing him, shoulders hunched forward, fists doubled, his firebrand slung into a corner where it began nibbling at the edge of the dresser. The arsonist grabbed him in a bear hug, his forward rush carrying them off-balance, and they fell to the floor, struggling.

As they rolled against the outer wall, the huge, muscular form of the attacker full atop him, Calico concentrated all his strength to thrust both knees upward, catching the man unprepared and launching him in a backward somersault over his head. There was a shattering of glass and a long, wild scream as the man catapulted backward through the window and plunged three stories to the street below.

Calico scrambled to his feet, still not fully comprehending everything that was going on, or why. He had little time to reflect before he was knocked to his knees as the other intruder rushed past him toward the door to the hallway. Calico saw Josh throw himself at the man, who shot one large arm out and shoved him roughly against the wall then opened the door and dashed into the hall. Elbowing his way roughly through panicked guests aroused by the sounds of fighting and the smell of smoke, he raced toward the stairs and disappeared.

One side of the room was already engulfed in flame, and the heat was becoming intense. The bed, too, was burning, flames marching steadily toward

Sarah's thin nightdress. Calico got once more to his feet, rushed to the far side of the bed where the blaze had not yet reached and scooped her into his arms. Josh appeared at his side and followed him from the burning room.

Calico paused only long enough to set the awakening but groggy girl on her feet. Josh put his arm around her for support and to protect her from being jostled by the last of the fleeing guests. Then he ran back through the fire to retrieve his rifle from his and Josh's room. Shielding his face with his arm, he retraced his steps through Sarah's room and into the smoke-filled hallway. He and Josh took Sarah, now able to walk but unsteady, under her arms and half-carried, half-dragged her to the crowded stairway and, finally, out of the hotel.

They stood in the throng of guests and onlookers gathered on the street across from the hotel and watched the large structure burn to the ground despite the best efforts of the local fire brigade.

CHAPTER 4

As THEY STOOD WATCHING THE LAST SECTION OF WALL FALL INTO THE MOUND OF NOW mostly embers, a tap on Calico's shoulder made him spin around defensively, ready to fight.

"Sorry, mister," a heavyset man in a nightshirt, nightcap and slippers said. "I didn't mean to startle you. I gather from the looks of you that you were staying at the hotel?"

The twins turned to look at the stranger, who looked as though he, too, had been a hotel guest.

"Yeah, we were," Calico said, puzzled and still on the defensive.

"Well, my name's Foster McGivey, and I own that grocery store right over there. Me and my wife live behind the store, and when we heard the commotion, I hurried over. This is the biggest thing that's happened in Fort Collins in years! Anyway, my wife told me to see if anybody might need a place to spend the night, and it looks like you three qualify."

Calico wondered why they had been singled out from all the other guests, but the grocer went on to provide the answer.

"I couldn't help notice this lovely young lady here in just her nightdress, and we can't have her or you sleepin' in the street, now, can we?"

Calico noticed there were a number of townspeople making similar offers to other hotel guests. He also realized the man was right—they couldn't very well sleep in the street, and there were really few other practical options at the moment.

"Well, that's mighty kind of you, Mister...McGivey. I can sleep in your stable, but if you could provide a bed for Sarah and Josh, here, I'd be mighty obliged to you."

"I can sleep in the stable with Calico," Josh volunteered.

McGivey waved his hand. "No, no, that won't be necessary. One of our daughters just got married, and we got another spare bedroom besides that one."

Sarah was beginning to shiver, either from the cool night air or from the realization of what had just happened. Josh put his arm around her and pulled her close to him for warmth.

"Well, that's it, then," McGivey said with an assertive nod. "You just come with me."

The fire delayed their departure for two days The twins had lost everything, including the $150 in cash neatly hidden in the false bottom of the smaller of the two grips, now part of a mountainous pile of smoking timber and ash. Calico, fortunately, had lost nothing except his boots, jacket and hat; he still had sufficient money for the journey but not enough to re-outfit the twins.

A wire was sent to the twins' lawyer in Chicago requesting money from their trust fund and explaining the circumstances behind the need. While they waited, Calico, who had brought two extra horses with him from the ranch, went in search of a small wagon upon learning, to his barely concealed dismay, that Sarah only rode sidesaddle, a position designed neither for comfort nor practicality on long journeys over rough terrain, and which neither of the cowponies was likely to put up with in any case.

The grocer and his wife, with the help of their neighbors, managed to find clothing for the twins the morning after the fire, and extended hospitality for the following night. Calico, hesitant to check into another hotel out of fear for their safety, gratefully accepted.

Though both he and Josh had been greatly concerned for Sarah, she proved remarkably resilient; and Calico was impressed by the fact these were not just two addlebrained, pampered rich kids who fell apart at the first sign of adversity. That morning, over a huge breakfast served by Mrs. McGivey, Sarah told them she had been awakened by the sound of her door closing. Before she could react, a wet rag was put over her face—chloroform, Calico speculated when she described the sweet odor—and the next thing she knew Calico was carrying her out of the room.

After breakfast, while Sarah insisted on helping Mrs. McGivey clean up, he and Josh went to the livery stable to check on Dusty and the other two horses.

Josh, despite the trauma of the night before, was as eager as a puppy to learn everything he possibly could about the new world in which he now found himself. Calico was pleased to learn that, even though the twins had been raised in Chicago, they had spent time on a farm owned by their grandparents and knew at least something about horses.

They were talking with the liveryman when the local sheriff—Calico spotted him a hundred yards away by the badge on his shirt—approached them.

"You had the rooms where the fire started?" the lawman asked without any preliminary introductions.

"I'm afraid so," Calico admitted.

The sheriff nodded. "Then I think we better have a little talk." He turned to Josh. "You know anything about this, son?"

"No, sir," Josh told him. "My sister and I just got here yesterday."

"Well, then, why don't you go about your business and let…" He looked at Calico "Mr. Ramsay, is it?"

Calico nodded, wondering how the sheriff knew.

"…and I have our talk."

Josh looked at Calico questioningly, obviously hoping he would ask the sheriff to let him stay, but what Calico had to say he didn't want Josh to hear. He saw no point in bringing up Dan's death in the boy's presence.

"That's okay, Josh, ya head back to the McGiveys' an' I'll be along in a minute."

Making no attempt to hide his disappointment, Josh shrugged and turned away, deliberately kicking up small puffs of dirt as he walked back down the dusty street toward the McGiveys'. Calico and the sheriff remained silent until he was out of earshot.

"So," the sheriff said finally, "what's this all about?"

He did his best to tell the man everything he knew—which was precious little, he realized. He told him of Dan's unsolved murder, and of his current mission with the twins. When he finished, the sheriff studied him closely, lips pursed.

"So, if somebody might be out to kill you, how come they started the fire in the girl's room?"

It was a question Calico had asked himself more than once, and for which he had no answer.

The sheriff strongly recommended that Calico and the twins leave Fort Collins as soon as possible, though Calico wasn't sure whether the man's concern was for their safety or making his job easier by getting rid of a potential problem. At dinner that night at the McGiveys, he was grateful Mr. McGivey avoided mentioning the fire or what was a source of much gossip in the town—that the assailant Calico had tossed through the hotel window had died a short time after being carried to the nearby home of a doctor. The second man hadn't been seen since he disappeared into the crowd during the fire, and no one questioned knew, or at least admitted to ever having seen, either of the men.

Calico tried not to think about the fire, though he had a gut-feeling Dan's mysterious killer and these two unknown assailants were somehow connected. He had absolutely no idea of who they might be or what their motivations were. That Rebecca Durant might have been responsible for Dan's death because of his refusal to send the twins to her had crossed his mind in the days after the funeral, but on further reflection he found the idea inconceivable—regardless of her and Dan never having met and the story of Cain and Abel aside, it was incomprehensible to him that family would harm family.

And even if he might have had lingering doubts, they were all but erased by this latest attack. Rebecca was getting what she wanted; he was bringing the twins to her.

Early Tuesday, the second morning after the fire, the twins received word their lawyer had transferred funds to a Fort Collins bank, and part of the morning was spent buying new clothes for the twins. Sarah had no real idea of the kinds of clothes she would need, but Calico was once again impressed when she asked Mrs. McGivey to help her choose.

Josh eagerly sought Calico's advice, a gesture he was surprised to discover he found oddly pleasing. The boy wanted to buy a gun, too, but Calico drew the line—the journey promised to be dangerous enough without him being saddled with an inexperienced and possibly trigger-happy youngster.

Through the grocer's good offices, he had managed to locate a wagon suitable for their needs, and traded one of the ranch horses for one more accustomed to harness. Late that afternoon they bid their farewells to the McGiveys. Despite their hosts' insistence that they spend one more night and get a fresh start in the morning, Calico had decided it was best to heed the sheriff's advice and leave town as soon as they could. With Josh at the reins of the wagon and Sarah seated beside him, they headed out of town.

He deliberately took the wrong road, going the opposite direction from the one he wanted and, as he rode beside the wagon with the extra horse tethered to it, kept a watch behind to be sure they were not being followed.

They traveled for just over an hour until he was satisfied they were not being followed. Mr. McGivey, to whom he had explained his plan, had told him of a back trail that made a wide circle around the town. With sundown only a few hours away, they turned off to follow a small stream until Calico found a spot he was confident could not be seen from the trail and set up camp for the night.

He was a little less than happy when Sarah told him, as suppertime arrived, that she did not know how to cook. Other than helping her mother bake an occasional cake, she had never had to learn. He knew cooking was a skill she would definitely have to learn if she expected to survive on the frontier, but for now he didn't want to make an issue of it and prepared dinner himself.

This would also be the first time in the twins' young lives that they had not slept in a comfortable bed. After supper, they set up a makeshift bed for Sarah in the back of the wagon then Calico and Josh spread their blankets on the ground by the campfire. While Sarah was somewhat apprehensive of sleeping outdoors, Josh was exuberant. The fact he insisted on sleeping as close as he could get without their blankets overlapping was not lost on Calico, though he wouldn't allow himself to think about it—or his own subtle surge of pleasure at the prospect.

Instead, he concentrated on staying alert to possible danger. He kept his rifle close at hand, and he intended to sleep with one eye open.

The next morning, after breakfast, he let the horses drink their fill in the stream, hitched up the wagon and was about to tether the extra horse to it when Josh spoke up.

"Can't I ride him, Calico?"

"Who's goin' to drive the wagon?"

"Sarah can. Grandfather let her drive one on his farm a couple of times."

He hesitated, but then looked at Sarah.

"Well?" he asked. "Think you can handle it?"

She clambered up onto the wagon seat and leaned forward to pick up the reins.

"If Josh can do it, I can do it," she said firmly. "What's the horse's name?"

It had never occurred to him to ask the horse's name when he traded for it.

"Well, mine's Dusty, and the one I brought from the ranch is Belle. I don't rightly know what this other one's name is."

"Well, then, it's Daniel," Sarah declared.

He grinned. "Tell you what. Josh, you get up here and drive with her for a ways but let her hold the reins. When she gets used to it, you can ride Belle. Okay?"

Josh shrugged then returned the grin. "Sure," he said.

Calico saddled Belle and Dusty then tied Belle again to the back of the wagon and mounted.

"Okay, kids, let's move."

Sarah tentatively flicked the reins, and the wagon moved slowly forward. After about an hour, and several requests from Josh, they stopped to allow him to untether and mount Belle. When they set off again, Calico rode close alongside the wagon in case Sarah might have any problems. Josh stayed as close beside him as he could.

It took most of the morning to make the circle around Fort Collins and head off in the right direction, but Calico was taking no chances on their being followed. Though he still had no idea why, he was certain the incident at the hotel would not be an isolated one.

As they rode along, he searched his mind for a possible clue as to who might want to kill him. Try as he might, he could not think of even a remote connection between Dan's death and the attack in Fort Collins. Then again, if someone were after *him*, why had they set the fire in Sarah's room? Why not just gun him down from ambush, like they'd killed Dan?

The day was bright and hot, with puffy clouds building up on the horizon, portending a possible summer storm. Josh's enthusiasm for their adventure was evident in his frequent and eager questions about the animals, trees, plants, rocks and terrain they passed. Sarah remained relatively quiet, though she and her brother exchanged occasional comments on some aspect of the countryside, or the sudden bolting of a jackrabbit across the trail. Calico sensed that they knew each other sufficiently well that not many actual words needed to pass between them for each to know what the other was thinking. Rather like him and Dan, he thought, and felt the now-familiar surge of sadness that came whenever he thought of the older man.

From time to time they passed a farm or small ranch, but such signs of civilization became less frequent the farther they got from Fort Collins. Calico was aware of Josh studying him, and it still bothered him a bit how much he liked it.

By early afternoon, the air was stifling. Calico had to wipe the sweat from his eyes, and his untrimmed blond hair had reached the length where it lay matted to his forehead. The clouds were building up noticeably now, their bottoms dirty gray, casting thick shadows on the landscape. Every now and then, a low rumble of thunder could be heard.

In the late afternoon, just before the storm broke, they reached the small settlement of Parker, which was little more than a scattering of houses and a livery stable. There was no hotel, but Calico made arrangements with the owner for the three travelers to spend the night in the small stable. The first drops of rain, driven by a gusty westerly wind, fell as he and Josh unsaddled the horses and led them into their stalls. Sarah helped carry in the bedrolls, and Calico just managed to spread an oilcloth across the rest of the gear in the wagon before the storm broke full on them.

He and Josh pushed the stable doors closed against the strong wind and driving rain, and the three settled down to a cold supper from one of the saddlebags. The twins were exhausted from the long ride, and after eating they spread their bedrolls on the sweet-smelling hay—Josh again choosing a spot immediately beside Calico—and went to sleep, lulled by the sound of rain, thunder and wind.

During the night, Calico woke to find Josh's arm across him. Though it pleased him, he carefully lifted it and placed it beside the sleeping youth. Moments later, it was back, and this time he left it alone.

They arose with the dawn to a crisp, freshly laundered morning smelling of damp earth and green things. Sarah insisted on driving the wagon by herself, an idea Josh had obviously encouraged in order to ride with Calico. Calico was considerably more confident of her ability to handle the rig, though he still rode close by, just in case.

The clearly marked trail from Parker meandered first slightly north then toward the south, becoming less and less distinct from the various paths and trails that crossed it until it disappeared. Calico had to rely on his keen sense of direction and the general information on the lay of the land he'd picked up in Fort Collins and Parker and from the increasingly infrequent passing riders. He had a map, but didn't feel the need to consult it until they reached totally unfamiliar territory.

By early afternoon, the land began a gradual rise, turning from low, heavily gullied hills into steep-bluffed ridges. There was still something of a discernible trail, and Sarah had only minimal difficulty with the wagon, so he felt sufficiently at ease to ride ahead a hundred feet or so now and again to check out what was in front of them. The first few times, Josh rode with him, until Calico told him to hang back closer to the wagon in case Sarah needed help.

Josh's expression showed his disappointment at not being able to stay close, but he obeyed.

Again Calico was equal parts amused and disturbed by Josh's attention. Despite his best efforts, he found his mind wandering into those areas he'd kept suppressed. He knew how the world worked—well, how his part of the world worked. He knew the rules, and he played by them. He couldn't—wouldn't—allow himself to hope for anything else.

He wasn't, he told himself, the kind of man given to self-delusion. Josh's attentions were undoubtedly nothing but a fascination with the new and, for a young man from the city, the exotic. In any event, he could not allow himself to become too attached to someone from so different a world, who would not be in his life for any longer than it took them to reach their destination. In his world, to be vulnerable was to be weak, and he could not be weak and survive.

Then, just as he had convinced himself of the logic of his thinking, he would notice Josh looking at him, and he would clearly see something…more…in the youth's eyes. That he did not know for certain what the "more" meant was the most disturbing thought of all.

As the sun began its slow descent, the three travelers reached the crest of a high ridge with a steep, rolling upslope on one side, a sharp drop-off on the other. They would have to camp soon.

He called a rest stop, and he and Josh dismounted as Sarah brought the wagon to a halt. She let the reins fall onto the seat beside her and turned to reach behind into the bed of the wagon.

The quiet air was suddenly alive with a high, rusty whirring sound that froze Calico's blood. Rattlers! He surveyed the rocky, weed-covered ground to spot the source of the sound just as the wagon horse gave a panicked whinny and rose up on its hind legs, pawing the air.

The movement tumbled Sarah into the back of the wagon, and the reins slipped off onto the ground just as Calico located the familiar coils of not one but two large rattlesnakes, eight feet apart but not ten feet in front of the frightened horse. He grabbed his rifle, cocked it, took quick aim and fired, neatly blowing the head off the closest snake.

Before he could re-cock, the horse bolted and the wagon shot forward, with Sarah struggling to regain her balance and climb back onto the seat.

"Can ya shoot, boy?" he called to Josh, who stood riveted in the same spot and nearly the same position he had been in when they first heard the snakes.

"Sure. I—"

He didn't have a chance to finish. In one motion, Calico tossed him the rifle and bounded into the saddle.

"Get that second snake, and keep a lookout for others," he shouted as he spurred Dusty in pursuit of the runaway wagon.

Sarah had by now regained the seat, but with the reins trailing on the ground well out of her reach, there was little she could do but hold on. The terrified horse galloped blindly, the wagon bouncing over the rough ground, edging ever closer to the sharp edge of the bluff and a drop of nearly a hundred feet.

Calico urged Dusty forward, finally drawing up beside the wildly bouncing wagon, which threatened to go over the edge at any moment. When the two horses were neck-and-neck and just a few feet apart, he reached out and grabbed the reins trailing from the bridle. Pulling both horses up, he reached over to pat the runaway reassuringly, talking to it in a calm, soothing voice.

When the horse was calmed, he dismounted, collected the reins and tossed them to Sarah, who reached out automatically to catch them.

"Next time, tie the reins, don't just put 'em down," he said, not unkindly.

Sarah, her face drained of color, merely nodded.

"Now, ya hold right here while I go back an' get Josh," he said, but as he turned to remount he saw Josh riding toward them.

"I got it, Calico. I got it on the first shot." he called as he reined in beside the wagon, Calico's rifle in one hand. "It was…" He suddenly remembered himself and looked at his sister, somewhat embarrassed. "I mean, are you okay, Sarah?"

She glared at him. "No, silly, I was killed. And a lot you'd care if I were, Mr. Cowboy Josh."

Josh looked chagrined. "Hey, I'm sorry, Sarah, it's just…"

His voice trailed off as his sister firmly turned her back on him, staring out over the valley below. With a sigh, he handed Calico the rifle.

"Do you understand women, Calico?" he asked, dismounting—but not before giving the ground in the immediate vicinity a careful once-over.

Calico took the rifle and grinned.

"Heck, Josh, sometimes I don't think women really want men to understand 'em."

Then, as Sarah spun around to glare at him, he shifted his grin to her and gave her a big wink. Her anger melted, and she threw up her hands in the eternal female gesture of frustration.

"Well, now that we're all calmed down," he suggested, "let's move on for about another hour then make camp."

"Good," Sarah said with an exaggerated shudder. "I want to get as far away from rattlesnakes as we can get."

He refrained from pointing out that the two snakes they had killed were not the only ones in the West, but he and Josh exchanged a knowing look.

They made camp on a high rise overlooking the series of ridges and valleys through which they had come. Calico shot a rabbit, which he then skinned, gutted and put on a spit over the fire. Josh had watched with reluctant fascination, but Sarah studiously avoided even looking in their direction until the aroma of the cooking meat and her hunger got the best of her finer sensibilities, and she joined them at the fire.

"Do you do this often?" she said, standing beside the hunkering men.

"Do what?" Calico asked.

"I mean, just go out and shoot something when you're hungry?"

He looked up at her and gave her a gentle smile. "Ya know of a better way?"

She thought a moment then shrugged, gathered up her skirts and sat on the ground beside them.

After dinner, they talked as the sky grew dark. About the West, about the East, and the differences in the way of life between them. Neither Calico nor the twins had ever known any other world than their own, but he had the advantage since they were now in his world.

As they prepared their bedrolls for the night—Sarah still preferring to sleep in the bed of the wagon—he happened to spot, far behind them in the direction from which they had just come, a pinprick of light representing another campfire. The hair rose on the back of his neck, and he did not sleep much that night.

CHAPTER 5

HE AWAKENED THE TWINS BEFORE DAYBREAK. THEY HAD A QUICK CUP OF COFFEE AND some pan bread left over from the night before then broke camp and moved on, Calico setting a somewhat faster pace than they had been maintaining for the past few days. Though he was concerned about the far-off campfire, he saw no point in mentioning it.

From the map and the terrain before them, he knew they soon would have a choice of two routes through a particularly rugged piece of country, either of which would bring them out at roughly the same place. One led through wide-open range. The other, somewhat shorter, was through rough, hilly country. By moving very fast and taking the rougher route, they could put themselves farther ahead of whoever it was he was sure was following them.

But with a wagon—and one driven by a relatively inexperienced girl, at that—the smoother range route was far more practical, and less dangerous. Reluctantly, he opted for that, but was determined to make it through the open country as fast as possible.

As they moved out into the grassland he urged Dusty to a gentle trot. Sarah flicked the reins expertly, and the wagon picked up speed to keep pace, as did Josh. It was approaching midsummer, but the altitude and the protecting ring of high hills had made the area through which they were passing exceptionally dry—the storm they'd experienced two nights ago had either not hit this particular area, Calico mused, or had done it no practical good. The grass was long, thick and scorched brown by the sun. Only a few scrubby trees dotted the landscape, though he knew from the map a river ran just beyond and to the left of the rolling hills in front of them.

About three miles ahead, the range began to funnel through steeper hills until, at its end, there was only a narrow pass beyond which the alternate route joined to spill out onto the larger flatlands beyond. The deeper they got onto the rangeland, the more nervous Calico became, until even the twins noticed his constant backward glances.

"Something wrong, Calico?" Josh asked, drawing up beside him. A moment before, he had been riding beside the wagon, conversing with Sarah in tones Calico couldn't overhear—and hardly noticed, in his growing apprehension.

"Nope," he lied. "Just checkin' our distance."

Josh looked at him strangely.

"Oh. Okay," he said, then dropped back to converse once again with Sarah.

A stiffening breeze was blowing in through the narrow pass from the open land beyond, and though it was warm, Calico welcomed any movement of air. Though they were making fairly good time, it wasn't fast enough for him. He was well aware that a swift rider, taking the more rugged route, could still head them off.

As they drew closer to the pass, he switched his attention from behind to ahead, keeping a sharp eye for any sign of riders or, higher up, of movement among the rocks.

They were about a mile from the pass, riding into a strong headwind, when Sarah called out, "Look, Calico. What's that?"

His attention had been momentarily distracted, and when he looked, he saw two riders, motionless in the pass. His muscles automatically tensed as he reined to a halt and motioned for Josh and Sarah to do the same. They waited, the only sounds the occasional nicker of one of the horses and the low, soft rumble of the wind in their ears.

The two riders were doing something, though at this distance it was hard for him to tell exactly what. Whatever it was, he sensed it boded them no good.

Suddenly, the riders split off in opposite directions, moving up the two slopes of the pass. They were dragging something behind their horses. The two riders turned toward one another and did not appear to move for several seconds, though he still suspected they were up to something. Then, as if on signal, they galloped toward one another. They seemed to meet in the center of the pass then turned toward the open country beyond and disappeared. In their wake, they left a thin trail of dust that ominously grew thicker.

"What's the dust from?" Josh asked.

Suddenly, Calico knew.

"That ain't dust, it's smoke. Them bastards have set the valley afire!"

Inexperienced as the twins were in country living, it wasn't hard for them to recognize the danger. The long, thick grass was tinder-dry; the wind blowing through the pass would fan the flames, blowing them directly toward where they stood. They had never seen a range fire, but Calico had, and he knew how fast flames moved when driven by a strong wind.

As the smoke began to build, he could see tiny licks of flame and, through brief openings in the pall, the two riders, in the center of the pass and safely upwind, watching.

Behind was five miles of open flatland—to try to outride the fire was foolish, the odds a hundred-to-one they would never make it. Even if they did, he had the gut feeling somebody would be there waiting for them.

"What are we going to do, Calico?" Sarah asked, frightened.

"We can either get ya on Belle with Josh, or we can try to make it with the wagon. Ya think ya can manage ridin' double with Josh?"

"I suppose," she said hesitantly. "But what about the wagon and Daniel?"

"We'll just cut Daniel lose and let him fend for himself."

"Can't we try to make it with the wagon?"

Calico thought fast. Two riders on Belle would slow her down. The countryside was quite flat, and the wagon should be able to make top speed with little danger of either hitting anything or tipping over, even if Sarah should lose control.

"Okay," he decided, "we'll go with the wagon. Now, let's move."

He turned Dusty sharply and waited while Sarah wheeled the wagon around and urged Daniel to his top speed. Then he and Josh took off after her. He deliberately led them in almost a direct line back over the way they had come, though he knew that to try following it all the way out of the valley would be fatal—the fire would catch up with them long before they reached safety.

He also knew the river lay about a mile to their right, but he wanted to wait until the smoke grew thick enough to obscure them from the watchers at the pass, to convince them their victims were headed for disaster.

As soon as he was certain the smoke and flames hid them, he surged ahead of Josh and the wagon, motioning them to turn to the right. With a mile to the river, in a direct line, and the fire now less than that behind them and moving fast, their best chance was to run nearly parallel to the flames but at a slight angle, which would keep some distance between them and the advancing blaze.

Keeping close to the wagon, he set his eyes on the horizon, every now and again glancing toward the encroaching fire. The smoke was rising high in the air now, thin wisps of it reaching toward them like tentacles. They could already smell it—sharp, not unpleasant, but foretelling a deadly danger coming closer by the minute.

He detected movement in the grass between them and the fire—darting rabbits and prairie dogs, flutters of quail and other ground birds fleeing the flames, which now swept like a long, blackening scythe across the grassland.

The smoke dimmed the sun, and small sparks, like fireflies, drifted past. Over the creaking of the wagon and the pounding of hooves rose the distinctive sound of the fire—a hushed crackling.

They were almost to the rise now, the smoke a thickening fog, the earlier scent of burning grass now a cloying, acrid stench. Calico put his kerchief over his face and yelled at the twins to cover their mouths and noses, and for Josh to ride in closer lest he get lost in the smoke. Their eyes burned and watered, making it difficult to see where they were going.

After what seemed like an eternity, they capped the rise, and Calico could just make out the river about two hundred yards ahead. He also saw that the fire had already reached the riverbank and was rapidly closing the small gap in front of them.

A stinging sensation on his shoulder drew attention to a spark that had landed on his shirt and burned through to his bare skin. He slapped at it with his free hand.

It was a race, now, between them and the fire, and the fire was winning. But they could still make it, if only the horses didn't panic.

The flames had cut them off, and Calico knew there was only one chance.

"Right through!" he called, spurring Dusty forward. The distance to the fire narrowed; he felt Dusty tense, but he urged him on—straight through the conflagration to the burned and smoldering area on the other side, then on to the river's edge. He stopped only when the horse was up to his chest in the water then looked behind him, ready to return to the flames at any sign of trouble.

The wagon, something burning in its bed, appeared through the smoke and flames, moving fast; Josh was right behind. They'd made it!

As soon as the wagon reached the water, he and Josh leaped from their horses to throw water on the small fire, which turned out to be Josh's bedroll. Sarah, too, jumped from the wagon into the river and knelt in the shallow water, splashing water over her face.

When everyone had calmed down, they moved upstream about a hundred yards to a small, sheltered section of shore untouched by the fire to rest and eat. Calico felt they would be safe there for a time.

No one spoke much until they sat around a small campfire.

"Those men set that fire," Sarah said, staring at her plate and picking at her beans with her fork. "Just like in Fort Collins. They wanted to kill us." She looked up at him beseechingly. "Why, Calico? Why would anybody want to kill us?"

He shook his head. "I don't know, Sarah. I just don't know." He thought a minute then said, "I suspect it ain't us they want dead so much as it is me. You kids just got caught in the middle, I guess, an' I do apologize for that. It's got to have somethin' to do with Uncle Dan, somehow. Somebody killin' him like that. I never knowed him to have a enemy in the world, an' then somebody killin' him."

Seeing the surprised looks on their faces, Calico realized this was the first they'd heard that Dan had been murdered.

"Why didn't you tell us this before?" Josh demanded.

He shrugged. "I didn't see much point in mentionin' it," he said. "But then that business in Fort Collins...Why'd they want to kill me? Uncle Dan's already dead, an' any reason they might of had died with him. But if they're after me, I just wish they'd leave you kids outta it. It's none o' your affair."

"Well, we'll help you if you're in trouble," Josh said seriously.

Calico suppressed a grin and gave him a curt nod.

"I appreciate that, Josh. I surely do." His admiration for the twins—and particularly Josh—advanced another step.

"What are we going to do now?" Sarah asked.

Calico took another helping of beans and shrugged. "Keep on goin', I reckon. With three of us to keep an eye out, I don't expect they'll be able to surprise us again, now we know for sure what they're up to."

"But what about right now?" Sarah persisted. "What if they come after us now?"

"I don't expect they'll do that, Sarah. The fire's still burnin', and for all they know, we was caught in it an' killed, like they planned. Besides," he said, getting to his feet, "men like that, they'd just as soon avoid a face-to-face fight. They know we're on to 'em, an' that we're on our guard. I think they'll wait a bit before they take another crack at us."

"Are we going to move on right now, Calico?" Josh asked.

"No, I don't think so." He leaned forward to pick up their empty plates. "I think we'll rest here till after dark then move on. When they see our carcasses ain't fried out on the grassland, they're goin' t' suspect the river. By that time, we'll be long gone. They ain't got no way of knowin' just where we're headed, so come dark, we'll follow the river a ways beyond the pass an' turn inland. Now, what say ya help me clean up an' then we try to get some sleep?"

CHAPTER 6

THE SOUND OF CRICKETS WOKE CALICO, AND HE OPENED HIS EYES TO THE THICK BLUE haze of evening. The sky remained blurred by smoke, indicating the fire still burned far down the valley. He woke the twins who, unaccustomed to sleeping during the daytime, had had very little.

They saddled the horses and hitched Daniel to the wagon. Calico knew the ground was soft enough to leave tracks, especially through the soot and ash of the burned-over valley, but he hoped that by riding in the riverbed as much of the way as possible they would leave few signs of their passage, and that perhaps in the land beyond the pass they might be able to elude their pursuers.

They moved out into the shallow river and headed upstream in the gathering darkness, behind the ridge of hills that separated it from the range. For some distance after Calico judged by the reappearance of unscorched shrubs and small trees that they had come parallel to the pass they kept to the riverbed. He suspected their pursuers would be camped close to the mouth of the pass and wanted to avoid starting the journey inland until they were well away from it.

They rode in comparative silence, the twins still groggy from too-short sleep, until Josh, who had been trailing slightly behind the wagon, rode up beside him.

"Are you ever afraid of anything, Calico?" he asked, too softly for Sarah to hear.

Calico turned toward him and smiled reassuringly.

"Well, 'course I am, boy," he said. "Ya ever meet a man who tells ya he's not, ya know ya just met either an idiot or the biggest liar God ever put breath into."

"Are you afraid now?" Josh persisted.

"No, not right this minute." Then he added, "An' almost never when I'm pretty sure o' what's goin' t' happen next. But I'll admit there's been a few minutes the last couple of days when I wasn't so sure."

Josh stared at him for a long moment, and he returned the look until Josh looked away.

"I never imagined you ever being afraid of anything," he murmured, and Calico felt a warm flush sweep over him.

He sighed. "Yeah, well, I ain't no different from any other man...maybe just not so ashamed to say it. Don't you ever be, either. There ain't nothin' wrong with a man havin' feelin's. It's the man that don't have no feelin's I worry about."

"Ummmm," Josh said, staring at the reins in his hand. "You really think they're trying to kill us?"

Calico shrugged. "Sure looks that way, don't it? Though I can't figure out why, for the life of me. I been wrackin' my brain, an' I ain't come up with one good reason. Like I said earlier, I just wish you kids wasn't mixed up in it."

"I'm no kid," Josh said, defensively. "I'll be eighteen in less than two weeks."

Calico studied him then rubbed his hand over his chin.

"No, I reckon you're not a kid no more. Matter o' fact, I think next town we come to, we ought to buy ya a gun. Now we know for sure somebody's out to get us, it might be a good idea if there was two armed men to look after Sarah. If ya can keep from shootin' me an' everything else in sight, that is."

Josh's grin was nearly bright enough to light up the entire valley. Calico was afraid he was going to let out a whoop of joy that would be heard for miles, so he put his finger quickly to his lips to forestall that possibility. Josh nodded solemnly, but was so elated he practically glowed.

"Thanks, Calico," he managed to say after a moment then dropped back to the wagon to give the news to Sarah.

Calico, turning to watch him, shook his head and grinned before giving his attention once more to the dim outline of the hills.

When he determined they had gone a safe distance beyond the pass, he motioned for them to leave the riverbed and move inland. The night was one of those ghost-lit evenings when the stars burned pinholes of light in the sky, and the thin crescent of the moon sketched black silhouettes of the horizon. The land beyond the pass stretched out unburned and endless, looking in the dim moonlight like a great gray-brown quilt. No campfires, no movement, no sign of life. The night sounds missing in the burned valley were present here, but there was no sign of human activity, no indication they were not the only three people in the world.

"I think we'll be okay for awhile," he said, dropping back to the wagon. "I checked the map at the river, an' there's two towns—Jeffrey and Batwing Junction—both about two days' ride from here but in near about opposite directions. Once those bushwhackers figure out for sure we ain't dead an' we ain't turned back toward Fort Collins, they'll be after us again. Hopefully, though, we got a fifty-fifty chance they won't know for sure we're goin' towards Jeffrey. With luck we'll lose 'em for good.

"But we're goin' t' have t' move fast while it's still dark. The more distance we can put 'tween us 'n' them before daylight the better."

Riding at a slight angle from the river to put even more distance between them and the mouth of the pass, they picked up the trail a few miles down the flatlands just as the sky was beginning to lighten. As dawn broke, several head of cattle wandered across the trail ahead of them, telling Calico they had entered cattle country, and he was glad of it—the more cattle around, the easier it would be to disguise their passage. The trail was a mass of hoofprints, but fresh wagon tracks would be a dead giveaway to any pursuer.

Weary and saddlesore, they ate a hasty cold breakfast beside the trail, once again in sight of the river, which had meandered toward and away from them ever since they entered the flatlands. A mile or so farther down the trail, they encountered a large number of cattle, apparently broken off from a herd, moving across the river from left to right. When they started to parallel the trail, Calico briefly considered joining them, at least until they were far enough from the river to make it impossible for them to be followed, but then thought better of it. Staying with the herd would only slow them down.

"We should be safe come mid-afternoon, if ya can hold out," he said, again dropping back to the wagon.

"We'll make it," Sarah said in a firm tone.

Though she had said practically nothing since the fire, her quiet acceptance of their plight had impressed him. So, of course, had Josh, but Josh was almost a man, and men were expected to accept hardship calmly.

They caught sight of a few random cowhands from time to time, and Calico guessed that the main body of the herd wasn't far off. They had left the stragglers some time before and, stopping briefly a few times to rest the horses and themselves, were now well out into open range country again. Ahead of them lay another long, funnel-shaped valley and a range of substantial-looking hills. To their right, just beyond a low rise, they could see the dust and hear the lowing of the main herd—a really big one, he judged.

Rather than attempt going any farther—they had, he estimated, been on the move for sixteen hours—they left the trail to circle a small hill and pulled up to make camp beneath a huge old oak at the foot of a larger hill that separated them from the main herd. A small stream a hundred yards or so away provided them with fresh water, and Sarah took the opportunity to seclude herself behind some low scrub at the stream's edge to bathe and wash out her soot-stained clothes.

Josh and Calico were next, and he longed for the feel of the fresh, clear water flowing around his tired muscles. He tried to resist—and failed—looking at Josh as the young man got undressed, admiring his body, his smile, his laugh, the way he moved. He was equally and pleasantly aware that Josh watched unabashedly as he removed his clothes.

He didn't have much time to ponder the significance of the young man's attention, however, since Josh, plunging into the water, suddenly laughed and slapped his hand in a wide arc into the chill water, sending a small wall of it over Calico's chest. Exuberant as a puppy, Josh splashed about noisily, laughing and trying to engage him in some rough horseplay.

Calico took it all in good-natured silence until Josh got a little too playful and tried to dunk him. They wrestled for a moment, until he felt Josh's hand accidentally brush against his naked crotch. The young man's touch—and the thought the contact might not have been accidental—disturbed him, made him both nervous and pleased.

He rose just far enough out of the water to grasp the boy by the shoulders and force him down into a sitting position.

"Now soak," he growled.

Josh was suitably cowed, and Calico was careful to hold him at arms' length lest he notice the response to his touch.

Though there was ample game in the area, Calico chose not to hunt in deference to the huge herd's proximity—he knew how skittish a herd could become at the sound of gunfire. Instead, Sarah helped him prepare a hearty meal from the staples they'd brought with them, the first really good meal they'd had in several days.

Just before sundown, a lone rider appeared briefly at the top of the rise separating them from the herd—one of the cowhands, they assumed. The man waved, and they returned his greeting. Then he disappeared back down the hill.

Daylight gave way gracefully to a magnificent evening, leaving a spectacular sunset as a souvenir. As they sat talking by the small fire, Calico was aware that this was the kind of evening that reaffirmed his conviction he wouldn't change his life for anything city life might have to offer.

A warm, lazy breeze carried the lowing of cattle from the other side of the rise as they prepared for sleep. Even Sarah opted to trade the bed of the wagon for the softness of the grass-cushioned ground.

The twins drifted off to sleep, and Calico was just about to join them when five shots, crisp as freshly bitten apples, tore through the air from behind the rise. Several more shots followed—just how many he couldn't tell because a new sound muffled them, the sound of whinnying horses, bellowing steers and, most ominous of all, a low, growing thunder.

He was on his feet in an instant, throwing his blanket off and reaching for his rifle. Josh and Sarah, startled, sat upright, confusion revealed on their faces by the flickering light of the campfire.

"Get up, quick!" he shouted.

The thunder was becoming louder, a long, low, steady rumble; and it was headed their way. He could feel it in the ground beneath his stocking feet.

"What is it?" Sarah asked, fear in her voice.

"Stampede," he said, racing to untether the horses then slapping them on the rump to start them running. Instinctively, they headed away from the approaching roar.

There was no time to flee—the herd was too close, and he had seen stampedes before. He looked around quickly for any possible shelter.

"The tree!" he called, his voice almost lost in the rising thunder. "Get in the tree!"

The twin stood as if hypnotized, staring in the direction of the rise, where they could now see a broad black mass sweeping toward them. Calico snatched up his rifle, and grabbing Sarah by the arm climbed with her onto the wagon, which stood beneath the lowest of the giant tree's branches. Josh jumped up beside her then scrambled easily onto a thick branch and reached down to help her.

In her long nightdress, Sarah was having trouble getting her leg hooked over the branch. Calico boosted her just as the first of the charging animals smashed into the wagon with a resounding jolt that nearly sent him sprawling onto the ground. Josh hoisted his sister onto the branch just as another huge beast struck the wagon another shuddering blow. There was the sound of splintering wood, and the wagon rocked crazily.

Calico handed his rifle up to Sarah then threw himself at the space between Josh and the trunk of the tree. A stampeding steer smacked his dangling legs with tremendous force, almost causing him to lose his grip. Clinging on with grim determination, he managed to pull himself onto the limb and safety.

The sounds of splintering wood and snapping boards as the wagon was crushed beneath the rushing herd were lost in the roar of hooves and bellowing. Eventually, the tide ebbed, its last trickles joined by the frantic forms of cowboys attempting to halt the stampede. They rode past, not even seeing the three forms huddled in the oak tree.

When the thunder had died to the hush of distant surf, Calico lowered himself from the tree and reached up to help Sarah down. Josh jumped lightly to the ground. Around them was desolation. Nothing of their camp remained; the wagon was a jumbled mass of broken boards and bits of wood trailing off in the direction of the departed herd. There was no sign of the horses, though Calico was sure Dusty at least would return in the morning, and he could then go out and find the others.

Until then, there was little they could do except try to rest.

CHAPTER 7

THE WHINNYING OF HORSES BROUGHT CALICO AWAKE LIKE A SHOT, HIS HAND REACHING for his rifle even as his eyes opened.

"Easy, Mister...easy," someone said, and he discovered three mounted riders looking down on them with mild curiosity.

Josh and Sarah were by now awake, Sarah brushing at her clothes self-consciously, Josh rubbing the sleep from his eyes.

"These your horses?" the man on the right, the same one who had spoken before, asked. Behind him stood Daniel, Belle and Dusty.

"Yeah, they're ours."

The three cowhands relaxed, and their spokesman leaned forward to hold out the reins.

"We found 'em this morning, figured they must be yours, though t' be honest with ya, we really didn't expect to find ya alive—not after last night." He gestured toward the scattered ruins of the wagon. "Ya oughtta be mighty thankful for this here tree."

Calico, rising and taking the reins, brushed himself off with his free hand.

"We sure are," he said. "An' we're mighty grateful to ya for bringin' our horses. I was figurin' on settin' out after 'em on foot."

"Y'all save anythin'?" the man in the middle asked in a deep Southern drawl, indicating the shattered wreckage of the wagon.

Calico glanced around. "We ain't had much time to look, but I'd say just about all we got's our hides, an' that's plenty enough for me, considerin'."

"Well, leastways ya got your saddles," the leader said, pointing to the base of the tree. Calico looked in the direction the man was pointing and remembered he and Josh had put the saddles at the base of the tree—fortunately, on the opposite side from the path of the stampede. He was vastly relieved to see his vest, which contained his father's pocketwatch, still draped over his.

"Where you headin'?" the third man asked. He was smaller than the others, with a round chubby face that reminded Calico of a chipmunk.

"Jeffrey."

"Well, y'all should be able to make there by tonight," the Southerner said.

"I reckon ya might like a cup o' coffee," the leader added, swinging down from his horse and reaching into his saddlebags.

"We sure could!" Josh volunteered.

"Sarah, why don't you an' Josh build us a little fire? Ya shouldn't have no trouble findin' firewood," Calico said with a wry smile.

The twins set off while the other two riders dismounted.

"Name's Calico. Calico Ramsay," he said, extending his hand to the leader of the cowhands.

"Mitch Evans," the man said, grasping it firmly. "This here..." He indicated the Southerner. "...is Sam Downing. The feisty one there's Hank Garrison. We're out o' Brandy Pass, headed for the rail line in Fort Collins with our herd...or what's left of it."

Josh and Sarah returned with the wood, and Josh began preparing the fire, a chore at which he had become fairly proficient over the past several days. Mitch handed Sarah a sack of coffee while he fished a battered coffeepot from his bulky bedroll. Josh took it and headed to the stream for water.

While Sarah tended the fire, the four men sat down beneath the tree, Mitch and Sam rolling and lighting cigarettes.

"Ya have any idea who started that ruckus last night?" Calico asked as Josh came running back with the water, not wanting to miss anything. Sarah set the pot on three large rocks in the center of the fire then joined the men.

"Not a clue," Mitch said, shaking his head. "Stupid fool thing to do—they stampeded the damned critters..." He shot a glance at Sarah, reached his fingers hastily to his hat. "Sorry, Missy. Anyway, they stampeded the whole herd up the slope. If they'd o' been any kind o' rustlers they'd o' swept 'em down the slope, where they could o' gotten off with a whole mess of 'em. Pretty stupid, if ya ask me. As it is, they just charged 'em right past ya up the slope a ways, an' that slowed 'em down so they just sort o' swept off in two slow arcs in either direction. We got most of 'em back already, 'cept for them what fell and got trampled."

"Any of your men hurt?" Calico asked.

"Nope, luckily. The good Lord must o' been on our side. I just can't figure out why anybody'd pull such a dumb-fool stunt like that."

Calico had a fairly good idea but kept it to himself. Josh was enjoying the whole thing immensely, while Sarah seemed lost in her thoughts.

"What do ya need in the line of supplies?" Mitch asked. "We ain't got much to spare, but you're welcome to what they is."

"That's mighty good of ya," Calico said sincerely. "I don't rightly know what we'll really need till we can look around a little an' see if your cattle missed anything." He suddenly realized that he, Josh and Sarah were all without shoes. "Sure hope we find our boots, though," he said with a grin. "This's the second pair of boots I lost in the last week. Danged if I ain't gonna tie the next pair 'round my neck."

They all laughed, Calico relieved to see that even Sarah had come out of her reverie and joined in.

"Tell ya what, though," he continued, "if ya can spare us enough vittles to get us to Jeffrey, we'd be much obliged."

"No trouble atall," Mitch said. "Sam here'll bring ya some grub from our chuckwagon. Wish we could help ya out on whatever else ya might need, but we're travelin' a little light ourselves."

"I know," Calico said, finishing his coffee and handing the cup back to Sam. "We're much in your debt as it is. We can get whatever we need in Jeffrey, like as not. They got a hotel there?"

"Finest hotel this side o' Batwing Junction," Hank said. "Great food, too," he added, patting his more than ample stomach appreciatively. "They got two roomin' houses, too, case the hotel's full o' cowhands An' then, o' course, there's Miss Daisy's."

He gave Calico a broad and knowing wink that was not lost on the twins.

Calico held back a smile, nodded and said, "Much obliged."

"What's Miss Daisy's?" Josh asked, looking directly at him.

His sister's arm shot out, and she hit him on the shoulder.

"Don't you be so nosy, smarty," she snapped.

Josh looked with bewilderment at Calico, who winked and gave him a half-smile.

"Later, boy," he said.

"Well, we got to be gettin' back," Mitch said, rising to his feet. He was followed by the other cowboys, who poured their remaining coffee on the fire.

"Oh, two things," Calico said as the visitors mounted up. "If you're plannin' to push through Master's Pass up yonder, I suggest ya go around. There's been a range fire, and there's not a stick of fodder for a day's ride. An' if ya should meet up with anybody askin' about us, would ya tell 'em we're headed f'r Batwing Junction?"

He sensed that Mitch wouldn't ask any questions, and he didn't, merely tipped his hat and said, "Thanks for the tip, Calico. I'll send Sam back with the grub. Good luck t' ya."

With a wave, the three cowboys rode off.

Calico picked up a large board from the ruins of the wagon and scooped dirt over the fire, stirring the ashes to make sure it was completely out.

"One range fire's enough," he said.

The three shoeless adventurers then set out to see what, if anything, remained of their supplies. At the creek's edge, partly in the water, Sarah found the battered remains of the valise containing her clothes, and she shouted in delight at the discovery. Josh found one of his boots and the leather vest he'd bought in Fort Collins, heavily trampled but still usable. A few moments later he let out a warwhoop as he came upon the small pouch containing the money wired by their lawyer. All three rejoiced in this find, since it meant they could get whatever they needed in Jeffrey without undue delay.

By the time Sam rode up with a satchel filled with supplies, they had gathered everything they could find that was still usable and put it in a pile beneath the tree. Calico had salvaged six bullets from his cartridge belt—and fervently hoped they would encounter no further trouble before they reached Jeffrey.

As Sam was getting ready to mount up for the return to the herd, he motioned Calico closer with a jerk of his head.

"Ah see y'all only got the one rifle," he said.

Calico nodded.

"Well, it 'pears t' me y'all might need somethin' extra." He reached into his saddlebag and withdrew an ivory-handled pistol. "It ain't much—Ah won it in a poker game from some fancy dude a while back. I don't cotton much to pistols, but it does shoot, an' it's better than nothin'. You're welcome to it," he said, extending it by the barrel.

Calico took it with a nod of thanks—he knew better than to offer to pay for it. Sam returned the nod and got on his horse.

Sarah and Josh joined Calico in expressing their thanks once again. Sam wished them well and rode off, back toward the reassembled herd.

Calico and Josh saddled Bell and Daniel, gathered their meager belongings and put them and the food Sam had brought in makeshift saddlebags made out of pieces of clothing they'd found, tying them to Josh's and Sarah's saddle horns.

Then Calico turned to Sarah.

"Well, Sarah, it looks like you're about to become a cowboy, whether ya want to or not. Think ya can do it?"

"I can do anything I put my mind to," she said, her jaw set with determination.

Calico smiled at her warmly.

"I just bet you can," he said.

She had surprised him when she stepped behind the tree to change, and emerged in an outfit she had bought in Fort Collins—a divided skirt made for riding. She couldn't have known at the time she'd be needing it so soon. He twined his fingers into a makeshift stirrup, and she stepped into it so he could hoist her up into the saddle. When she was seated, she leaned forward to take the reins Josh handed her.

"Daniel's more a wagon horse than a ridin' horse," Calico told her, "but he'll be okay once the two of ya get used to one another."

Though few western horses were broken for both saddle and harness, the livery man had told Calico his kids would miss Daniel because they had used to ride him around the farm. He had accepted the saddle easily and now bore his rider without protest.

"What are you going to do, Calico? You don't have a saddle," Sarah said.

"Heck, girl, Western boys don't need no saddle, they're just a luxury. I was ridin' bareback when I was five, so don't ya worry 'bout me, thanks." To prove his point, he jumped easily onto Dusty's back, reaching forward to pat him on the neck affectionately while holding the jerry-rigged halter he'd made from pieces of the wagon harness.

Josh, too, mounted up, and they started off toward Jeffrey.

For a girl who had only ridden sidesaddle, Sarah proved herself readily adaptable to riding Western style. They traveled abreast through open country broken only by occasional clumps of oak. Calico preferred the open range, where he could see far enough in any given direction to be warned of possible danger—there was nowhere four men could hide without being seen. Just to play it safe, he steered well clear of any stands of trees.

"Calico," Sarah said, after a considerable period of silence, "how do you suppose they were able to follow us, after all the trouble we took to be sure they wouldn't?"

It was a question that had been in the back of his own mind since the stampede.

"I don't rightly know," he admitted, and then a thought struck him like a winter breeze. "Unless..."

"Unless what?" Josh asked.

"Unless they know where we're goin'."

"You mean Aunt Rebecca's?" Sarah asked, sounding incredulous.

"'Fraid I do." It was the first time the idea had occurred to him, and it was a bone-chilling one. The question of how they knew opened all sorts of possibilities in his mind...and possible dangers. If their pursuers knew where they were going, they could not be sure of being safe anywhere. Whoever the unknown attackers were, all they'd have to do was stay ahead of them and set up ambushes at their leisure—there was only one practical route to Bow Ridge from where they were.

Calico wished he had more than a pistol and six spare bullets for his rifle—he had a feeling he might need them, and soon...

CHAPTER 8

THE RIDE TO JEFFREY WAS WITHOUT INCIDENT, THOUGH ALL THREE TRAVELERS WERE ON edge, eyes and ears alert for the slightest hint of trouble. The countryside grew progressively rougher as they neared the foothills. Several times, as they approached sites of possible ambush, Calico had the twins stop while he rode ahead to check it out.

Jeffrey was located at the base of the most-used pass through the mountains for a hundred miles in either direction. It acted like the mouth of a funnel, through which wagon trains, trappers, miners and travelers poured. Calico knew from consulting his map that only three towns now lay between them and their destination—Jeffrey, Toohigh and Clantonville. Between Jeffrey and Toohigh, a single rugged trail was the only link; there were no alternative routes he could even consider with the twins along when there was none even experienced mountain men would attempt willingly.

Toohigh stood just beyond the crest of the ridge. From there, the going should be easier into Clantonville; and once they hit Clantonville it was only a matter of thirty or forty miles to Bow Ridge and the Rebecca Durant.

Though he constantly watched for danger, Calico couldn't keep his mind from pondering the unknown source of their troubles, and from the fact that after the twins had reached their destination he was going to miss them. The days they had spent together had given him a growing admiration for both; he regretted the probability he'd never get to know them better

That he would particularly miss one of them was a feeling/thought he struggled to ignore. There was something that grew inside him every time he looked at Josh, and despite his earlier determination that he was misinterpreting Josh's interest, he was increasingly sure his feelings were reciprocated.

They reached Jeffrey shortly before nightfall. It was not, as so many plains towns were, specifically geared to serving the needs of cattlemen—ranchers preferred to drive their herds the long way around rather than risk losing them on precipitous mountain trails. As a result, there was a certain absence of the chaos usually associated with cowboy-centered towns—not quite so many bars, more merchants devoted to the needs of travelers.

With only a small amount of daylight remaining to them, Calico checked out the one hotel and the two rooming houses, all located within sight of one another, finally selecting the hotel only because its location and relationship to surrounding buildings provided the best protection from ambush. There was also a livery stable a few doors down, and he wanted to be able to ensure the horses were well fed and looked after.

The hotel clerk seemed to find it not at all unusual to have three barefoot travelers check in. Calico specifiied rooms at the back on the second floor—which, he had seen from the street, looked out on a deep gully and would therefore make access difficult for any would-be assassins.

Sarah, bone-tired from unaccustomed Western riding all day, went immediately to her room, escorted by Josh, who was to stand guard outside the door to the bathroom at the end of the hall while she took a bath. Calico led the horses to the livery stable and made several inquiries as to the condition of the trail between Jeffrey and Toohigh. He knew it would be pointless to ask about suspicious strangers, since Jeffrey was a town full of transients, quite a few of whom could easily be classified as "suspicious."

The general store was closed, so boot buying would have to wait for the morning. He returned to the hotel and, while Josh had his bath and before taking his own, made arrangements with the cook to have their supper sent up to their rooms. It was the first kitchen-cooked meal they'd had since Fort Collins, and they relished every bite.

There was no door connecting the rooms, but the windows closest to the dividing wall were only about three feet apart. After dinner, Calico went with Sarah to her room, closed and locked the door from the inside then slid the heavy dresser in front of it. Sure she would now be safe from intruders, he bid her goodnight, crossed to the window, opened it and swung out and across into the open one in his and Josh's room. After repeating the barricading precautions, he began to remove his outer clothes for bed.

"Aren't you going to go see what Miss Daisy's is all about?" Josh asked, and Calico was mildly surprised by the serious look on the young man's face.

"I know what Miss Daisy's is all about," he said, punching him playfully on the arm. "An' I think you do, too."

"I'm not a kid, Calico," Josh said quietly. He then moved to the far side of the bed, sat on it with his back to Calico and began removing his shirt. "Do you have a…a woman friend at home, Calico?" he asked, without turning.

Calico looked over at him, his brow slightly furrowed.

"No, Josh, I don't," he said. "How about you? You leave a lot of brokenhearted gals missin' you in Chicago?" He intended it as a teasing remark, and was surprised by the flatness of his voice.

Josh had removed his shirt, and now stood up and turned to face him.

"No," he said. "I didn't."

Calico turned away quickly, making a pretense of adjusting the angle of his rifle, which leaned against the headboard of the bed. He couldn't fool himself into thinking he didn't know exactly why his heart was beating so fast, why he wanted so badly not to have turned away, why he wanted to continue to look—no, to stare at the half-naked youth, to reach out and touch him.

"Well," he said, a little gruffly, "you'll grow into it in time."

Slowly, he turned and forced himself to look at Josh again. His gaze moved slowly up Josh's body, over the velvet-smooth torso and the developing musculature that clearly showed the rapid transition from youth to manhood. The ache in his chest making it impossible for him to break his stare, he continued his slow survey to the broadening shoulders and the young man's solid neck and chin, then up the face until he came to Josh's eyes, which were looking directly into his.

When Josh spoke, his words were so soft Calico wasn't sure he heard them correctly.

"I'm almost eighteen years old, Calico, and I know a lot more than you think I know. No, I will not grow into it. Did you?"

Calico turned away again abruptly and sat. He said nothing, but felt lightheaded as he leaned down to take off his tattered socks. He forced himself not to look at the youth again, though he knew Josh was removing his pants, and remained with his back turned until he felt the bed move as Josh climbed under the sheets.

"Well, we best get some sleep, I reckon," he said, reaching to turn down the lamp and feeling like an idiot for having made such a lame remark.

When the room was dark, he stretched out, fully clothed, on top of the covers, close to his edge of the bed.

After a moment of silence, Josh said, "You didn't answer my question. Did you grow into it?"

He was very careful not to look at him, instead staring through the darkness at the ceiling.

"No, Josh, I didn't."

"Goodnight, Calico," Josh murmured.

"'Night, boy."

He did not find sleep easily.

As evidence of their exhaustion, the twins were still sleeping at seven-thirty. Calico, who awoke with the dawn as usual, got up and studied the map carefully, looking for possible areas of particular danger, and for alternate routes once they passed Toohigh. He found his eyes drifting from the map to Josh, and he watched the young man sleeping until a pressure—the now-familiar soft ache in his chest—forced him to reject the path his mind was taking and turn again to the map

He was anxious to get out and get going but knew the twins deserved and needed the rest. It again occurred to him how totally different a world they were now in. The realization of the vast gap between the pampered Eastern life they'd led until just a few days ago, and the far more basic, danger-filled life they'd now entered, made him even more appreciative of their spunk and spirit.

Josh awoke just as Calico had decided to go over and wake him. The lanky teenager propped himself up on his elbows, blinking his eyes at the day.

"It's been so long since I've been in a bed I'd almost forgotten how good it feels," he said.

Calico grinned and nodded.

"From the way ya was goin' at it, I figured ya planned to stay there indefinitely. Ya realize it's almost eight o'clock? You city folks sure don't see much daylight."

Josh threw the covers aside and sprang out of bed.

"Aw, come on, now, Calico, it's not that bad."

"I guess not." Calico chuckled, following Josh's every movement. "Maybe I'm just a mite jealous. Now, ya get dressed an' go over an' knock on Sarah's door to see if she's up. If she is, I'll cross over and open up her room so she can get out."

"How come you let us sleep so long, Calico? Shouldn't we be starting out? Especially since those men are after us."

"Well, one day ain't goin' t' hurt," he said, pushing the dresser away from the door and back to its original position. "'Sides, the way I figure it, they ain't after us, exactly. Right about now they're probably waitin' for us, an' it'll do 'em some good to just sit an' wait a spell."

He watched as Josh pulled on his pants and hopped, one leg at a time, into his socks.

"What are we going to do?" Josh asked, reaching for his shirt.

"Well, first thing is some breakfast—I imagine you're ready to eat again."

He nodded.

"Then we get the supplies we need, includin' some boots. Then we're goin' t' get ya a gun." Calico paused, relishing the young man's obvious delight. "But I want ya t' understand a gun ain't no toy. I hope we're never in a spot where ya have t' use it, but if we are, I want t' be sure ya got your wits about ya." He looked around the room to be sure he had everything back in its proper place. Sensing rather than seeing Josh's eyes on him, he shrugged. "Still, I guess you're a pretty sensible young fella...an' I'm glad you're on my side."

He could practically hear Josh's grin.

"Now, suppose ya go check on your sister so we can get t' doin' what's gotta be done."

Buying boots, a change of clothes for all of them, blankets, food, saddlebags, tack for Daniel and a new rifle for Josh put a large dent in both the day and their pooled assets. Sarah, after her experience riding Daniel in the split-skirt dress and to Calico's unspoken pleasure, sought out a pair of women's riding breeches.

It was nearly one-thirty before they were on their way up the heavily traveled mountain trail. In the space of two hours, they saw at least three groups of travelers: a family in a Conestoga that apparently had broken off from a wagon train and was returning to Jeffrey, two riders with mules laden with stacks of beaver pelts, and a lone rider who came up fast behind them, making Calico extremely nervous, but passed them without a word and disappeared up the trail.

All this traffic both comforted and worried him. On the one hand, he reasoned, with so many people coming and going, whoever was after them might think twice about an ambush; on the other hand, never having had a good look at their pursuers, he viewed each person they met along the way as a potential enemy.

Nearing sundown, as the increasingly rough terrain began to be bathed in long shadows, they came upon a large wooded area on relatively smooth ground. Leaving the trail, they located a spot Calico considered safe, sheltered by three large boulders and a large stand of pine, and made camp, building a small fire close to one of the boulders to minimize chances of its being seen. Sarah, for the first time since the journey began, volunteered to make supper alone, a gesture that pleased Calico as further evidence of her adjustment to Western living, and also freed him of an unwelcome chore.

The smell of frying meat and potatoes and the aroma of coffee put them all in a mellow mood and helped relieve some of the tension of their long journey. Calico talked of his life with Dan, relating stories of his first ranch experiences and various adventures in learning to become a cowboy, to Josh's complete fascination. Sarah asked him about social life for girls her age, but his responses, centered around church socials, barn raisings, picnics and square dances, left her less than enthralled at the prospects of her future life.

"What sort of a woman's your aunt Rebecca?" he asked, in an effort to bring her interests more into the conversation.

"We don't know her all that well," Sarah answered. "She got married and moved away when we were very small. No one ever said it in so many words, but I don't think anyone in the family—especially Grandmother—approved of the marriage, though I can't imagine why. The only time we saw her after she got married was the time she came to visit after Grandmother passed away and..." Her voice dropped and went flat. "...and there was the fire that killed our parents."

"I didn't like her much," Josh volunteered.

"Why's that?" Calico asked, rather sorry he'd brought up the subject.

"Well, she came back home just after Grandmother died, in May, and she was sick a lot, so we didn't see much of her. Kept mostly in her room. Then, when she started to get better, she'd come down to dinner and spend some time with us, and I guess she was okay then."

Josh stirred the fire with a long stick, gazing into the coals in a way that reminded Calico of Dan staring at the end of his cigar. Then, as if suddenly recalling he was not alone, he threw the stick into the fire and continued.

"She was even kind of nice, I suppose. And then her husband, Uncle Mike, came to get her, and boy, did she change! Started acting real funny—"

"She did not!" Sarah interjected. "She just had a relapse of her illness, that's all. That's what Momma told me."

"Well, what sort of man's her husband?" Calico asked, hoping to head off a sibling argument.

"Oh, he's ever so nice," Sarah said. "So handsome, and friendly. He was very kind to both of us."

"Father didn't like him very much," Josh said. "He never said anything, but I could tell. And the funny way Aunt Rebecca was acting—"

"Grandmother had just died, Josh. And she was sick!" Sarah insisted.

"Okay, okay, she was sick," Josh said, throwing his hands in the air. "Anyway, they all had a big argument the night...the night of the fire. You were asleep, but I heard them. Mother and Father and Aunt Rebecca and Uncle Mike—Granddad was away on business." He was once again staring into the flames, talking now more to them than to Calico or Sarah. "I couldn't hear what it was all about, but I knew they were arguing from the tone of Father's voice. Then after a while it was quiet, and I went to sleep.

"About an hour later, I guess it was, we heard the maid screaming. Sarah and I both ran out into the hall at the same time, and the house was on fire. The stairway between our rooms and our parents' was already burning—we couldn't get to them. We yelled and yelled, but they didn't answer. The drapes in the hall caught real easy, and it was like looking through a solid wall of fire, rolling toward us like it was on wheels."

Calico could see the reflection of that other, long-ago fire in Josh's eyes. His voice was low, without emotion—a chilling effect reinforced by Sarah's own facial expression, one that showed plainly she was with her brother, right that moment, in a burning house in Chicago.

"Sarah and I ran into her room and slammed the door, then crawled out her window onto the porte-cochere. Granddad's coach came up just as we climbed out of the window. The servants had a big blanket, and they held it up for Sarah to jump into. I climbed down some vines then jumped the rest of the way.

"Aunt Rebecca was standing there with Uncle Mike, just staring through the open door into the house, watching everything fall down. Granddad asked where Mother and Father were, and Uncle Mike just nodded toward the house. He tried to go in, but the servants held him back. In a little while, the roof fell in, and the walls fell down. Two days later, they found Father's gold watch, all melted, and...and some other things. And that's how we got to be orphans."

The silence around the campfire was broken only by the sound of crickets and, far away, the cry of a wolf.

"And your aunt Rebecca?" Calico prompted gently.

"She and Uncle Mike went back to Colorado right after the funeral," Sarah said, almost visibly pulling herself back into the present. "We got a couple of letters, but we haven't seen her since."

"Calico?"

"Yeah, Josh?"

"Why do we have to go to Aunt Rebecca? We'll be of age soon, and able to do what we want. I mean, why couldn't we just stay with you? Uncle Dan was going to take us. Why couldn't you?"

Calico pursed his lips and rubbed his nose. "I'm real pleased you'd want me to, Josh," he said, painfully aware of how much he meant it, "but..."

"It's not just me," Josh insisted. "Sarah'd like that, too—wouldn't you, Sarah?"

Sarah looked confused and embarrassed, avoiding Calico's eyes. She said nothing.

"No, Josh. You belong with your own kin, somebody who can give you a real home. Your aunt wants you...you belong with her." Calico knew what he was saying was the truth, but that he was saying it as much to convince himself as Josh.

There was a long silence, during which he tried to think of something reassuring to say, but as usual, he found it difficult to put his feelings into words. Finally, he got up, brushed himself off and went to check on the horses.

Returning to find the twins still in silence, Calico cleared his throat awkwardly, and said, "Well, I s'pose we'd best think of gettin' some sleep."

They fixed their bedrolls under the stars, in the shelter of the three boulders, lulled by the sounds of the crickets tufting the thick quilt of the night. As he drifted off to sleep, Calico was haunted by the reflection of the fire in Josh's wide blue eyes.

CHAPTER 9

THE SUN WAS WELL UP IN THE SKY WHEN CALICO AWOKE TO THE SMELL OF COFFEE. Sarah was by the campfire, adding some twigs to revive the coals into flames. Josh was nowhere to be seen but soon appeared around the side of the largest of the boulders with an armload of firewood. He beamed at Calico and said, "'Morning."

Calico shook the cobwebs of sleep out of his head and grunted an unintelligible greeting. He was a little perturbed with himself. Not only was this the latest he'd slept in more than a year, but—far more dangerous under the circumstances—he'd actually slept through the sounds of people moving around him.

Sarah was wrestling with a large slab of bacon, trying to cut slices for the heavy iron skillet they'd purchased in Jeffrey. He struggled into his pants, cursing the necessity to dress and undress under a blanket, then got up and went over to her.

"You're goin' t' take a healthy slice out o' yourself that way, girl," he said, reaching for the meat and extending his other hand for the knife. "See, ya do it like this...cut across the thin side, not down through the top." He sliced a strip expertly then handed both bacon and knife back to her. "Ya'll catch on soon enough," he added with a smile, which she returned.

He turned to Josh. "Josh, what say you an' me go behind the boulders with your rifle, an' ya can show me just how good ya are with it." He realized as he suggested it he wanted to be alone with him as much as determine his level of skill.

Sarah looked up, startled.

"But what about the men who are after us? Won't the sound of shooting tell them where we are?"

Calico picked up his rifle from beside his bedroll, hefting it in his hand as though it were the first time he'd ever handled it. He looked at her, automatically assuming the defensive stance of cowboys everywhere, ready to move instantly in either direction.

"Don't worry," he reassured her. "There's lots of travelers in these parts. An' it's daylight. If they want t' know where we are, they'll know. 'Sides, like I said yesterday, they're probably up ahead of us a ways, waitin' on us. We'll just let 'em."

Josh was like an excited young colt, still with the awkwardness of youth but showing clear signs of emerging adulthood. Calico felt a flush as he looked at him, at the thought that Josh was as eager to be alone with him as he was to be with Josh. With effort, he shoved the thought aside.

They moved around the boulders and down into a narrow gulley with a small stream at the bottom. The stream had worn away the land around it, creating a horseshoe-shaped bluff about ten feet high. Calico didn't want to get too far from Sarah and the campsite, so he pointed out a small tree from which a broken branch still dangled by a strip of bark, halfway down the face of the small bluff and about a hundred feet from them.

"Think you can hit that?" he asked.

Josh smiled, took a left-foot-forward stance, cocked the rifle and raised it to his shoulder. The shot cracked through the still air, muffled somewhat by the surrounding foliage, and the broken branch jerked. Calico was impressed, but said nothing.

Josh recocked the rifle, took aim and fired again, the sound of the shot reminding Calico of ripping cloth. A splinter of wood leapt off the branch.

"Not bad for a city boy," he said, his face showing no emotion. "Let's see how you are with somethin' that moves."

He strode forward, picked up a forearm-sized chunk of driftwood and threw it into the stream. It hit the water, disappeared momentarily, then bobbed to the surface and began riding the swift current. Josh cocked, took aim and fired, recocked without lowering the rifle and fired again, then a third time. Small plumes of water and broken bits of wood spattered into the air.

"Okay, okay!" Calico said in mock exasperation. "Save some bullets for when they might do some good."

Josh grinned, lowered the rifle then turned and headed back up the hill toward camp. Calico put his arm around the youth's shoulders as he passed and walked in step with him. Josh shifted the rifle from his left hand to his right and slipped his arm around Calico's waist. Neither said anything, but Calico was almost painfully aware of how natural it felt.

Breakfast was waiting. As they ate, Calico's attention was drawn to Sarah where she sat with her back against one of the boulders, eating quietly. It struck him he had possibly been unfair by focusing most of his attention on Josh. Even though he knew better, in his heart, he told himself it was partly because he'd had relatively little contact with girls Sarah's age—and little interest in girls or women of any age, he now allowed.

Even so, he could readily acknowledge that Sarah was on the brink of becoming a woman as truly beautiful as her brother was handsome. A wisp of hair toppled over her forehead, sweeping past and just above her bright-blue, long-lashed eyes. Her complexion was flawless, and the outdoor living of the past few days had enhanced the healthful glow of her cheeks.

They were going to be some couple, Josh and Sarah, when they finally matured, and no man or woman would be immune to their charms. He thought it something of a shame that Sarah's beauty would be wasted on a small Colorado ranch. Josh, he knew, he needn't worry about—a man could make his way anywhere and under any conditions; but a woman as lovely as Sarah was sure to be…

He forced himself out of his reverie, finished his coffee and reached for Josh's empty plate.

"Gimme these an' I'll take 'em down to the creek for washin'. While I'm gone, ya can saddle the horses while Sarah packs stuff away."

He took Sarah's proffered tin plate and the forks and tin cups, moving down to the stream without looking back. He was aware that a part of him wished Josh would follow but knew it would be best if he didn't—he didn't fully know how to deal with what was happening between them, and he needed time to sort it all out.

It was a peaceful day, and he hoped it would stay that way. He regretted having to leave this idyllic setting and move out into a world of unknown dangers, but dangers were a part of life and had to be faced. When the time came, he would face them, and he'd win.

The trail became narrower and steeper, the landscape more jagged. Huge boulders, in the ages-long process of splitting off from overhanging cliffs, towered menacingly above them, as if waiting for the right moment to tumble down.

Their route began to alternate between narrow, deep gullies barely wide enough for a wagon to cliff-hugging pathways with sheer walls of rock rising above on one side and dropping away dizzyingly on the other. Ruts worn in the center of steeper portions of the trail indicated where men, horses and oxen had formed chains to haul wagons up or ease them down particularly difficult sections. In at least three places, looking over the edge, Josh called attention to, far below, the remains of the ones that didn't make it.

They finally reached Toohigh, a small cluster of weathered buildings on the saddle of a ridge that marked the crest of the mountain range, about four in the afternoon. Already the shadows from surrounding peaks were growing long, like ghostly fingers reaching out to engulf them.

A wagon train from Jeffrey was camped on a small flat of land about a quarter-mile outside of town, and Calico had a momentary pang of memory as he watched people moving about in the center of the rough circle of wagons. The usual bustle and distant music usually associated with wagon trains was missing, the travelers too exhausted from the long climb to do anything but eat and sleep in preparation for the equally long descent. It had taken the train three days to make the climb; it would take another two to reach the level country beyond.

Of the twenty-odd buildings making up Toohigh, five were saloons. There was one dormitory-style "hotel," one general store, one livery stable/blacksmith. The rest were unidentifiable as to either purpose or inhabitants.

With two hours of daylight before them, Calico debated whether to try moving beyond the town, then decided not to risk being caught by nightfall on a section of unfamiliar mountain trail. Besides, he reasoned, they would probably be safer with other people nearby, even though their pursuers might be among them.

They set up camp in a small clearing between the town and the wagon train. After unsaddling the horses, Calico set up the campfire, urging Josh and Sarah to wander down to the train in search of young people their own age. Josh made it clear he would prefer to remain at the campsite, but Calico was well aware the twins had enjoyed no other company than his since leaving Fort Collins and insisted he go with his sister. Perhaps, he told himself yet again, much of what he perceived to be going on between him and Josh was largely his imagination responding to Josh's natural need for male companionship—

that if he had the opportunity to associate with other people, especially other young men his own age, he'd lose interest. But even as he thought it, a large part of him didn't believe it.

Loneliness was a fact of Western living, and Calico had long since grown accustomed to it, even to the point of enjoying being solitary most of the time. But for active youngsters used to the bustle of city life and a social circle unimaginable to him, the crushing loneliness of vast open spaces and few people would be a heavy burden.

Josh returned alone shortly before sunset.

"Where's Sarah?" Calico asked.

"She's at the wagon train, with one of the families," Josh replied. "They've got a son just a little older than us."

"What about girls?" Calico asked. "Wasn't there any girls there your age?"

"None that I saw, except one, and she was married and had a baby. But, then, I wasn't looking for girls." Looking for a reaction and receiving none, he hunkered down beside Calico at the fire. "Sarah wants to know if its okay if she stays to supper with that farmer and his folks. I told her I'd come back and get her if it wasn't."

Calico shrugged. "Sure, it's okay with me. Didn't they ask you to stay, too?"

Josh stared into the fire, picking up a stick to push a few unburned pieces of wood into the flames.

"Yeah," he said without looking up, "but I said I had to get back. I'd rather be here with you."

Calico remained silent a moment, filled once again with the sense of a developing relationship. He wasn't sure he was ready for it.

"Well," he said, reaching into the saddlebags for food, "we might as well have our supper. Then, later on, you go back to the train an' fetch Sarah. Close as it is, I don't want her walkin' back here alone."

But neither of them seemed to be in any great hurry, and Josh plied Calico with questions about life on the range, about ranching, raising cattle, dangers commonly encountered and a myriad of other subjects of interest to a city boy suddenly thrust into a new and, to him, adventure-filled lifestyle. Throughout their talk, though, Calico sensed Josh had something else on his mind.

Finally, after a slight pause in the conversation, he said, "What do you think of me, Calico?"

Caught by surprise, he was at a loss. After a moment, he said, "I'm not sure what you mean, boy."

Josh was staring at him, and it made him once again both nervous and…

He couldn't pin it down, but the sensation was warm, and good, and like he'd never felt before Josh entered his life.

"That's just it—*boy.* You really do think I'm still a boy, don't you?" His tone was a combination of frustration and anger.

Calico started to speak, not having any idea at all what he was going to say, and was relieved when Josh continued.

"You think I'm a kid who isn't old enough to know what I want."

Calico knew exactly what Josh was getting at, and he had known they would have to address it at some point. But now that the point had come, he was more nervous than he'd imagined he could or would be. Rather than say anything, he shrugged, hoping Josh would continue.

"I do know what I want, Calico. I've known what I wanted since I was six years old. It's not something I'll grow out of. It's not something I've ever been ashamed of, or felt I have to be ashamed of. It's who I am—who I've always been and who I'll always be. I always knew what I wanted, but I never found it until…"

He paused, staring into the fire, then turned to face Calico, who had been watching him intently, unable to take his eyes off the young man.

"Somehow," Josh continued, keeping his eyes locked with Calico's, "I've felt since the day you met us at the train station you understood that. Sarah thinks so, too. If we didn't, I couldn't be talking to you now. You do know what I'm talking about, don't you, Calico?"

Calico felt almost dizzy. He was flooded with feelings that were both familiar and alien. He realized they had been with him all his life, but he had never been in a position to fully acknowledge them before.

He nodded.

"Yeah, I think I know, Josh."

"Did you ever…do you…feel the same way, Calico?"

The older man sighed deeply, a little embarrassed at the thought that even Sarah had seen something he had so carefully hidden all his life.

"Yeah, Josh," he said finally, "I guess just about everything ya said's pretty much the same fer me, 'cept you're a lot more aware of it than I been. I always just figgered I was different'n most men. Not that it ever bothered me much, or that I ever thought there was anything wrong with it, but feelin's are kind o' private out here—folks, 'specially men, don't show 'em all that much.

"So, till you come along, I just sort o' kept everythin' inside. I gotta tell ya it feels kind o' funny puttin' words to things I never spoke out loud about before in my whole life."

They sat in silence a long moment, Calico staring at the fire, trying to sort out the flood of feelings washing through him.

Finally, Josh spoke again. "You think there might be a chance, Calico?"

He looked up, thinking, but again not quite sure, he knew what Josh meant.

"A chance?"

"For…for you and me." Josh said quietly. "To…to be together."

Calico ran one hand over his face and thought another long moment before replying.

"Ya sure do know how to bowl a man over, bo—Josh," he said with a weak grin. "I'd be lyin' if I didn't say that a big a part o' me wants t' say yes. But it ain't that easy. Out here, the law means a lot to decent folks, and by the law you're still a kid." He raised his hand quickly to forestall the anticipated response. "But it ain't just that. Certain other…things…ain't looked on kindly by most folk." He said nothing for a moment then sighed deeply and continued. "We're talkin' about somethin' that's mighty hard f'r me t' find words for, Josh. I thought about it a lot, I guess, an' I guess it's somethin' I wanted all my life, too."

"Have you ever…you know…been with other men?"

Calico said nothing as he studied Josh's handsome face.

"That's somethin' I don't feel comfortable talkin' about right now," he said at last.

Josh looked at the ground.

"I'm sorry," he said. "I didn't mean…"

"It's nothin' t' be sorry about," Calico said. "It's just that I don't think this is the time or the place fer a conversation like that."

Josh scowled, and his voice reflected his frustration.

"When will be?" he asked. "And—by the law—I'll be an adult in a week, and nothing will have changed except that I'll be at Aunt Rebecca's and you'll be somewhere between there and your ranch and we might never see each other again."

That had been in the back of Calico's mind long before now; but like so many things actually being spoken about for the first time in his life, the impact only now registered.

He nodded. "What you say about your just about bein' an adult in the eyes of the law is true enough. But ya ain't quite there yet. When ya are, then you're free to do whatever ya want. You an' me only knowed each other less than two weeks, an' 's much of an adult's ya might be already, ya still got a lot o' livin' t' do, and I don't want t' stand in the way of your doin' it." He smiled a lot less sincerely than he'd intended, and raised his hand again to forestall Josh's objections. "If there's one thing I learned, it's that it's lots better t' *grow* inta somethin' than t' jump inta it."

"But we'll be at Aunt Rebecca's soon, and you'll be leaving us there!" Josh persisted.

"True enough," Calico said "An' that'll give ya time t' think. I got nine years on ya, Josh. I never put words t' it before, but I think I been waitin' all this time, too. So I reckon I can wait a while longer. I just want ya t' have the time t' be sure ya know that what ya really want is what ya think ya want now. Ya understand me?"

Eyes downcast, Josh nodded.

"An' one more thing—'bout me callin' ya 'boy.' My Uncle Dan called me 'boy' right up t' the day he died, an' I know he didn't mean no disrespect by it. I think I know now it was his way o' lettin' me know he cared about me." Calico stirred the fire with a stick then looked into Josh's face. "Ya just keep that in mind if I should call ya 'boy' again sometime."

The two sat in silence until Calico said, "Well, it's 'bout time we had our supper an' then ya c'n go get Sarah."

The meal was prepared and eaten in awkward silence; neither Josh nor Calico had much of an appetite. Calico was very much aware that in his entire life he had never put as many of his inner thoughts into words as he had just done. It was both liberating and exhausting.

When he finished eating and had cleaned his plate as well as he could with leaves for later washing, Josh rose without speaking and turned toward the wagon train. Calico stopped him.

"Josh?"

He turned around.

"About there maybe bein' a chance for us t'...well, ya know...I think I'd like t' find out. But let's take our time, okay?"

Josh's face brightened, and he nodded.

"Okay, Calico," he said, and moved off into the growing darkness.

"Hey, Josh," Calico called again. "Don't forget your rifle."

The younger man, beaming, returned to pick up his rifle and gave Calico a smile that made the bigger man feel weak in the knees.

Calico sat alone by the fire, drinking coffee, still somewhat awestruck over their conversation. His thoughts had always flowed like a wide river, slowly and deliberately. Now, they were like a wild rapids, roiling and churning and leaving him with a sense of having no control over where they were taking him. Josh had opened floodgates within him, and it was only with great effort that he forced them into calmer channels. What would happen would happen, he told himself, and somehow, he knew it would come out all right.

It suddenly struck him that he was alone—really alone—for the first time since he had met the twins. He realized he had never before associated loneliness with the absence of a particular person. He'd never thought much about loneliness at all, for that matter—the last time he'd even given it a conscious thought was in regard to the twins being lonely for social contact. For him, the very concept of loneliness had been a general one.

He had always been something of a loner, even before the death of his parents. Dan had encouraged it, and Western life made the ability to be satisfied being alone a strong asset.

He reflected on Josh's question, and realized one reason he hadn't answered was that he didn't know how he could explain it so Josh could understand. Josh had no idea of the isolation of being on the range for long periods of time. Despite their vehement denials, it was not at all uncommon for men to find release with one another during those periods. And those infrequent contacts had been Calico's only outlet—his only chance to, as Josh had put it, *be with other men.*

But there were strict rules, which he abided by. It was never spoken of, even though it might, rarely, be repeated; and it was for physical release only—any emotional involvement was strictly taboo. Calico had played the game, though he had never allowed himself to initiate it, under those rules, more than once. But he had cheated. On more than one occasion, he had felt something more, but never allowed himself to express it.

But with Josh…

Always before, Calico had managed to be alone without being lonely. This new-for-him awareness of being lonely was not one he enjoyed.

His musings were interrupted by the awareness of someone watching him, and he was immediately alert. He darted a glance to the left without turning his head. In the darkness at the edge of the firelight, he could see a pair of scuffed boots and the cuffs of a very dirty pair of pants. Very slowly, he moved his hand toward his rifle.

"No need for that, son," a voice said from the darkness above the boots. "Your name Calico?"

He turned, and looked up into a tangle of wild whiskers topped by a nondescript shape he took to be a hat of some sort. Between the hat and the whiskers, two bright eyes sparkled in the firelight.

"It might be," he answered casually. "Who wants t' know?"

The night air was split by a high sound somewhere between a laugh and a cackle. It was unnerving, but not frightening, and somehow familiar.

"It might be!" the voice said, the words broken by the laughter. "He sits there lookin' at me with one blue eye and one brown eye, and he says *it might be.*"

In a motion so swift Calico could hardly follow it, the bewhiskered form hunkered down beside him, his bearded face not two feet away, his eyes riveted on Calico's, looking from one to the other.

"Now, how many young men be there this side o' the Mississippi you know got one blue eye an' one brown?" The back of a wrinkled, tanned hand shot out and slapped him on the shoulder. "Huh? How many you figure?"

Calico stared intently at the face before him, trying to picture it without the whiskers. The voice...he knew the voice.

"Don't recognize me, do ya," the whiskered visitor said. Then his brow furrowed and a dirty sleeve rose to vigorously rub the vicinity of a nose. "Well, no reason why ya should, I reckon. Ya was but a lad." The sparkling eyes fixed on the coffeepot balanced on the edge of the fire. "Ya got s'more o' that coffee?"

Calico nodded, tossed the remaining contents of his cup onto the ground to one side and, using his neckerchief as a hot pad, poured the old man a cupful and handed it to him. It was accepted with a curt nod.

As he raised the cup to drink, Calico noticed the man's right index finger was missing.

"Zeke!" he yelled in sudden recognition. "Zeke Cramer!" Leaning forward, he embraced the older man in a bear hug that sent the coffee sloshing onto the ground, just missing scalding his arm. The two men laughed and slapped each other on the back until Zeke started coughing wildly. Calico immediately released him and sat back, alarmed.

"You okay, Zeke?" he asked, concerned.

The coughing subsided, and Zeke wiped his eyes with the heel of his hand.

"'Course I'm okay, ya overgrowed puppy. Jes' not as young's I used t' be. Wild women an' watered booze'll do it every time, boy."

He motioned with his now-empty cup, and Calico refilled it.

"Sorry I can't offer ya nothin' stronger," he said, and Zeke waved his hand as if to dismiss the apology.

"Don't think nothin' of it, boy. We could take a stroll up to the saloon yonder if ya've a mind t' a bit later. Get a little somethin' for snakebite."

"Sure, Zeke," Calico said with a grin. "But what the hell ya doin' here?" Then he slapped his leg with a resounding smack. "You're with the train! Hell, I should o' knowed. But I thought ya'd o' quit all that nonsense years ago."

Zeke gave him a wide grin, showing an almost toothless mouth. "Hell, boy, ya know the only way I'm ever goin' t' settle down's in a pine box. An' even then, they're goin' t' have t' nail the lid on mighty tight."

Just then, Sarah and Josh moved into the firelight and sat down by the fire, Josh placing his rifle carefully at his side, as he'd seen Calico do. He looked at Calico and smiled.

"Mr. Cramer," Sarah said by way of acknowledgment, giving the older man a charming smile.

Calico looked at all three of them. "Ya mind lettin' me in on all o' this?" he asked.

"No mystery, son," Zeke said. "I met this here young beauty this evenin' after supper. Seems she'd been impressin' the Fletcher boy an' his folks with talk of some recent adventures, an' when she mentioned the name Calico Ramsay, I knowed it had t' be you. So when this young buck brother of hers come t' fetch her, I jes' had t' set out t' find ya."

"Mr. Cramer is one of the guides on the wagon train," Josh volunteered with no little degree of respect in his voice.

"Heck, lad, I been leadin' wagon trains 'bout as long as they been comin' West. That's how me an' Calico here met."

"Really?" Josh asked, eyes wide. "How did that happen?"

"Well," Zeke said, setting his coffee aside so as to have plenty of room to punctuate his tale with arm-waving. He leaned forward conspiratorially, causing the twins to automatically lean forward, too. "I was workin' a train out o' St. Joe. It was a big 'un, an' a spell o' sickness had delayed our settin' off for a couple o' weeks. This here youngster," he said, nodding at Calico, "an' his folks was part o' the train. Everybody knowed him 'cause o' his eyes, an' he was constantly gettin' into fights with t' other boys, who'd make fun o' him an' call him names.

"Well, it was gettin' so close t' fall that we couldn't wait much longer t' start, but there was still a lot o' sick folks, so the train was broke into two sections. The wagonmasters all flipped coins t' see who'd go with which half, an' I got the second section. Calico an' his folks, bein' well enough t' travel, left in the first section."

Zeke broke off his story to fumble around in his shirt and pants pockets for a pipe and tobacco. Watching the twins carefully, he made a grand production out of tapping out the bowl, filling it with great deliberation, lighting it with a burning twig from the fire, sucking carefully to be sure it was drawing, then slowly refolding the tobacco pouch and putting it back into his vest pocket. By this time, Josh was squirming restlessly, and even Sarah looked anxious for him to continue.

Finally, Calico spoke up.

"Oh, go on, ya ol' coyote, ya got 'em just where ya want 'em."

The two men exchanged grins, and Zeke continued.

"Well, I reckon ya know what happened. The first section turned in through Indian territory an' got itself massacred, 'cept for Calico, here. Him an' his uncle Dan joined up with the second section right after Dan found him, an' ya can be sure we steered a wide circle around that part of the country. Did send a burial detail in, though, so's them folks'd be laid t' rest proper.

"I knowed his uncle Dan for a long time before that...an' after. The old trail used t' run fairly close t' Grady—that's where Dan's ranch's near—an' I used t' stop by whenever I could t' see how young Calico here was doin'. Then the new trail opened 'bout ten years ago, an' Calico an' me ain't seed each other since." He tapped his pipe out on a rock. "An' now if you young'uns 'll excuse us, Calico 'n' me's goin' t' mosey into Toohigh an' see about a little snakebite cure. Right, Calico?"

Calico rose to his feet and offered his hand to help pull Zeke up.

"You say so, Zeke." He looked carefully around the campsite to make doubly sure it was safe, and decided it would be all right to leave the twins alone for a short time. "You kids..." He gave Josh a wink not lost on Sarah. "...get ready for sleep. I'll be back in just a bit."

Josh looked hurt at not being asked along, but Sarah seemed not to mind. Her thoughts, judging from the small smile and far-off expression she wore, were back at the wagon train.

"Josh, ya take care of things while I'm gone," Calico said, noting the immediate change in attitude at his words. "Keep your rifle close by, an' if there's any sign o' trouble at all, ya fire two shots in the air—an' I mean *in the air*. Ya got that?"

He nodded, and Calico's gaze lingered on him a bit longer than he intended.

He forced himself to turn to Sarah.

"And in the mornin', young lady, I'm goin' t' expect a full story on that

Fletcher boy." He gave her another wide wink, and she blushed.

"G'nite, young'uns," Zeke said, with a wave.

"Goodnight, Mr. Cramer," the twins echoed.

As they moved away from the firelight toward the yellow-lit windows of Toohigh, Calico kept glancing back to watch them spreading their bedrolls.

"Stop playin' mother hen, boy," Zeke said. "They'll do all right without ya bein' there ridin' herd on 'em every second."

Calico shifted his rifle from one hand to the other. "Yeah, I s'pose you're right, Zeke. But we been havin' some mighty peculiar things happenin' to us lately."

"So I hear tell."

They walked in silence for a moment, the only sound their own movement. Then Zeke spoke again.

"I was right sorry t' hear 'bout Dan, Calico."

More silence; then Calico's quiet "Yeah."

They reached the saloon, which despite the proximity of the wagon train was almost empty. Calico ordered drinks, which they carried to a table in one corner and sat down.

"Calico, ya got any idea what's goin' on? With Dan, I mean, an' all this other stuff the girl was tellin' us?"

He shook his head and stared into his drink. "I'm afraid I might be gettin' an idea, an' I don't like it one bit."

"So, who ya figger's after ya...and why?"

"Not sure exactly who, an' sure as hell no idea why. How many, though, I got some idea."

"Four?" Zeke asked.

Calico looked at him intently, and when he spoke his voice was low. "Sarah tell ya that?"

Zeke polished off his drink and set the glass carefully on the table, pushing it off to one side.

"She didn't have t'. Ya don't spend most of your life herdin' wagon trains without bein' pretty sharp-eyed," Zeke said. "Day before yesterday, four riders passed us by. I never seen none of 'em before, but I recognized one from his poster—Jessie Riles, one of the meanest sons-a-bitches in six states. The other three didn't look much better sorts.

"That Jessie Riles, he's got hisself quite a reputation. He don't like face-to-face fights if he can help it. He's more a shoot-'em-in-the-back man. That an' settin' fires. Jessie just loves t' set fires, I hear. Sound familiar?"

Their eyes met and held.

"Yeah," Calico said, "it sounds familiar. How long ago ya say ya saw 'em? Day before yesterday?"

Zeke nodded.

"That means they must be down in flat country by now, settin' somethin' up for us."

"Either that or on the way," Zeke amended. "I know this country, Calico. It ain't easy in the best of times or conditions. There's not many places for ambush, but there's some. An' if I know about 'em, ya can be sure Jessie Riles an' his boys know about 'em, too." He wiped his mouth with the back of his hand. "Let's have another drink."

Calico went to the bar, returning with a bottle, which he set in the center of the table.

"What we don't drink ya c'n take along for the trip," he said.

Zeke gave a curt nod of thanks.

"Now," Calico said, taking his seat, "c'n ya tell me where these ambush spots'd be?"

Zeke uncorked the bottle, poured them both a stiff drink, took a big swallow from his then nodded again.

"Yep, but I got a better idea. You an' the kids stick around an' ride down with the train. We'll be restin' here through tomorrow then headin' down next day. Ya ride with us, ya'll be safe."

Calico gave a wan smile and shook his head. "Thanks, Zeke, I 'preciate it. But ya got a couple dozen people on that train, an' neither you nor me can risk puttin' 'em in any danger. The three o' us can move faster by ourselves, an' if ya can tell me where the danger spots are I c'n handle 'em one at a time."

Zeke sighed, drained his glass, then poured and picked up another drink. "Ya always was a bullheaded 'un," he said in grudging admiration. "Ya got somethin' I can draw a map on?"

Calico reached into his vest pocket for his map, unfolded it on the table, face side down, and ironed the creases out with the flat of his hand. From another pocket, he withdrew a badly chewed pencil.

"I borrowed this from the bartender," he explained. "Figured I might need it."

Zeke shook his head in mock exasperation then reached for the pencil.

"Okay, now, there's three places most likely to be trouble," he said, and started drawing.

CHAPTER 10

THEY BROKE CAMP SHORTLY AFTER DAWN, WHILE THE AIR WAS STILL CRISP ENOUGH TO show their breath. A flat meadow of fog and mist spread out below them, the tops of jagged peaks rising from it like islands from a ghostly sea. People were just beginning to awaken in the wagon train, and a few solitary figures moved about attending to early-morning chores.

Calico had studied Zeke's rough map of the downward trail, and he patted his vest pocket to make sure it was still there as he climbed into the saddle. As he looked back at the wagon train a short, bearded figure rose from beside one of the campfires within the circle of wagons and waved slowly. He returned the wave, and the figure was soon lost behind the canvas arch of a wagon.

They rode slowly, the fog and mist evaporating before them, Calico instructing the twins to keep a sharp eye out for any possible signs of danger. Both he and Josh rode with their reins in one hand, their free hand at their side within easy reach of their rifles. Sarah rode between them, her head moving casually from side to side as her eyes traced every outcropping of rock in front of them.

"You think they'll try anything today, Calico?" she asked.

His eyes on the trail ahead, he shrugged without looking at her.

"Sure wish I knew, Sarah," he said. "I kinda doubt it, this trail bein' so heavily traveled. Leastwise, now we know where the most likely trouble spots might be. Zeke's been over this route with more wagon trains'n ya can count, an' he says there's only three places we should have t' worry about. That don't mean I ain't goin' t' worry 'bout ev'rythin' in between, o' course," he added with a chuckle. "An' now we know f'r sure there's four of 'em. It's always nice t' know how many you're up against."

"Do you suppose there might be a gunfight?" Josh asked, not quite able to hide the excitement in his voice.

"Don't ya be too hasty to want shootin', boy," he replied, again without turning. "People get themselves killed that way, an' you're a long time dead. From what Zeke says, the one of 'em ain't much f'r showdowns when he can avoid it, an' that's been pretty much bore out by our run-ins with 'em."

The trail meandered down the slopes and across the sides of several large hills, varying in steepness and width. All in all, the downhill part of the trail was less rugged than the uphill portion.

A ranch wagon carrying two men approached them, headed for Toohigh, and Calico rode ahead to meet them. They stopped to converse for a moment then moved on, waving as they passed Josh and Sarah.

"They ain't seen nothin'," Calico said as the twins caught up with him. "No four riders, anyhow, which might mean either they're already down on the flats, or up here somewheres pretty much hid."

They rode on without much conversation, their attention directed at the trail and terrain ahead. Calico was aware, from time to time, of Josh watching him, and it was with considerable effort that he kept himself from looking at the youth more often than he did. Now wasn't the time, he knew, to let his heart start distracting his head.

About ten that morning they neared the first danger spot on Zeke's rough map. The trail, cut into the side of a steep incline, took a sharp S-turn among some rugged boulders. The far side of the turn afforded ideal cover for anyone with ambush in mind.

Calico signaled for the twins to stop just short of the first curve, then dismounted and handed his reins to Josh. Taking his rifle, he scrambled up the steep slope, his feet sending small rivers of stones bouncing down onto the trail.

About fifty feet above the trail, he found a position from which he could see down the other side of the S-curve and to the rocky wall beyond. He scanned the facing slope carefully, eyes straining to catch any sign of movement or other indication of men in hiding. After two or three minutes of careful surveillance, he was satisfied the road immediately ahead was clear, and half-walked, half-slid back down the slope to the waiting twins. He and Josh exchanged a long look as he mounted up without a word, the leather creak of the stirrup strained by his weight the only sound.

Turning to the twins, he said, "I'm goin' t' ride ahead a ways. Josh, ya wait right here at the turn. Keep as much outta sight as ya can till I signal ya both t' come on. Sarah, ya keep right where ya are, hear?"

She nodded, and Josh dismounted, leading his horse to the edge of the curve, his back against the sheer side of the boulder that marked the turn.

Calico clucked Dusty forward, rifle at the ready, and moved around the turn. He gave his full attention to every detail of the area ahead as he moved up the slight incline of the trail, around the bottom curve of the S and outward again toward the second bend. Without looking back, he raised his left hand above his shoulder as a signal, hoping Josh would get the message and keep his eyes on the opposing curve, of which he had a better view than Calico.

Just before rounding the curve, he once again dismounted and moved cautiously toward the bend on foot. The slope at that point was too steep to climb, though the jumble of rocks above could have hidden several men.

Peering around the bend, he saw the trail began a long, meandering downward slope, fairly clear for at least half a mile.

Turning back, he waved to Josh. The youth disappeared momentarily only to reappear on horseback, followed by Sarah.

Ahead of them, the valley that separated the parallel mountain ranges narrowed and finally squeezed between two vertical cliffs, which rose hundreds of feet on either side. Zeke had warned Calico of this narrow pass. In winter, it was totally blocked by snow, and in spring and summer it was given to flashfloods following heavy rains. Fortunately, there had been no rain in recent days, though the stream they had seen rushing below them at several points along the way shared the pass with the trail.

Immediately beyond the pass, the trail took a sharp turn to the right, again affording an ideal spot for ambush. There was no way Calico could climb those sheer walls to see if danger lay ahead; the only way was to go right on through, be alert and hope for the best.

As the pass loomed before them, the three travelers stopped for their noon meal. Josh and Calico ate heartily, but Sarah barely touched her food. Calico noticed, but said nothing. They could hear the sound of the rushing stream now—the trail had worked its way down to the valley floor, running side by side with the stream through the pass, then climbed steeply again for a distance before resuming its downward path, circumventing a series of spectacular waterfalls that poured the stream onto the flatlands below.

Remounted and moving once again, Calico was about to halt once more at the mouth to the pass when Sarah cried out, "Look, Calico, there's something in the pass!"

Lifting up in his saddle for a better look, he saw, at the far end of the pass just where the trail took its turn, a large, bulky shape with several figures milling around it.

"What is it?" Josh asked.

Calico grinned in sudden recognition. "It's the stagecoach from Clantonville t' Jeffrey. Looks like it lost a wheel."

"Do you think it's a trick?" Sarah asked apprehensively.

The same thought had occurred to him, but he replied, "Naw, I don't think so, but I'll ride on ahead just to make sure. You two stay here, an' if there's any kind of trouble, ya both hightail it back toward Toohigh an' join up with Zeke an' the train."

"But—" Josh began.

Calico cut him off with a glare. "No buts about it, youngster. This ain't the place for no heroics. If somethin' should happen to me, ya got your sister to look out for, an' I expect ya t' do just that."

Josh looked disgusted, but he nodded.

He left them side by side in the middle of the trail. As he got closer to the disabled stagecoach he could see a small cluster of men on the downward side trying to lever it high enough by the use of a long pole to enable the wheel to be put back on. Two women passengers sat on the rocks beside the stream with parasols raised, though they were in no direct sun.

One of the men waved as he saw Calico approaching, and Calico returned the greeting. Pulling his horse up a short distance from the group of men, he holstered his rifle, dismounted and tied the reins to a deadfall. Without speaking, he took his place at a vacant spot on the pole and helped the straining men to lift.

The stage grudgingly righted, with several creaks and groans, and two of the men released the pole and lifted the heavy wheel into place. After considerable jockeying to get the stage's axle aligned properly, a thick peg was driven between the hub and axle to secure the wheel. With a collective sigh, the remaining men released the pole.

"Much obliged, stranger," a man Calico took to be the driver said, extending his hand.

He took it and shook it strongly.

"No trouble."

"Well, we surely do appreciate it," the man said. "Danged if I know what this country's comin' to, though."

"What d' ya mean?" Calico asked.

"Well, hell, son, we done passed four bastards up the road a piece, just settin' out behind some boulders, an' I damn well know they saw the wheel fall off—they could o' heard it three counties away—an' I'll be gol-damned if I didn't see 'em headin' off in the opposite direction like a bunch of scared jackrabbits! What the hell they was thinkin' of, not even offerin' t' help, I'll never know."

"Hey, driver," one of the men, apparently a passenger, called. "We goin' t' get movin', or should we start buildin' a cabin for the winter? I got important business in Jeffrey."

The driver gave him a curt wave. "Okay, okay. Everybody git aboard." Turning again to Calico, he said, "Thanks again, stranger." Then, leaning forward so only Calico could hear, he added, "If ya should see them four varmints, kick 'em all in the ass for me, will ya?"

Calico grinned. "I sure will, friend. I sure will."

The driver checked the horses, took another look at the wheels, climbed onto the seat and flicked the reins.

"Next stop, Toohigh," he called, and the stage moved off in a flurry of dust and sound.

A few minutes later, as the dust began to disappear, Josh and Sarah rode up.

"Did you find out anything, Calico?" Josh asked before his horse had drawn to a complete halt.

"It seems our friends was waitin' for us here, but the stage scared 'em off," he said as he swung into his saddle.

"What does that mean?" Sarah asked, looking nervously up the trail.

"It means that if they're goin' t' try for us, there's only one more likely spot, an' that's about three miles down the trail," he told her, urging Dusty forward.

Despite his reassurances, however, he removed his rifle from its scabbard and rode with it in his left hand.

The trail rose sharply for half a mile then took a sharp turn to the left and began an equally steep descent. The sound of a nearby waterfall filled the air, and Calico imagined he could feel the spray, though the actual falls were obscured behind an intervening rise. Allowing his horse to drop back almost abreast of the twins, he still had to raise his voice to be heard over the roar.

"Our last trouble spot's in another gorge, pretty much like that last 'un," he said as the twins strained forward to make out his words. "Accordin' to Zeke, the gorge is a little wider than the one we was just through, but the hills are steep an' rocky, with lots o' places to hide. Then there's a stretch a couple hundred yards long, straight as an arrow, dead-endin' at an almost straight-up cliff. Lots o' big rocks an' boulders at the base, fell down from above, an' any one of 'em big enough to hide a man an' his horse. Then the trail makes almost a right-angle turn, even sharper than the last one."

"What do we do?" Sarah wanted to know, and Calico took a deep breath, which he let out in a long sigh before replying.

"We'll see when we get there," he said.

In silence, they rode past two more waterfalls, neither as large nor as loud as the first, and then the trail moved away from the stream's course, not to rejoin it until they reached the flatlands below.

"That's it, isn't it?" Sarah said, pointing.

Two mountains swooped dramatically down and together, the wall of a third affording what seemed an impenetrable barrier between them. He nodded, and the three riders slowed, each automatically studying the terrain.

The mountains were forbidding, a mixture of soaring cliffs and jumbles of precariously balanced rocks and overhangs looming above a narrow pass barely wide enough for one wagon.

Calico signaled for a halt.

"Okay, we'll do it like before. I'll go on ahead, an' when I see the way's clear I'll signal ya t' come." He looked over at Josh, who was opening his mouth to speak, and raised his hand to silence him. "I know, I know...ya want t' do somethin' t' help. Well, this time ya can. See that pile o' rock down there?"

He pointed to a jumbled formation almost in the center of the narrow valley floor that looked directly down the mouth of the pass toward the massive wall of the center mountain.

Josh nodded.

"Okay. Ya leave your horse here with Sarah, an' if you're careful, ya can work your way down there without bein' seen. It should give ya a clear view of the pass, an' of anybody who might be at the other end. Once you're down there, an' ya signal me it's clear, I'll move on through." He turned to Sarah. "Sarah, ya wait right here an' watch Belle. When I signal okay, ya take the horse down t' him, an' both of ya come on through. Got that?"

Both nodded, and he noted they looked a little scared, though they were trying to hide it.

"Okay, Josh, get goin'. An' be careful."

Josh dismounted, took his rifle from the scabbard and handed the reins to Sarah. Then he scrambled down the slope beside the trail, keeping low, moving from tree to boulder. Calico and Sarah watched as his figure grew smaller, disappearing from time to time behind obstacles.

At last they saw him dart across the small open clearing to the pile of rocks. He cautiously peered around first one side of the pile then the other, then turned and raised his arm. Calico returned the signal and turned to Sarah.

"I'll see you in a while," he said, smiling, and rode forward, rifle in hand.

It was the quiet he noticed first—no birds, no crickets, not even the sound of the wind. But there was danger in the air, and he recognized it. Dusty moved slowly, deliberately, as if sensing his rider's caution.

Calico remained totally focused as the pass grew narrower, the slopes and overhangs more menacing. No sound. No movement save his own. He passed Josh's hiding place without acknowledging his presence.

Scanning swiftly from side to side, he surveyed the steep slopes. To the right, several hundred feet up, the mountain became almost a mesa. Hard for a man to reach, but not impossible, and once there…

He entered the pass, riding close to the right-hand wall, making it difficult for anyone on the flat area above to shoot down on him, and also affording Josh a more open view from behind him. The boulders at the base of the sheer cliff ahead were closer now. No sign of movement from behind them.

Calico raised his rifle slightly from his lap, waiting. He moved his horse among the large boulders on the right face, muscles tense, eyes and ears straining.

A shaft of light lying across the base of the cliff announced the trail's right-angle turn. It was only yards ahead now. He stopped and swung silently from the saddle, rifle at the ready. Patting Dusty's neck, he dropped the reins and moved, back to the cliff, to the turn. He could see behind some of the boulders against the opposing cliff now. Nothing. No one.

Peering around the corner, Calico saw the walls of the gorge, steep and piled with rock. The sun, now moving down in the sky, was directly in the center of the narrow pass, but he could tell the hills fell away just a bit farther on. Aside from the deep ruts made by wagons and the tracks of countless horses on the floor of the pass around him, the desolation and sharp sense of aloneness made him feel as though he might well be standing somewhere at the start of time. Shielding his eyes against the sun, he could see an eagle making a swooping bridge between and above the two steep slopes.

Rifle in both hands, he dashed across the open trail to the far wall, taking refuge behind a boulder. From his new vantage point, he surveyed the area again. Still nothing. Dusty stood quietly across the trail, head low, reins trailing on the ground.

Looking up, he surveyed the slopes for any sign of life. Nothing. Advancing through the pass by moving from boulder to boulder, he satisfied himself he was alone in the narrow pass.

But his gut told him danger was still very near. He sprinted to his horse and jumped onto the saddle, riding out onto the trail and around the corner, out of Josh's view. He rode slowly for another hundred yards, looking for the unseen danger he sensed was present.

It wasn't, he knew, a matter of alternatives. There was only one way through the pass, and they had to take it. Either that, or wait several days for the wagon train to come through. And even then, they would have to move through the pass.

Reluctantly and still wary, he turned back. Positioning himself beside a large boulder that would afford him a view of both the twins and the trail ahead, he signaled toward the pile of rocks Josh had taken as vantage point. He saw Josh wave then dart away from the rocks toward the trail and Sarah. About five minutes later, the twins rode into the narrow gorge.

They were less than a hundred feet away when he heard the rustle of stones, and a light shower of pebbles fell just in front of him. The hair on the back of his neck rose as he looked up.

A large boulder at the edge of the mesa was tipping slowly toward the trail.

Calico jabbed Dusty with his spurs and wheeled around. More stones were falling now, making a sound like heavy rain that quickly crescendoed to that of rushing water. The twins looked up, startled.

"Get back!" he shouted, racing toward them.

They yanked on the reins, causing their mounts to rise up on their hind legs, whinnying. Calico was momentarily alarmed that Sarah would fall, but she held her seat.

"Get back!" he yelled again, his voice now lost in the rumble of falling rocks.

By the time he reached them, they had turned their horses and were heading at full gallop back in the direction from which they had come. They didn't stop until they were well out of the pass then turned to peer into the rising cloud of dust that filled the entire gorge.

Gradually, the noise died, and the dust cleared enough for them to see, though it still hung thick in the air. The clearing haze revealed a wall of rock and dirt fifty feet high, completely blocking the gorge.

"I think that was meant for us," Sarah said, scooping her hair back from her forehead with one hand.

Josh stared at her in wide-eyed disbelief then broke out laughing. His sister joined him, and their laughter filled the dust-choked air.

Calico stared at them and shook his head. "I think you're both plumb loco," he said.

CHAPTER 11

RATHER THAN TRY TO MAKE IT OVER THE MOUND OF RUBBLE BLOCKING THE PASS—AND face the possible dangers that lay beyond—in the daylight remaining to them, Calico decided to camp for the night in the valley near their present location.

"Unless they was watchin' real close, which I doubt they could with all that dust, they don't know for sure whether or not we're under that avalanche," he said, "and we don't know that they're *not*." He pointed to the mesa from which the avalanche had started; much of it had crumbled away. "So, rather than take any chances, we'll spend the night up the valley a ways, then go over tomorrow."

They turned off the trail and down onto the narrow valley floor. About a half-mile from the pass they found a grassy area with ample fodder for the horses, hidden from the trail, where they set up camp.

"We better go without a fire tonight," he said, "just in case they might still be alive an' come up the trail lookin' for us."

He hobbled Belle and Daniel to keep them from wandering too far, but left Dusty free, just in case. He knew his horse would stay close.

"Shouldn't we take turns keeping watch?" Josh asked, as Sarah handed around pieces of beef jerky and some dried fruit from one of the saddlebags.

Calico smiled and winked at Sarah as he took a piece of jerky.

"You're a step ahead of me, Josh," he said. "I don't really think there's any danger tonight, but t' be on the safe side, I think maybe you an' me should take turns stayin' awake, just in case."

Sarah gave them both a scathing look but said nothing. Calico was sure he knew the reason.

"I'll take the first turn," Josh said eagerly.

"Okay," Calico agreed. "It's just about sundown. There's that clump of trees we passed…" He pointed with the remains of his jerky. "…just beyond them rocks. Anybody comin' up this way'd have to come the same way we did. There won't be much of a moon, with them clouds out tonight, but there should be enough. Here," he said, reaching into his vest and taking out his father's watch, "ya take this so's ya c'n keep track o' the time."

It was the first time he had ever let the watch out of his possession, and he could tell by the way Josh took it carefully and put it in his own pocket that the significance of the gesture was not lost on him.

"You wake me 'bout eleven for my shift," Calico said.

"And what about me?" Sarah demanded, her voice edged with sarcasm. "I'm just a girl, I suppose. My eyes aren't sharp enough to see what a man's eyes can see."

Josh looked at Calico and raised his eyebrows. "Oh-oh," he said resignedly.

"Well, now, what's all that supposed to mean?" Calico asked, though he knew full well what she was getting at.

"It means that Sarah wants to have a turn at lookout, too," Josh said. "She thinks—"

"Don't you tell me what I think, Mr. Cowboy!" Sarah snapped. "I can do anything you can do, and I can do it just as well as you, and you know it! I'm tired of always being treated like some porcelain doll just because I'm not a man!"

Calico raised his hand to curtail the tirade.

"Whoa, now, Missy. No sense in gettin' your dander up like that. Nobody's been treatin' ya special 'round here that I noticed." He deliberately slowed and lowered his voice to a conciliatory tone. "Ya want a turn at lookout, ya take it. As a matter of fact, ya can just be first. An' ya shouldn't go snappin' at your brother like that. He's been treatin' ya like a lady, an' ladies don't usually stand lookout."

Sarah appeared pacified.

"Well," she said, her voice calmer, "this isn't exactly the place for ladies, and as long as I'm here, and doing the things you two are doing, I don't want to be treated any differently." She got up from the log on which she'd been sitting and dusted off her pants carefully. "Now give me your rifle, Josh, and I'll be going."

She held out her hand to her brother, palm up.

Josh's automatic reaction was to hug the weapon closer.

"You ain't going to use my rifle," he said defensively.

"The word is *aren't*," Sarah corrected, "and, yes, I am." Her voice was calm but determined.

Calico thought briefly about offering her the pistol Sam had given him after the stampede but thought better of it.

"I don't think ya'll need a gun, Sarah," he said, then hesitantly added, "'Sides, do ya know how to use one?"

"Have I had the chance to prove otherwise?" she replied, hand still extended. "I'm just as good a shot as Josh, and he knows it. Granddaddy was my granddaddy, too." She stared hard at her brother. "Tell him, Josh. Tell him I'm just as good as you with a rifle."

Josh's eyes darted from his sister's face to Calico's then back again, and finally to the ground in front of him. His shoulders sagged, and his head drooped to his chest.

"She ain't..." His eyes flicked to her face then dropped again. "...isn't so bad, I guess."

Calico shrugged. "Then give her your rifle," he said, and Josh grudgingly thrust the gun in the direction of his sister's hand. She took it, and Calico noted a look of triumph, quick as summer lightning, flash across her face.

"Thank you," she said.

"And she'd better have the watch, too," Calico said.

Josh looked at him then reached into his pocket and handed the watch to her. She took it and turned to give Calico a warm smile.

"Thank you, Calico." Placing the watch carefully into a pocket of her breeches, she gave a brief sigh of satisfaction. "I'll see you both later," she said as she moved off toward the clump of trees he had indicated earlier.

"Oh, Sarah," he called after her. "Now that there's three of us on guard duty, we'll each have shorter shifts. So ya come wake me 'bout ten 'stead o' eleven."

She nodded, waved and disappeared behind the rocks.

When she was out of sight, Josh, head still down, said, "Why'd you have to let her do that, Calico?"

He walked over and put one hand on the young man's shoulder.

"Because she's right," he said simply.

Josh looked at him out of the corner of his eye and shrugged.

"An' now that that's over with, let's get us some sleep. I'll take second watch, you c'n have third."

Twilight was growing thicker, the increasing cloud cover hastening the darkness. Calico made a production out of straightening his bed, adjusting his saddle as a pillow and settling in for the night. Josh, too, had prepared for sleep—again placing his bed as close as he could get; and Calico waited, eyes closed, until he could tell by the young man's steady breathing he was asleep. Then, he slid out of his bed, took his rifle and, rising noiselessly, moved toward the large clump of trees where Sarah stood guard.

He found a large tree from behind which he could make out her huddled form and beyond, down the valley toward the pass, and there he stayed until the position of the moon between the clouds told him it was just about ten o'clock. Quickly, he retraced his steps and got back into his bed just as Sarah approached the camp. He waited for her to bend over and shake him then pretended to wake up.

"It's okay, Sarah," he whispered, so as not to awaken Josh. "I'm awake. Ya get some sleep now." He rose once again, making a point to wipe his forearm across his eyes as if to rub the sleep out. "Ya did a good job…thanks."

He gave her a warm smile and could tell, even in the dim light of the suddenly appearing moon, that she blushed as she returned the smile. Then she reached into her pocket and handed him his father's watch.

Around two a.m., with no sign of intruders or anyone moving on the trail above, Calico returned to the camp and woke Josh.

"Your turn," he whispered as he gave him the watch and crawled gratefully into his bed. Within seconds he was in a deep, dreamless sleep.

Sarah woke him to broad daylight and the sound of birds.

"Do you suppose it's all right if we have a fire now, Calico?" she asked. "I can fix some breakfast, and we could all use some hot coffee."

"Sure," he said, sitting up and running one big hand through his hair. "Now it's light, there's no point t' hidin'." He looked around the campsite sleepily. He was once again irritated with himself for not having awakened before anyone else. "Where's Josh?"

Sarah was taking supplies from the saddlebags.

"He's off exploring to see if he can find some water," she said.

At that moment, Josh strolled into camp looking as though he had been born in and bred to the wilderness. He grinned broadly at Calico.

"Good morning," he said, brightly.

"Good mornin' yourself," Calico said, pulling on his boots. "You didn't happen t' bag yourself some firewood while ya was out roamin', did ya?"

Josh tapped his forehead with an index finger.

"Ah-hah! I'm ahead of you again," he said, gesturing toward a small pile of twigs and pieces of broken branch he'd collected while Calico slept. "And," he added, "I found a blackberry patch that's just loaded with berries. We can have some for breakfast."

Both embarrassed for having overslept and pleased by Josh's initiative, Calico just wrinkled his nose, rubbed it vigorously with one finger and grunted.

While Calico cleared a small area, Josh gathered rocks to make a circle for the fire. Using dried grass for tinder, They soon had a fire started, and Calico joined Josh gathering blackberries in the tin coffee cups.

When the cups were full, they started back to camp, but Josh suddenly stopped and set his cup carefully on the ground.

"I forgot," he said, reaching into his pocket to retrieve the watch.

When Calico reached out his hand to take it, Josh carefully put it in his palm with one hand then closed Calico's fingers over it with the other. When he did not release his grasp, Calico looked at him, puzzled.

Then he saw the expression on the young man's face, and he impulsively leaned forward and kissed him.

Immediately startled by his action—he had never in his life kissed another man—he broke away and mumbled something about getting back to camp. Josh merely stared at him, smiling.

"Sure," he agreed.

Calico deliberately walked several paces ahead so Josh couldn't see how flustered he was. His heart was racing, and he felt lightheaded. He had no idea what it boded, but he knew this was a feeling he had never had before, and that he was exhilarated by it.

When they reached camp, the smell of coffee filled the air. After breakfast, they broke camp, carefully extinguishing the fire, and made their way to the blocked pass. The mound of rock and dirt looked no less forbidding in the light of a new day, but Calico knew it wouldn't present too serious an obstacle for them—although it undoubtedly would cause a delay for the wagon train behind them. Still, such minor disasters were commonplace to wagon travelers, and this one, like all others, would be overcome.

Checking both sides of the pass to make sure another landslide—manmade or natural—was not imminent, he walked his horse cautiously up the new slope, sending small rivulets of loose dirt and rock cascading down toward the twins, who stood safely back. Reaching the top, he checked the other side then motioned for them to come ahead.

Once they were beyond the avalanche, the trail widened and began a fairly steep descent. Ahead, through a saddle of two mountains, they could see the flatlands spread out before them.

When the trail became wide enough for them to ride abreast comfortably, they did so. Though still cautious, all three were in good spirits. Their journey was nearing its end, the clear, sun-bright day made danger seem remote, and the sadness of parting—a parting Calico was increasingly reluctant to see—would come later. Still, none of them was completely free of concern for their continued safety.

"Do you think they were killed in the avalanche, Calico?" Sarah asked, glancing back over her shoulder toward the blocked pass now far behind them.

He pushed his hat to the back of his head with his thumb and shrugged.

"No way o' tellin'," he said. "There's an awful lot of rock back there, an' I don't imagine they was expecting the ledge t' fall away like it did. If they was standin' anywhere near the edge of that mesa, there's a good chance they went down with it. But then again…"

He repeated the shrug. His gut feeling told him the chances of their pursuers being dead were extremely remote; but he kept his opinion to himself.

"Have you figured out yet who they are…were…and what they were after?" Josh asked.

"Nope," he said, shaking his head, but despite his protestations, he was coming to the painful conclusion that the only possible explanation lay in Bow Ridge with the Durants. He saw no point, however, in sharing this conclusion with the twins. "But whoever they are, they sure been mighty persistent. An' while I don't wish no man no harm, I sorta hope the whole thing ended back there at the pass."

They reached the flatlands by late afternoon, and could see smoke from the chimneys of Clantonville on the horizon. It was still a two-hour ride into town, but the twins—and especially Sarah—were eager to be among people again and to sleep in a real bed, so Calico agreed to ride on. They passed several ranches and farms, the part of the flatlands closest to the mountains being fairly well populated. Too much so for Calico's taste.

Clantonville was a good-sized town with a population of just over 700, laid out with the same casual unconcern as most Western towns that, like Harriet Beecher Stowe's Topsy, "just growed." There was, however, the obligatory main street lined with more saloons than an Eastern town of equivalent size might have.

There was only one hotel of any note, and out of deference to Sarah, Calico chose it over the other small, dirty-looking "hotels" and rooming houses. It was obviously new, gleaming in bright yellow paint with pristine white trim he estimated would remain white only until the dust storms of late fall and the everyday passage of traffic along the unpaved streets could do their work.

He requested, and got, what had become the usual two adjoining rooms on the second floor at the back. A quick check had shown this location to once again be the least vulnerable to intruders, thanks to the steep banks of a small stream that ran directly behind the hotel—another similarity to the hotel in Jeffrey. Both rooms could be securely locked. What was more, this time there would be no need for him to do any climbing between windows. Sarah was delighted, and he relieved, to find that the hotel's modern conveniences included bathrooms shared, as in Fort Collins, between two rooms, so they did not have to be entered from the hallway.

It was nearly six o'clock when they checked into the hotel; Calico asked the clerk for the best place to eat in town and was, not surprisingly, referred to the hotel's own dining room, which, he was told, remained open until eight o'clock. Once they were in their rooms, he made a close check of them, the hallway and, by looking out the windows of both rooms, the buildings nearby. Everything seemed in order, and he fervently hoped there would be no trouble.

Returning to the room he shared with Josh, he noted the door to the shared bath was open. Sarah stood by the large iron bathtub, running her hand lovingly along its rim.

"They have running water," she said when she saw him. The fact there was only one spigot, for cold water, didn't matter. A pot-bellied stove in one corner of the room came equipped with a large kettle for heating water, and Sarah had already filled it and lit the stove.

Josh, who had been sprawled across the bed, looked unimpressed by her discovery.

"I'm starved," he said. "When can we eat?"

"Well," Sarah informed him, "you're just going to have to starve until I've had a bath."

"Now?" he asked, incredulous. "Can't we eat first?"

"No, we can't. At least, I'm not going to. Do you think you could get away with not cleaning up before dinner if Momma were still alive? Or even Granddaddy? Now, you go do whatever it is you want while I take a bath."

And without further comment, she closed the door firmly.

Josh propped himself up on his elbows and shook his head.

"Women!" he said disdainfully.

Calico merely grinned and sat on the edge of the bed to clean his rifle.

"Maybe you and I could go out and look around town for awhile," Josh suggested.

Calico looked up from his cleaning. "I don't think that would be such a good idea right now, Josh," he said. "It's about dark, an' we still don't know whether we might have somebody out there waitin' for us. I think we should stick together, don't you?" He motioned to Josh's rifle with a nod of his head. "'Sides, it wouldn't hurt for ya t' clean that thing up a bit. Out here, the better ya take care of your gun, the better it can take care o' you."

With a sigh, Josh got up and picked up his weapon.

It was nearly eight o'clock before all three were ready to go down to the dining room, Sarah having completed her bath and closed herself in her own room while Josh and Calico took turns washing up then changing clothes. Calico made a deliberate effort not to watch Josh as the young man dressed, but as he stood bare-chested in the process of changing his shirt, he glanced up to see Josh studying him. The young man made no attempt to look away, and Calico wondered if the expression on Josh's face reflected the same intensity he felt himself whenever he saw Josh undressed.

Once again, he felt a wash of warmth sweep over him, and he hastily put on his shirt, self-conscious but excited.

Since he knew carrying a rifle into the dining room might create a bit of a stir in such a fancy hotel, Calico carefully slipped the pistol into the waistband of his pants, where it would be hidden by his vest.

When Sarah opened the door to join them, he had to look twice to believe his eyes. Though he had recognized her potential while they were still on the trail, he was struck by the beautiful young woman before him. Her hair was swept back and neatly tied with a bright red ribbon she must have bought in Jeffrey, the style accenting the soft oval of her face and her slender neck. Her complexion was smooth as velvet, the tan from many days' exposure to the sun only heightening her beauty.

She noticed him staring and gave him a warm, totally feminine smile that made him blush. Suddenly, he felt like an awkward teenager.

Josh, oblivious of his sister's charms, saved the day by announcing loudly, "Are we going to stand here all night or can we go eat now?"

Having earlier moved the heavy dresser in Sarah's room in front of her door to the hall, Calico now locked both doors to the bathroom. Then, when they were in the hall, he carefully locked his and Josh's door and slid a matchstick into the upper left corner.

"What's that for?" Sarah asked.

"So Calico'll know if anybody's gone into the room while we're downstairs, dummy," Josh said in a superior tone.

Calico shot him a stern glance.

"Don't call your sister names," he ordered, and Josh rolled his eyes at the ceiling and sighed.

Calico placed a hand on each of the twins' shoulders, grinned broadly at both of them. "Well, what're we waitin' for? I'm hungry!"

His arms around both—but far more aware of one—and their arms around his waist, they strode down the hall to the stairway and the dining room.

Though it was close to closing time for food service, the combined dining room and bar was fairly crowded. Calico's glance darted around the room, looking for any face that might be suspicious. He smiled to himself when he saw that Sarah's beauty was turning heads all through the room as they entered, and Sarah wore a pleased little smile.

He and Josh ordered steaks. Sarah, being informed by the waitress that the cook had just returned from a fishing trip, ordered freshly caught trout. Throughout the meal, He—and Sarah—were aware of the stares she was receiving from appreciative men.

Josh was aware only of the food in front of him, which he polished off in short order, topping his meal with two huge pieces of blueberry pie.

"Tomorrow," Sarah announced as they rose from the table, "I'm going to buy a dress."

Calico was surprised to find himself increasingly nervous as bedtime approached. After saying goodnight to Sarah and making sure everything was secure, he returned to the other room to find Josh already under the covers. He noticed that Josh's nightshirt still lay at the foot of the bed—the young man was naked under the sheet.

He forced himself to take a moment to deal with the rush of feeling sweeping over him, pretending to look out the window at the moon. Finally, he moved around to Josh's side of the bed and sat down beside him.

Josh drew one arm from beneath the sheet and reached toward Calico's chest. Calico caught it before it could touch his shirt and held it.

"Josh," he said softly, "what happened this mornin' caught me completely by surprise. I'm not sorry it happened. And I'm not sayin' I don't want it to happen again. But right now we got men tryin' t' kill us, an' we gotta keep focused on that.

"Just about all I been able to think about all day is what happened this mornin' and how good it was an' how there's so much more I want t' do with ya. An' right now, that's downright dangerous 'cause it takes my mind off how t' keep us alive until we get t' your aunt Rebecca's. We got our whole lives ahead of us, Josh, so for now, let's just take one thing at a time. D'ya undertand what I'm sayin'?"

Josh nodded. "Yes."

They remained silent and motionless for a long moment, Calico not wanting to let go of Josh's hand, until Josh said, "Can we do it again now, Calico? Just one?"

Calico sighed and shook his head. "Josh, you an' me both know that it wouldn't be just one. I'm havin' a hard enough time keepin' control o' myself as it is. Ya sorta stampeded my herd, an' I gotta get 'em back under control. Okay?"

Josh sighed then nodded. "Okay."

Calico released his hand, got up and moved around to his side of the bed, where he again lay down fully clothed on top of the sheet.

They all slept late the next morning; even Calico didn't waken until he felt the bed move as Josh got up and entered the bathroom. He was not unaware that Josh left the door partially open while he bathed, and it was with great effort he forced himself to sit up and keep his back to the door as he once again cleaned his already-clean rifle.

When it was his turn in the bathroom, he took care to close the door completely, though he didn't want to. He allowed himself a nice, long soak that drained the tension from his muscles—he didn't leave the tub until he heard movement in Sarah's room indicating she was up.

When all three were dressed, they went once again to the hotel dining room for a huge breakfast, after which they went on a walking tour of the town. There wasn't much to see, but Sarah did spot a couple of stores into which she insisted on dragging them. At the general store, she found several dresses that appealed to her, and she insisted on trying them on, to their dismay, leaving them to stand around awkwardly, trying not to appear bored.

As she disappeared into the dressing room for the fifth time, a small boy ran into the store and directly up to Calico.

"You Mr. Ramsay?" he asked, panting.

"Yeah," Calico acknowledged, exchanging puzzled glances with Josh.

"Desk man at the hotel sent me to fetch ya. He says to tell ya there's somebody goin' through your rooms."

Josh looked sharply at Calico, who said, "You stay here with Sarah. I'll be right back."

Without waiting for acknowledgment, he bolted out the door and up the street toward the hotel. Racing through the lobby and up the stairs, he slowed in the hallway long enough to remove the pistol from his waistband then crept toward their rooms. He mentally cursed not having brought his rifle—he was a keen shot with both, but pistols always struck him as somehow less than a real man's weapon.

There was no sign of activity as he eased swiftly and silently down the hall. Sarah's door was closed. The dresser was still blocking it on the other side, he knew, but he cautiously tried the knob anyway. It was locked. He continued toward his and Josh's room, his back to the wall.

The door was closed, and as he reached one hand toward the knob, he glanced up and saw that the matchstick was still in the crack.

"Jesus!" he cursed, the realization of what was happening striking him like a hammer.

He ran back down the hall and took the stairs four at a time into the lobby, where he nearly collided with Josh.

"What the hell are you doin' here?" he demanded.

Josh stared at him, wide-eyed.

"Some guy came into the store and said you needed help," he said then smacked the side of his forehead with the palm of his hand as the truth struck him. "It was a trick!" His eyes widened farther. "Sarah!"

Together, they ran out and back down the street, oblivious to the startled glances of passersby. They tore into the general store abreast, nearly colliding again as they both tried to make it through the door at the same time.

In the corner, on the floor, was the crumpled form of the storekeeper. Sarah was nowhere to be seen. Calico raced to the dressing room, threw aside the curtains and stared at a shambles of overturned chairs and clothing. Sarah's riding clothes were in the pile on the floor, but the room was otherwise empty. At the open window, the curtains fluttered in a slight breeze…

CHAPTER 12

Josh!" Calico called. "Go get the sheriff—we passed his office a few doors back. Tell him Sarah's been kidnapped. Then go back t' the hotel an' get our gear. I'm goin' after them now, before they c'n get too far."

Josh headed for the door then paused, as if seeking some sort of reassurance. Calico noted the frightened look on his face and gave him what he hoped was a confident smile.

"It'll be okay, Josh. Ya just do like I say, an' then follow me. I got a feelin' they'll be headin' toward Bow Ridge."

"But that's where Aunt Rebecca—" Josh began, but Calico cut him off. There was no time for explanations, and he wasn't sure whether or not he could even put his suspicions into words.

"I know. Now get goin'."

They pushed through the crowd forming at the front door. The shopkeeper, Calico noticed, was picking himself up from the floor and rubbing a sizable welt on his left temple.

As Josh took off to the sheriff's office, Calico ran back to the hotel for his rifle, angry with himself once again for not having carried it with him when they went out. At the livery stable, he told the attendant to saddle the other two horses for Josh, hastily saddled his own then leaped on and galloped out the door, heading in the direction of Bow Ridge.

A short distance outside of town, he came upon a freight wagon heading for Clantonville and pulled up in the middle of the trail, causing the wagon driver to do the same.

"Ya seen some riders—probably four—pass this way? They'd o' had a girl with 'em." Dusty danced and pawed the ground, eager to be off.

The wagon driver spat out a long stream of tobacco juice then nodded.

"Yep. Come up on me a ways back, but they had the good sense to pull off the trail 'stead o' tryin' to run me down like you done. They headed off thattaway," he said, turning and pointing off the trail to Calico's left.

"Was there a girl with them?" he asked.

"That there was," the driver agreed. "She was ridin' with the big 'un, an' she didn't look happy about it. Thought it kinda funny, her wearin' a dress on a horse, 'specially as fast as they was ridin'. But then, I mind m' own business."

"Much obliged," Calico said, feeling Dusty's muscles tense, anticipating his command to break into a gallop. He held him back long enough to say to the driver, "There'll be a young fella comin' along this way in a few minutes with an extra horse. I'd be in your debt if ya'd tell him which way I went."

"Sure thing," the driver said as Calico whipped the long reins on Dusty's flank. The horse reared then galloped off in the direction the freight driver had indicated.

Wooded hills lay to the left of the trail—ideal country for the kidnappers to lose themselves in. He could only hope to find and follow their trail.

That wasn't, as it turned out, too hard a job, and the trail indicated all four horses were moving fast. He followed through several groves of trees, fully aware that any one of them would provide perfect cover for an ambush. The abductors were aware he'd be after them, and it was logical at least one of them might be lying in wait for him.

He heard the first shot, and saw the spurt of dust it raised about three feet to his left. Automatically, he ducked and began to rein in. He didn't hear the second shot, but he felt it—a bright pain across his left temple, and then darkness.

The next thing Calico knew, he was looking up into Josh's wide blue eyes, from which fear was only beginning to fade. Then his vision was obscured by the wet kerchief Josh was using to wash off his forehead. His head burned, and it seemed that every bone and muscle in his body ached.

"Boy!" Josh said. "I was afraid you were never going to wake up. When I first got here, I thought you were dead for sure. I never saw so much blood!"

With an effort, Calico raised his hand to the cloth pressed against his forehead. There was blood on his shirt, and he could feel wetness—whether blood or water from the wet kerchief he had no idea—on his neck.

Josh grabbed his hand and forced it down to his side.

"Leave it alone," he said sternly. "You were really lucky—the bullet just grazed your forehead. The bleeding's just about stopped."

He did as he was told, taking mental note of his other various aches and bruises.

"Anything broken?" Josh asked.

"Not's I can tell," he managed to mutter, his head throbbing with every word.

He started to sit up, only to be forced back down by Josh's surprisingly strong hands.

"Where's the sheriff?" he asked.

"Fishing," Josh answered. "He took off for a few days. The deputy said he'd ride out and find him, but by the time they get here, it could well be Christmas."

Calico painfully raised himself off his back, supporting himself on his right elbow. "Come on, then, help me get up. We got t' get movin'."

Josh scrambled to his feet then did as ordered, steadying him as he managed to stand.

"You sure you're all right?" Josh's voice showed his concern.

Calico straightened up slowly, every muscle protesting.

"No, I'm not sure I'm all right," he said, rubbing a particularly sore spot on his hip. "But we ain't got much choice 'cept for me t' be." He looked up at the sky, seeking the position of the sun. "How long ago'd ya find me?"

"About fifteen minutes," Josh said.

Suddenly remembering his father's watch, Calico reached apprehensively into his vest pocket to retrieve it and was relieved to find it hadn't been broken in the fall. Holding it to his ear, he was further reassured by the steady ticking.

"Must o' been around ten-thirty when they took Sarah. It's near one o'clock now."

As he leaned over to pick up his rifle, pain turned it into a very slow process. Josh started to reach for the weapon, but he waved him off.

"Gotta get used t' usin' these muscles again sooner or later," he said. "I was just tryin' t' figure out how far ahead o' us they are by now. We better get movin'."

He whistled, and Dusty, who had been grazing about a hundred yards off, obediently trotted toward him, reins trailing the ground.

"Do you want some help mounting up?" Josh asked.

Calico glowered at him. "Hell, boy, I ain't no cripple. I sure feel like it, but I ain't. The sooner I get ever'thin' in workin' order the better, an' I can't do that by gettin' help all the time."

Josh shrugged and went to untether the other two horses from a nearby tree. With maximum effort, Calico made it into the saddle, grunting in pain. Josh rode up beside him, leading Sarah's horse, and looked at him impassively. Calico was suddenly aware his face was fixed in a grimace, and he forced it into what he hoped was a more natural expression.

"Feel better?" Josh asked. He was close enough for him to throw a punch at, but Calico knew better than to try.

"Let's move," he said instead.

They picked up the kidnappers' trail beyond the next clump of trees—the ones from which he'd been shot. The tracks indicated the riders weren't moving quite so hard now, apparently satisfied Calico had been killed. He had the impression the kidnappers also knew pursuit by the sheriff was unlikely.

The closer he and the twins had gotten to the end of their journey, the stronger his suspicions grew concerning who was behind the numerous attacks. It was a thought he did not relish, but he was convinced Rebecca Durant was somehow involved.

But why? If, for some reason, she wanted him dead, why risk the twins' lives as well? And—his mind fought against the idea—if it was the twins who were the real targets...?

No, he couldn't accept that. After all, he was bringing them to her, as she'd demanded in the letter to Dan. Why go to all the trouble of sending men after them when, if she intended them harm, all she had to do was wait until they were in her care? It didn't make any sense.

He shook his head to clear it, and Josh, who was riding close behind him and had been watching him, he knew, out of the corner of his eye, asked anxiously, "Are you all right, Calico?"

He nodded. "Sure."

It was beginning to grow dark, the shadows of trees and jutting rocks inching across the ground. Calico grew more alert, sensing they had nearly closed the gap between themselves and Sarah's abductors. As long as the outlaws were still riding, it was a good bet Sarah was still all right. It was when they stopped that had him worried, but he wanted no confrontation until he was sure they were down for the night. It was then that Sarah would be in the greatest danger, but it was also then he hoped the element of surprise would be on his side.

Ahead was a large grove of trees nestled between two medium-sized hills, and he detected the pinprick flicker of a campfire. He raised his hand to signal to Josh and slowed Dusty to a walk. Josh followed suit, sensing the reason and squinting for any sign of movement ahead. They were still too far away to be able to see anything clearly in the deepening twilight.

Motioning Josh toward a small stand of scrub and trees about fifty yards away, he nudged Dusty in that direction and, reaching it, dismounted. Josh did the same.

"Look yonder," Calico said in a low voice, pointing toward the distant trees. The small speck of light could be seen more easily now as dusk turned to dark. "It looks like they decided t' make camp."

Josh's voice, too, was low. "What are we going to do, Calico? We can't stay here all night. God knows what they might do to Sarah."

He rested one big hand on the younger man's shoulder.

"Calm down, Josh." He kept his voice low and, he hoped, reassuring. "We're just goin' t' wait till it gets a little darker—won't be but a few more minutes. Then, what I'm goin' t' do is t' leave ya here…" He raised his hand to ward off Josh's expected objection. "Let me finish, boy. I'll leave ya here while I circle around behind them hills. I figure that'll take me about ten minutes. By that time it should be pretty near dark." He pointed off to the left and slightly ahead. "You see that little gully there?"

Josh nodded.

"Okay, ya wait here till it gets dark enough so's ya can't be seen. Leave the horses here, then ya move on down to that gully an' get as close to their camp as ya can. They'll probably have a lookout posted, watchin' this way, but chances are he won't be able to keep watch on both the gully and up the valley.

"Like I said, get as close as ya can, but f'r God's sake, don't let 'em see ya. Then ya just wait there, ya hear?"

He paused and looked hard at Josh's handsome young face until the youth nodded. Then he continued.

"Okay. Now, I don't know zactly what's goin' t' happen, but when it does, ya wait till they move out after me then get in there an' grab Sarah. But don't do nothin' until I'm ready, ya understand?"

Josh nodded again.

"An' I don't want ya usin' that rifle unless it's absolutely necessary. Ya just get Sarah an' run. Head for the gully an' follow it back here. Soon as ya see the coast is clear, you an' Sarah get on them horses an' hightail it back t' Clantonville. I'll catch up t' ya on the way."

Realizing he still had his hand on Josh's shoulder, he gave it a strong squeeze and released his grip.

"Now, ya do like I told ya, an' don't wait on me. If I ain't caught up with ya by the time ya get to Clantonville, ya find that sheriff an' be sure he sees to it ya get t' your aunt okay."

Josh looked as though he wanted to say something but didn't, and merely nodded.

"See ya later," Calico said, and moved off into the darkness.

He walked his horse until he could no longer see the spot of light from the campfire then, with effort, mounted and began a slow circle around the nearest hill. There was very little light now, and he rode slowly to avoid making any more noise than was necessary.

Wending through clumps of trees, brush and rock in the near-total darkness and in unfamiliar territory took all his concentration. His concern for Sarah's safety urged him to move faster, but his head and gut told him caution was the best procedure. He prayed Josh wouldn't get anxious and start off too soon, that he wouldn't be seen and that he'd wait until Calico make his move before trying to rescue his sister.

It took nearly fifteen minutes to work his way around the hill, and when he reached the point where he could see the light of the campfire—much nearer now—he dismounted and tied Dusty to a tree. Rifle in hand and ignoring his aching muscles, he crept forward in the darkness toward the fire and the sound of voices.

As he moved from tree to tree, his heart jumped with relief when he had crept close enough to see Sarah seated on the ground in front of the fire. Around her were three men, drinking and talking loudly. The fourth man was nowhere to be seen, but Calico assumed he was on lookout somewhere at the far side of the grove, watching for pursuers.

The biggest of the three men leaned forward and offered his canteen to Sarah, who shook her head, eyes fastened on the fire.

"Come on, girlie, have a little drink," the man said, hunkering down beside her, thrusting the canteen at her again.

She pushed it away.

One of the other men, ugly and squat with a black, unkempt beard, laughed as he reached for the large coffee pot on the fire.

"Seems like she don't care much for you, Granger," he said.

The man called Granger took another deep swig from the canteen then wiped his mouth with the back of his forearm.

"Sure she does, Tom, sure she does. Why, this little lady knows it was me what saved her life. Jessie woulda slit her purty little throat back there in Clantonville, but it was me what talked him outta it." He grinned broadly at Sarah, showing a mouth full of jagged, discolored teeth, and reached for her arm.

She slapped his hand away and started to get up, but Granger pulled her back down roughly. Calico's hands tightened on his rifle.

"Come on, now, Granger," the third man—a tall, skeletal figure dressed entirely in black—said soothingly. "Don't get rough with the lady. Not just yet, anyways. As soon as Jessie gets back we'll all have us a little fun."

Granger was not to be put off.

"Well, I think we done waited long enough. There ain't nobody followin' us. Not since I knocked off that pretty boy back there this afternoon. Only one there'd be's that snot-nosed brother of little Miss Eastern Gal, an' he's probably still tryin' t' round up the sheriff. We'll get him in time."

The skeletal man shook his head slowly. "Jessie won't take kindly t' us startin' without him. Ya know he always likes t' go first." He grinned down at Sarah, his tight-skinned lips spreading until his face looked like a skull. She looked up at him with fear in her eyes.

Calico knew he'd have to make a move—and soon; but he wanted to be sure he knew where the fourth man was before he started anything. He prayed Josh would be able to keep calm and do as he'd been told.

"Well, I'm sure old Jessie wouldn't mind if I took just one little kiss," Granger said, dropping his canteen and grabbing Sarah roughly by the arm.

Tom, standing by the fire, was just starting to pour a cup of coffee when there was a sudden movement in the trees at the edge of the firelight and Josh appeared, rifle raised and pointed directly at Granger. Calico suppressed a curse but remained hidden.

"You get your hands off my sister, you bastard, or I'll blow your ass from here to Kansas City. And you other two better not make a move, either."

"Well, well," the skeletal one said, "if it ain't Baby Brother come to join the party. Your ma know you're up this late, kid?" He gave Josh one of his skeletal smirks.

"You go ahead and grin, bastard," Josh said calmly, "but if you reach for that gun in your holster, I'm going to splatter your insides all over that tree behind you."

Despite his concern, Calico was grudgingly awed by Josh's behavior, and he sensed the three gunmen were, too. The youth was gone; the man had taken over.

"What about me, sonny?" Tom asked. "You mind I finish pourin' this cup o' coffee? The pot handle's gettin' mighty hot."

"You just stand there, fat man," Josh replied. "And we'll see how long you can hold it." He jerked his head in Granger's direction. "Now, you take your hands off my sister, like I told you. But do it very slowly, and put them behind your head."

Granger did as he was told.

"Sarah, get up," Josh said, and Sarah, her face reflecting a blend of confusion and relief, scrambled to her feet and ran to her brother's side.

Calico's focus moved rapidly from one kidnapper to the next, alert for the slightest movement. Josh had the situation well in hand; but he knew it couldn't last, and that one of the men would make a move soon.

He was right. Tom's extended left hand still held the coffee pot, but his right hand, holding a battered tin cup, was slowly dropping to his side...and his holster.

Josh and Sarah moved backward, a step at a time, Josh's rifle still trained on Granger. They were nearly out of the campfire's circle of light, the darkness flowing over them like a deep river.

Suddenly, the hair on the back of Calico's neck bristled. His looked to the side just in time to see the dull glint of a knife being thrust toward the small of his back.

With reflexes born of years on the range, he jumped aside, spinning around with his rifle still clutched in both hands. In one motion, as he turned he brought the butt up sharply, catching his assailant squarely in the neck.

As the man grunted from the force of the blow, Calico heard the crack of Josh's rifle, then the hiss of liquid on fire. The campfire light was snuffed out like a candle as the contents of the full coffeepot spread out over it.

Calico was aware of his attacker's body hitting the ground, and of shouts and scuffling sounds from around the campfire. He yelled into the darkness, "Josh! Get the hell out of there!"

As he charged forward toward the extinguished campfire, he heard the sharp crack of a revolver and Sarah's scream. Using his rifle as a club, he swung at a dark figure with a raised revolver—whether it was the man called Granger or the skeletal one, he couldn't tell.

There was the satisfying sound of wood on bone, and the man fell face forward. He could make out another form to his right with another gun raised, this one pointed at him. He dodged to one side as a bright point of flame appeared at the end of the barrel, and felt the bullet whizzing past his ear before he heard the actual shot, which was like a slice of thunderclap.

He swung his rifle again, up from the ground, and caught the man between the groin and the pit of the stomach. The man emitted a spray of vomit as he pitched forward.

The fourth man was nowhere to be seen, and Calico continued running toward the point from which he'd heard Sarah's cry. It was nearly pitch dark now, what little moon there was covered by a thick cloud. About fifty feet into the woods, toward the gully, he made out two forms huddled on the ground, one kneeling, the other on its back. He saw, as he drew closer, that the kneeling figure was Sarah. Josh lay beside her, hand clutching his shoulder.

Sarah looked up as he reached her.

"They shot Josh," she said, her voice small and unbelieving.

Calico, his stomach knotted with concern, knelt beside her and could feel more than see Josh's wide, frightened eyes studying his face.

"I've never been shot before," Josh said.

Calico ripped the young man's shirt away and saw the small, clean hole of the bullet just below his shoulder blade. A thin stream of blood pointed the way from the hole like a tipless arrow.

"Sarah, you wait right here and don't move," he said.

He rose and moved quietly back to the campsite. He could hear a low, steady moaning, and the sound of retching. The overhead clouds thinned sufficiently for him to make out the three men still on the ground—one motionless, only his legs showing behind a tree; one in a fetal position, rocking slowly back and forth, and the third lying flat, both hands on his head.

The fourth man appeared from the far side of the campsite and knelt beside the man holding his head, offering him a canteen. When he turned, still kneeling, toward the one behind the tree, his back was to Calico, who tiptoed up to him and tapped him on the shoulder. The man stiffened and began to turn, and as he did so, Calico brought his knee up sharply, catching him squarely under the chin. The force of the blow raised him up, knocking him over backward.

Satisfied that all four were out of commission for the moment, he untethered the men's horses, slapped each on the rump to send it off into the woods then hurried to where he'd left Dusty. Without mounting he ran back to where Sarah and Josh huddled; Josh was now sitting up.

"Sarah, I hope you're good at runnin' in a dress, 'cause that's what we're goin' t' do." He bent down and picked Josh up in his arms like a large sack of flour. "You think you can ride, Josh?"

Josh gave a weak grin, his face pale and contorted in pain.

"Sure," he said.

Calico helped him into the saddle then led them as fast as he dared through the darkness, following the lip of the gully back toward the twins' waiting horses, far down the valley.

They were a little closer to Clantonville than to Bow Ridge, and returning to Clantonville was probably the most logical choice. It was the larger of the two towns, and shared its sheriff with Bow Ridge. But the sheriff was off fishing, and Clantonville's doctor, he remembered hearing, was somewhere north of town tending to an outbreak of scarlet fever on several ranches.

So, he opted for Bow Ridge, hoping to find a doctor, and that their pursuers, once recovered, would assume they had returned to the nearer town.

They reached the tethered horses, and he urged Sarah to mount up as he set Josh on Dusty. Josh, who had said nothing during their escape, sagged on the saddle, and Calico feared he might fall off.

"Sarah, you take Josh's horse in tow. I'm goin' t' ride with him." He mounted, sitting behind the saddle and, putting both arms around Josh, took the reins. It was slow going, but at last they reached the trail and turned toward Bow Ridge.

He knew the route would be much shorter if they left the trail and cut overland, and that if they stuck to the trail their pursuers could, if he'd miscalculated their analysis of their quarry's destination, be there before them. But with Josh's condition, an overland route was out of the question, particularly at night.

Sarah rode close beside them, frequently asking, "Is he all right?" Each time, Josh would make an effort to straighten up, replying, "I'm fine. I'm fine." Calico held his arms close against the young man's sides, and when Josh suddenly slumped, his head dropping forward onto his chest, he moved Dusty off the trail and toward a dark clump of trees and rock, barely discernible, about two hundred yards to his left.

"We're goin' t' have t' rest some, Sarah," he said as they entered the grove.

She quickly dismounted—with surprising agility, he noted, considering she was wearing a dress—and he eased the unconscious Josh slowly forward until she could prop him up while Calico dismounted. Together they lowered Josh from the saddle and onto the ground.

Calico once again checked the young man's wound, noting the increased loss of blood. Still, he saw with relief, it appeared to be a clean wound and didn't seem to have struck his lung or done any serious damage. He was aware, even in the stress of the situation, of the warmth and softness of the young man's skin beneath his hand. For just an instant, his mind pictured the same skin, the same hand, in another place, in another time...

"Can't we do something, Calico?" Sarah asked, shattering his inappropriate reverie.

"Well, not much, I'm afraid," he said, drawing himself back to the present. "We can dress the wound to stop the bleeding, at least." He pointed to Josh's saddlebag. "Get me a shirt out o' there."

She hastened to do as he said, and when she handed him the shirt, he tore it into strips, folding two of them into a pad to place directly over the wound, then the rest to make a bandage to tie around Josh's torso to hold it tightly in place.

It was a stopgap measure, but at least it would slow the loss of blood.

"The bullet's still in there," he said, getting up from his knees, "an' I don't want t' risk tryin' t' take it out myself unless I absolutely have t'. Once we get him to a doctor, I'm sure he'll be all right. He's just sorta in shock right now. We'll rest here a spell then move on soon's it gets light enough t' see where we're goin'."

"Calico?" Sarah said after making sure Josh was made as comfortable as possible and had fallen asleep.

"Yeah?"

"Did you kill those men?"

He shook his head. "No, Sarah. Lord knows, they deserve it, but I don't believe in killin' unless there ain't no other way. I just wanted to get you an' Josh outta there, an' maybe teach 'em a lesson or two."

"But that means they'll still come after us, won't they?"

He sighed and shrugged. "Hard t' say. We're almost to your aunt Rebecca's, so if what they're tryin' t' do is keep us from gettin' there, they ain't got many chances left. An' I think they got a pretty good idea now that we ain't easy game." He wasn't sure, from studying her face, that she was satisfied with his answer. Neither was he.

Checking on Josh one more time, he gestured toward the bedrolls.

"What say we get some sleep?" He had planned to set his bed next to Josh, but when Sarah did so first he thought better of it, under the circumstances.

At the first light of dawn, he roused Sarah. Josh was feverish and disoriented, and while Sarah was able to get him to drink some water, he refused food. Both of them were more concerned with getting Josh to a doctor than they were with food, and didn't take the time to prepare breakfast.

With effort, they got Josh back in the saddle, and Calico remounted behind him. Sarah gathered her dress, swung easily into the saddle and reached for the reins of Josh's horse, which followed her dutifully as they moved off. There was no sign of their pursuers, but that fact provided little comfort.

The sun was fully above the horizon in the cloud-dotted sky when they topped a small hill and saw Bow Ridge before them, lined up against a row of hills on the far side of a small valley. The town was roughly T-shaped, with the top of the T following the foothills, the base running down into the valley.

Calico, who had been looking over his shoulder constantly for signs of their pursuers, suddenly noted a cloud of dust on the trail far behind them. Several riders—four, if he was correct—were coming up the trail behind them, riding hard.

"Sarah," he said calmly, "we're goin' t' have t' move some t' get into town before they catch up with us."

Sarah, too, was now looking back at the distant cloud.

"Can Josh take it?" she asked, nodding toward her brother, who had been in and out of consciousness since they'd left their resting place.

Calico shrugged. "Looks like he's goin' t' have t'."

They spurred their horses and galloped down the trail toward town. As they approached Bow Ridge, Calico sensed something was wrong. The town was too quiet. A few dogs roamed the streets, but there were no people. As they moved up the dusty main street, he strained his eyes and ears, seeking some indication of life.

As they passed a clearing between two houses, Calico heard far-off singing and, looking to his right, made out a group of buggies and horses clustered on a distant hill in what was apparently the town's cemetery.

A hell of a time for a funeral, he thought, but knew there was no time to try to detour and get to the people before their pursuers caught up with them.

They had reached the top end of the street. Looking behind him, he knew it would only be a matter of minutes before the riders crested the hill and crossed the valley into town. He rounded a corner to block them from the view of their approaching pursuers and pulled up.

"Sarah, move up close an' hold Josh."

When she did, he jumped down and sprinted across the street to the line of small stores and shops at the top of the T. He tried several doors, and all were locked, until he came to a general store located at the exact center of the T and facing straight down the main street. The door opened easily, and a quick check of the interior found it empty.

He ran back to Sarah, moving between the horses, and she let Josh slide down into his arms. Then she, too, dismounted, and they carried Josh across the street. Not, however, before Calico slapped the horses on the rump and sent them off in the direction away from the junction of the streets and, he hoped, out of sight of their pursuers.

Inside the store, he laid Josh carefully on the floor behind the counter, and Sarah at once knelt beside her brother, stroking his forehead with her hand. Calico shut the door and, as he looked out, saw four riders coming down the far hill toward town. They pulled off to the left just short of the main street, and he lost sight of them behind the town's farthest buildings.

"Isn't there anything we can do?" Sarah asked, the strain of the past several hours telling in her voice.

"Not at the moment, I'm afraid," Calico said. "All we can hope is that that funeral gets over mighty fast an' the people come back into town."

He took quick mental stock of their surroundings and decided they had selected just about the best place in town to make a stand. The front of the store gave him an unobstructed view of the main street, and he noted the lowest small pane of glass in the shop's display window was missing, affording him a clear line of fire without having to call attention to their whereabouts by breaking a window. The clutter of bolts of cloth, harness, butter churns and other paraphernalia in the window would serve as good cover.

A sudden movement to his left caught Calico's eye. From a narrow alley between two buildings about half a block down, a man appeared, gun drawn, and moved cautiously in their direction, sliding his back against the front of each intervening building. It was the skeleton-faced man, looking much bigger in the light of day. He glided along like a stalking cat, his eyes darting from side to side.

Calico knew what he had to do. The thought made his stomach weak, but when he thought about Dan, about Josh lying wounded on the floor, and of the hell he and the twins had been through in Fort Collins and since, the queasiness was replaced by a growing knot of anger. Suddenly, the man in front of him ceased to be human and became a symbol of their past troubles.

He eased his rifle into position. The man drew closer...only twenty or so yards away now. Calico drew a careful bead with his brown eye and squeezed the trigger...

CHAPTER 13

HE FELT A VAGUE SENSE OF PLEASURE AND VINDICATION AS THE THUNDERCLAP OF THE shot was followed by the appearance of a bright red stain on the stalker's dirty gray shirt. The man stood, unmoving, a look of surprise on his pockmarked face. His head turned slowly, as though seeking the source of the shot.

Then, the gun in his hand wavered and dropped to the ground. He opened his mouth as if to speak, and a small trickle of blood oozed out of the corner and ran down his stubbled chin. Like a felled tree, he toppled forward onto his face, raising a small cloud of dust as he fell.

"One down," Calico murmured, then strained his ears for any telltale movement in the surrounding buildings. All he heard was his own breathing, suddenly interrupted by the sound of Sarah's muffled sobbing. He turned sharply, raising a finger to his lips to silence her.

"He's not moving," she sobbed, indicating the curly dark head of her brother, cradled in her lap.

"He's just passed out," Calico whispered reassuringly, though the knot in his stomach reflected his concern for the young man's condition. "He'll be all right. 'Sides, he ain't feelin' any pain's long as he's out."

He hoped he sounded more confident than he felt. He could see Josh only by looking in a large full-length mirror on the wall beside the end of the counter. The youth's face was drained of color, and it was only by staring at his chest, bared to dress the bullet wound, that Calico could see the almost imperceptible movement of his breathing.

But at the moment, he had other things to worry about, if the three of them were to get out alive.

Movement to the right, behind a window facing the balcony of the saloon three buildings down on the main street caught his eye, and he quietly and smoothly cocked his rifle. The window opened and a black-hatted man crawled through, belly-down, onto the balcony. The black hat appeared over the low railing, followed by the dark moon of a face that turned from side to side.

Calico's location could be fairly easily determined from the position of the dead gunman in the street below. A rifle barrel snaked over the railing as the man cautiously raised his shoulders and arms into view. Calico followed the man's gaze as it swept from the fallen figure up the street toward the general store. The man turned slightly to someone still on the other side of the open window behind him. His lips moved, and Calico squeezed the trigger.

The man was carried backward by the force of the bullet, the crash of his body onto the balcony unheard in the singing echo of the shot reverberating down the row of storefronts.

"And one makes two," Calico said aloud, re-cocking his rifle. They'd know where he was now, no question.

Not taking his eyes from the street, he began talking in a low, calm voice.

"Sarah, you leave Josh here and move over to that back door, ya hear?"

She started to say something, but he cut her off.

" I don't want to spend all day arguin', so ya just do like I tell ya. Josh'll be all right. Ya move over to that door real quiet...and keep down low to the floor."

Once again scanning the buildings in front of him, he heard rather than saw her movement across the rough wood floor to the door.

"Now, ya open it, just a crack, okay?" He heard the rustle of her dress as she raised her arm to the doorknob and turned it slowly. The door opened with a slight creak. "Keep your head close to the floor and peek out. Can ya see anything?" More rustling. "Is anybody out there?"

He could see, reflected in the large mirror, that the back of the shop opened onto a small, scruffy backyard with only a clothesline, an outhouse and a low stack of wood between the building and the sharp rise of the foothills. Her view was unobstructed for several hundred feet in either direction.

"I don't see anyone," she said in a small, frightened voice.

Still watching the street, Calico grunted. He was pretty sure there were only the four pursuers who'd been on their trail for the past several days: two dead, one probably still in the saloon, and the fourth one likely trying to circle around behind them right now. It would be a gamble, sending Sarah out, but he had to risk it.

"Good," he said, trying to make his voice as natural and conversational as possible. "Two doors down on the left—your right—there's a haberdashery, remember? You go down there and see if ya can get in. Hot as it is, chances are the owner's left a window open, at least. There's no spaces between the buildings, so ya won't be seen."

"But what about them?" Sarah asked, her voice a little more steady.

"I think there's only two left, and I doubt as they've both had the time to get around back—it'll take quite a while to circle around without bein' seen. Even so, I 'spect one'll come at the front while the other tries the back." He glanced at her and was relieved to see her staring at him intently, obviously listening to his instructions.

"Now, when ya get in there," he continued, "I want ya to keep low so's ya can't be seen from the street. Get up as close to the front as ya can, find yourself a place to hide where ya can't be seen from either the front or the back, an' wait there. The saloon's off to the left, so I suspect one of 'em 'll come down this side of the street, huggin' the storefronts. If he does, you wait till he gets past ya, comin' this way. Then ya count t' five and throw whatever ya can get your hands on through the front window. Then ya duck back outta sight and stay there till I tell ya to come out. Ya understand me?"

"Yes. But what about the other one?"

"I wager he'll work his way around so he can come down the back from the other direction, so when ya get inside, ya be sure the window's closed and the door's locked behind ya. We'll take care of him when the time comes. Now, ya better get a move on. Remember what I told ya, hear?"

"I'll remember. Don't let anything happen to Josh."

Calico tossed a wave over his left shoulder without turning around. "Ya know I won't. Now get goin'...and shut the door behind ya."

He heard her leave, and the door click shut. He wished there was some way to block it against an unwelcome intrusion, but he couldn't leave the window. He waited until he was sure she'd had enough time to make it into the haberdashery. Then, cautiously, he moved closer to the front door and crouched behind a cracker barrel. The door opened out, he noted, and would easily give with his weight.

On the floor behind the counter, Josh had regained partial consciousness and was moaning softly. Calico could no longer see him in the mirror, but whispered, "Quiet, Josh. It'll all be over in a few minutes."

The moaning stopped. It was so quiet he could hear his ears ring. The seconds seemed like eternity. Why didn't...?

A board of the wooden sidewalk creaked somewhere to his left. He edged out from behind the cracker barrel and closer to the door, his insides coiled like a spring. He risked extending his neck to see down the street to his right. It appeared clear.

Crouched low by a large crate beside the door, his leg muscles so tense they ached, Calico waited, his rifle clutched in both hands—one on the barrel, one on the trigger guard.

And then it came—a shattering crash from the direction of the haberdashery. He sprang forward, threw his weight against the door and burst out onto the street.

He saw the stalker, gun drawn, in the awkward stance of one who's started to spin around in one direction only to stop halfway and turn back. Still in motion himself from the momentum of his crash through the door, Calico pulled the trigger and saw the man lifted off his feet by the force of the blast, his raised gun flying through the air like a startled bird. Automatically, Calico re-cocked his rifle.

That same instant, the back door of the general store burst open. He spun and, aiming almost by instinct, pulled the trigger, re-cocking immediately. The corner post of the back door splintered, and he got the fleeting image of someone ducking away behind the shop. He ran through the store after him, leaping over the counter and narrowly missing landing on the wounded young man behind it; but by the time he got to the rear door, the intruder was disappearing around the corner of a building several doors down. A moment or two later, he heard a horse whinny and the sound of hoofs heading off down the street to the right.

Still holding his rifle, Calico pulled a kerchief from his rear pocket and mopped his forehead. He felt as though someone had dumped a bucket of ice water on him, and his knees felt weak. Then he remembered Josh, and went back into the general store. He knelt over the wounded youth, whose eyes were now open and fixed on his own, and grinned.

"Looks like you'll live."

Josh gave him a weak smile and whispered, "Why do I always miss out on the fun?" He raised his good hand, and Calico, setting his rifle at his side, took it, holding it with both of his for a moment. Then, freeing one hand, he pushed a lock of curly hair back from the boy's forehead, noting that there didn't seem to be a fever. The now-familiar feeling—a tightness in his chest that came each time he touched Josh—washed over him, and he had to force himself to concentrate on where they were.

Releasing Josh's hand, he picked up his rifle and called an all-clear to Sarah. In seconds, her footsteps announced her return. She threw herself down on her knees near her brother.

"Are you okay, Josh?" she asked, repeating Calico's act of brushing the hair from his forehead.

Josh made a weak attempt to wrinkle his nose in disgust at being fussed over.

"'Course I'm okay," he murmured. Then his eyes closed, and he was quiet.

Sarah looked up at Calico in concern.

"He's fine," he reassured her. "Just out again. We'll see if there's somebody in town who knows enough doctorin' to look after him."

Sarah put a bolt of cloth under her brother's head then rose and motioned Calico to follow her out into the street. She pointed to the rag-doll form of the dead gunman draped half on the sidewalk, half in the dusty street.

"He's the one who shot Josh," she said.

"Yeah, I know," Calico said, recognizing the dead man for the first time—in the heat of the gunfight he hadn't had time to identify which of the attackers was who, other than the skeletal man.

The sound of approaching horses and carriages alerted him to the return of the townspeople. As Sarah went back into the general store to see to Josh, he sat down on the edge of the sidewalk, two dead men within fifteen feet of him, a third a hundred feet away, and pondered just how in hell he'd ever gotten into this mess.

CHAPTER 14

CALICO WAS STILL SITTING ON THE SIDEWALK, RIFLE AT HIS SIDE, WHEN THE FIRST OF THE townspeople arrived. He looked up at the tall man in the saddle.

"Is the doc in town?" he asked.

The man looked at the two bodies sprawled in the street.

"Don't look like they need no doctor," he replied. "Looks like you might, though."

Calico got wearily to his feet. "No, I'm fine, but I got a friend in there how does."

He motioned with his thumb, and as he did, Sarah appeared in the shattered doorway of the general store behind him. A crowd had begun to gather, forming two wide circles, one around each of the bodies. A small boy pointed up to the balcony of the saloon, where an arm dangled between two rail posts and a steady trickle of blood oozed between the boards and dripped down onto the wooden sidewalk below.

Sarah edged over to Calico, her face still pale.

"He's awake again," she said, ignoring the staring crowd.

He nodded, rose and moved toward the door, then turned again to the man on the horse.

"I asked you about the doctor," he said.

The man swung down from his horse, touched his hat in greeting to Sarah and followed Calico into the store.

"Doc Smith's over in Clantonville lookin' after a scarlet fever outbreak," he said, confirming what Calico had suspected about the towns sharing the doctor. "We can send somebody after him, but let me take a look at your friend first."

Josh was where Calico had left him, face pale, but his eyes were open as he watched their approach. He managed a weak smile as they knelt beside him; Sarah hovered nearby.

"This here's Mister…" Calico turned his head, realizing he didn't know the man's name.

"Anderson. Sam Anderson." He reached to examine Josh's wound. "Hmmmmm," he said, lips pursed. "Looks like you just might live, son," he pronounced finally then broke into a wide grin. "Hell, I seen gophers shot worse'n you run clean across two counties."

Both Josh and Calico grinned, and Sam's eyes moved quickly from one to the other.

"You folks kin?" he asked.

Calico blushed. "Not exactly. I'm takin' Josh an' Sarah to their aunt. Maybe you know her. Rebecca Durant?"

Sam spun away and got to his feet. "Don't think the boy needs a doctor. Joe Potter, he's mighty good with a knife. He can get that bullet out in no time. I'll go fetch him."

He left the shop without another word; Calico, squatting on the floor, stared after him, puzzled by his sudden change in attitude. When he turned back to Josh, he saw his own confusion mirrored in the young man's eyes.

Sarah stood beside him, hands at her sides, watching the crowd peering through the window and doorway. Yet no one entered until a tall, thin man with gray hair and a goatee pushed through and came into the shop, followed by a mousy little woman in a brown dress.

"You the one what broke my window?" he demanded of Calico.

Calico rose to his feet.

"If you mean the haberdashery two doors down, you're right."

Sarah's eyes widened, and she looked as though she were going to speak; but he shot her a glance that made her keep silent.

"That's right. That's my store an' I want t' know who's goin' t' pay for my window."

His bold manner was belied by his frightened eyes, particularly as he looked up and down Calico's imposing frame.

Calico smiled, and the man relaxed ever so slightly.

"I'll pay for any damage, sure." he said. "What'd you say your name was?"

The man smoothed his goatee with a bony hand.

"Pitt. Ezekiel T. Pitt." He indicated the mousy woman beside him with a sideways nod. "An' this here's Miss Arabella Boggs. Her pa's the owner of this here store, but he's laid up with a broke leg."

Arabella Boggs, nervous little eyes darting from side to side, looked up from under her eyebrows and flashed a tiny smile a blink would have missed, then bobbed her head like a quail in what Calico took as a sign of greeting.

"An' I'll sure pay for the damage t' your door, Miss Boggs," he added, receiving another blink-quick smile in return.

Sarah came over to kneel beside Josh, and Calico was suddenly aware of the crowd at the windows and in the doorway. They stared, for the most part, in silence, though he could detect a buzz of whispered conversations, like the sound of distant bees.

"My name's Calico," he volunteered, trying to capture Miss Boggs's gaze and failing. "Calico Ramsay. This here's Josh and Sarah Howard. I'm takin' 'em to their aunt, Rebecca Durant."

He said the last name carefully, watching for the reaction, and got what he expected—a nervous exchange of glances between the shopkeepers. He was also aware of a sudden silence from the townspeople gathered near enough at the door to hear.

Ezekiel Pitt cleared his throat nervously.

"Well...ah...I got t' get back t' my store, t' see what else might be broke. I'll get a bill ready for ya."

In unison, he and Miss Boggs turned and, by squeezing their shoulders together, managed to pass through the door at exactly the same time. The townspeople made way for them and, like metal shavings drawn to a magnet, followed as they disappeared from Calico's line of sight.

"What was that all about?" Sarah asked.

"Danged if I know," he replied, shaking his head. He stood, legs apart, hands on hips, and, one by one, engaged in a staring contest with the few people still peering in the window, pleased as the force of his stare made them look away.

One young girl, however, continued to stare at him so intently he could almost feel it. He gave her a slow, deliberate wink, and her face blossomed into the brightest grin he had seen in days. Giggling, she turned and ran off in the direction the rest of the townspeople had taken.

A few moments later, Sam Anderson re-entered the shop, followed by a husky young man about Calico's age who carried what looked like a doctor's bag in one hand and a bottle of whiskey in the other. Nodding curtly to Calico and Sarah in turn, he hurried to Josh and knelt beside him. Sarah moved out of the way, rising to her feet and backing up to the counter.

"Name's Joe Potter. You a drinkin' man, son?" the man asked.

Josh's puzzled glance darted from the man's face to Calico's then back again.

"Not exactly," he said.

"Well," Potter replied, pulling the cork out of the bottle with his teeth, "I think it's about time you learned, don't you?"

He spat the cork onto the floor and handled the bottle to Josh, who took it with his good hand.

Josh's attention was on the bag on the floor beside him.

"Are you going to cut me?"

The man shrugged, then nodded.

"'Less you know some other way t' get that bullet out."

Calico knelt on the other side and lifted Josh's head so he could raise the bottle to his lips. Josh took a long drink then began coughing wildly, spraying much of the liquor around the room, a trickle running down his chin.

Joe Potter paid no attention, just nodded to Sam, who moved to the door and began talking to the remaining townspeople in a low voice.

In the meantime, Joe extracted a sharp-looking knife from the bag, took the bottle from Josh long enough to soak a cloth in a stream of whiskey and wipe the knife blade with it. Then he handed the bottle back.

"Have another," he ordered.

Josh tilted the bottle to his mouth. He drank more slowly this time, and though he started to cough again, he fought it back and continued drinking until Joe pulled the bottle away from him.

Joe turned to Calico and grinned.

"Your friend here's goin' t' be quite a man," he said.

Calico returned the grin.

"Young lady," Joe said, "why don't you go over there an' see if you can find some white cloth we can use as bandages."

Sarah, wide-eyed and staring at the knife in his hand, nodded and edged away, her back still against the counter.

"Like I said, I'm Joe Potter," he repeated to Josh gently. "I always think it's a good idea t' know the man who takes a bullet out o' ya, don't you?"

Josh grinned weakly, the alcohol beginning to take effect.

"Sure," he said.

Joe turned to Calico. "You mind helpin' Sam move the rest of those people away from the window? I need enough light so's I can see what I'm doin'."

Calico turned to find that all but two or three people had moved away. Lowering Josh's head, he stood, picked up his rifle and went to the door. Immediately, the hangers-on scattered. Satisfied, he returned, leaned his rifle against the counter and knelt beside Joe.

"Anythin' else I can do?"

Joe, who had been examining the wound, turned his head and looked into Calico's eyes, his focus moving from one to the other. Calico just shrugged and grinned.

"Interestin'," Joe said.

Josh snickered. Joe handed him the bottle again.

"Just one more, for the road," he urged, and Josh lifted his head high enough to drink without spilling it and took another long chug while Calico and Joe exchanged glances.

"There *is* somethin' you can do," Joe murmured to Calico. "This may sting a bit, an' your young friend here might get a little rambunctious. Maybe you can sorta make sure he don't move around too much." To Josh he said, "You about ready?"

Josh squeezed his eyelids tight then opened them to blink several times rapidly, as if trying to focus. Finally, he nodded.

"Miss," Joe called to Sarah, who had been standing at the end of the counter, a bolt of white sheeting in her hand, her eyes fixed on his every movement. "Would you cut off a piece o' that 'bout the size of two kerchiefs an' bring it here? I seen a scissors just about right there behind you."

Sarah did as she was told, rushing over with the swatch of cloth then backing away. Joe took the material and folded it several times. When he had a small wad about an inch thick, he handed it to Josh.

"You might want t' put this in your mouth—it's always good t' have somethin' t' chew on when you're thinkin' 'bout things."

Josh took it with his free hand, moving rather clumsily, and did as suggested.

Joe turned again to Sarah.

"It's gettin' a mite stuffy in here, Miss. Why don't you go outside an' get some air?"

Sarah stared directly into his eyes and shook her head. Joe shrugged then lifted the whiskey bottle over Josh's wound and poured some directly into the opening.

Josh's eyes flew wide, his entire body stiffened and he sucked his breath in through the cloth. Then his eyes lost focus and closed, and he went limp.

"So much f'r that," Joe said, exchanging a knowing look with Calico. "You hold him, now. This shouldn't be too hard."

He raised the knife and lowered the point to the wound. Calico glanced up at Sarah and saw her turn her head away sharply. He held Josh's arms gently but firmly, although the young man was unconscious and made no movement.

The only sound in the shop was that of breathing.

With a slight grunt, Joe slowly removed the blood-covered tip of the knife from the wound, tilted at a slight angle. As it emerged, it brought with it a lump of yellowish lead. With his free hand, he plucked it from the wound and rubbed it with the whiskey-soaked rag he'd used to sterilize the knife.

"Maybe he'd like it for a watch fob," he said, handing it to Calico.

They grinned broadly at one another, and Calico felt the tension flowing from his muscles. He released Josh's arms and ran one large palm over his own forehead, which was wet with sweat.

"I c'n use some more of that cloth now, Miss," Joe said, watching as Sarah, too, seemed to turn from stone back to flesh. She'd been clutching the bolt of cloth so tightly to her stomach her knuckles were almost as white as the fabric. Now her hands relaxed, and she hurried over with the bolt and scissors. Joe expertly and swiftly cut several long strips then handed both back to her.

"You see any cobwebs around here?" he asked.

Both Calico and Sarah searched the rafters of the small shop. In one corner, Calico spotted several up close to the ceiling and went to get them. Sarah watched, looking puzzled, as he moved a barrel to stand on then scooped the cobwebs into one hand with large, sweeping motions. When he had them all, he hopped from the barrel and returned, open-palmed.

"This do it?" he asked.

Joe nodded, and Calico carefully lowered his open palm over Josh's wound and pressed the cobwebs gently into it. He looked up at Sarah, who observed him with a mixture of puzzlement and shock.

"Stops the blood," he said.

After wiping Josh's blood from his hand, Calico raised him gently into a sitting position and held him while Joe wound strips of cloth around his chest and shoulder. When he was done, Calico lowered him again to the floor while Joe wiped his knife off carefully and put it back in his bag. Then he got to his feet and dusted off his pantlegs.

"How about you?" he asked, indicating Calico's bloody shirt and the graze on his temple. "Need me to look at that?"

Calico shook his head. "No, thanks, I'll be fine."

Joe shrugged. "I'll go fetch Sam, an' we'll see about findin' y'all someplace t' spend the night," Joe said. "We got a hotel o' sorts, but I think you'd be better off someplace a little more quiet."

With a nod to Calico and a smile for Sarah, he turned and strolled from the shop as casually as though he'd just come in to check the time.

"He's wonderful," Calico heard Sarah say, and looked up to see her staring after Joe's departing figure. He smiled at the starry look in her eyes.

"Yeah, I guess he is," he agreed.

"Is he a doctor?" she asked in an almost reverent tone.

Calico shook his head. "Not as I can tell. He's just mighty good with a knife. That's a handy thing t' be in a town like this."

Sarah just nodded, her eyes still fixed on the door, a small smile on her lips.

Calico did a close visual check of Josh then, satisfied he was still unconscious and in no seeming pain, rose, placed his hands on his hips and did a back stretch. His muscles still ached from his fall, but he'd been too tense until just now to notice.

He then took advantage of the wait for Joe's return to leave Josh in Sarah's care and fetch the horses. Before he headed back, though, he took his spare shirt from his saddlebag and put it on to eliminate any more inquiries into his health.

A short time later, a small farm wagon pulled up, driven by a matronly looking woman. She was accompanied by both Sam and Joe. Joe dismounted quickly to help her from the wagon while Sam crossed the street and disappeared into one of the stores.

Calico greeted them at the door, noting that the gunslingers' bodies were gone; only the blood pools remained to show they had ever been there.

"Calico…ah…" Joe began.

"Ramsay," he supplied.

"…Ramsay, this is my mother, Mrs. Potter. We'll take your young friend home with us for the night. You an' the young lady are more'n welcome, too, if you'd like."

Calico and Mrs. Potter exchanged smiles, and he liked her at once.

"Mrs. Potter, I'd like you to meet Sarah Howard. Her brother Josh's the one your boy just took a bullet out of, an' we're mighty grateful to him."

Mrs. Potter turned her eyes to Sarah, still standing beside Josh. Sarah smiled shyly and curtsied. Mrs. Potter, her feet hidden under her long dress, seemed to glide, like a ship under full sail, through the doorway and up to her.

"My, aren't you the pretty one?" she said warmly, and Sarah flushed and looked down at the floor. "Why don't you come help me set up a bed in the wagon so we can get your brother into a real bed, where he belongs?"

Taking Sarah's arm, she maneuvered her smoothly out the door.

"Soon's we get Josh settled, what say you an' me go have a drink?" Joe suggested.

Calico nodded and wiped the back of his hand across his mouth. "I'd say that was 'bout the best idea I heard all day," he said.

Mrs. Potter motioned to them, and they went to the still-unconscious Josh—Calico suspected the fact he was not yet awake was more due to the whiskey than to his injury. Carefully sliding his arm under Josh's shoulders while Joe took his legs, he raised the young man up slightly; then they carried him to the wagon. As they put him onto the makeshift bed of hay bales draped with a blanket, he noticed both Ezekiel Pitt and Arabella Boggs standing in front of the haberdashery. When they saw him looking at them, they turned away and disappeared into the store.

He glanced quizzically at Joe, who gave him a raised-eyebrow look that said "later."

Sam Anderson emerged from the store across the street and came over to join them.

"I'll be sending someone ahead to the Durants'," he said, and Calico noticed a long, meaningful glance pass between him and Joe. He started to say something then thought better of it—he and Joe had a lot to talk about.

He offered Sam his hand. "We're grateful f'r everything you done," he said. "An' tell Mr. Pitt an' Miss Boggs I'll arrange to pay 'em as soon as they tell me how much I owe."

Sam tipped his hat to Sarah and Mrs. Potter then mounted and rode off in the direction from which he'd come. Joe tied his horse to the back of the wagon and joined Calico on the wagon's bench seat. Mrs. Potter and Sarah remained in the back with Josh, who was finally awake and apparently suffering from a severe headache.

The townspeople stopped and stared in silence as the wagon moved past them and up the rutted street toward the foothills behind town. Calico saw a young man leading their three horses toward the livery stable.

The Potters' house was at the extreme west end of town, a weathered clapboard building with a picket fence immediately behind which a scraggly row of petunias peered out at the world like prisoners behind bars. They pulled up in front of the house, and Joe jumped off to tether the horse to a hitching post, then untied his and led it to a sagging barn beside and slightly behind the house. Calico dismounted to help Sarah and Mrs. Potter to the ground then, when Joe returned from the barn, climbed into the wagon bed. Together, they got Josh, who insisted on walking, out of the wagon and into the house.

Realizing that the alcohol, blood loss and shock had taken their toll, Calico supported him with an arm around his waist, even under the less than pleasant circumstances savoring the opportunity to be close as, he sensed, did Josh.

Mrs. Potter led the way to a small bedroom off the kitchen. A large brass bed nearly filled it, making it difficult for Joe and Calico to maneuver the uncharacteristically quiet Josh onto the mattress. Calico carefully removed Josh's boots before covering him with the quilt folded at the foot of the bed.

"Now, you rest awhile," he ordered, and Josh nodded weakly.

He and Joe went back into the kitchen, closing the door behind them. Mrs. Potter was outside drawing water from a bright red hand pump, and Sarah sat at the table. When she saw them, she rose to go into the bedroom, but Joe stopped her.

"There's nothin' you can do right now, Miss. Why not just let him sleep a spell, while you an' Ma have some coffee an' talk?" He gave her a warm smile, which made her blush and look away.

Calico smiled to himself.

Mrs. Potter returned with the water, which she set on the table and ladled out into the coffeepot with a large dipper.

"Ma, Calico an' me's goin' t' take a walk down t' Reb's for a drink. You an' Miss Howard can get acquainted while we're gone. We'll be back in time for supper."

Busy at the stove, she waved acknowledgement without turning around.

With a nod from Joe and a wink from Calico, both aimed at Sarah, the two men left the house and walked out into the dusty street.

CHAPTER 15

THE HEAT OF THE DAY SETTLED OVER THEM LIKE AN INVISIBLE QUILT, AND THEY KICKED up little clouds of dust as they headed toward the main part of town. People they passed seemed to draw away from them and suddenly become very busy with other things, but Calico felt their eyes on him.

"Joe, ya mind tellin' me what's goin on?" he said at last. "Why is everybody actin' so strange? I ain't never been in a town where people acted so peculiar."

Joe looked at him and smiled.

"You been in a lot of towns where you killed three men in the street before?" he asked, and Calico broke into an embarrassed grin.

"Nope, can't say as I have," he admitted. "But I got a gut feelin' it goes beyond that."

"Well, it might be partly 'cause you're strollin' down the street with your rifle—not that I don't understand why, given what you been through. But mostly I think it's account o' they know who you are." Joe answered calmly.

Calico stopped abruptly, forcing Joe to do the same.

"What's that supposed t' mean? How the hell could anybody 'round here know who I am? Ain't like I was some gunslinger with his picture on every fence in town. I ain't nobody special."

"Maybe not, but you're the one who brought the Howard twins to town, and they *are* special. Leastways, 'round here."

Calico was thoroughly puzzled and wanted to know more, but sensed Joe would explain in good time. For the moment, he just shook his head and continued walking.

They approached the main street, passing by the general store and the haberdashery, where Ezekiel Pitt was busy with a hammer and a stack of boards, nailing up the broken window. He didn't look around as they passed, though Calico knew he was watching their reflection in the unbroken glass of the next pane. Little knots of people were clustered around in various places along the street; their conversation cut off as if by a knife the minute the two men got within earshot, resuming the minute they passed.

Joe headed for the balconied saloon, but Calico nudged him with the back of his hand and, glancing up at the place where the gunman's body had dangled, said, "Ya mind if we go someplace else?"

Joe followed Calico's glance, smiled weakly and said, "Sure," then turned diagonally toward a smaller saloon across the street.

They entered the dim, stale-smelling bar, where a group clustered at the far end broke off their conversation like a snapped twig.

"A bottle, Jack," Joe called, and steered Calico to a table in the farthest corner of the bar.

Calico chose to sit with his back to the wall, facing the rest of the room. Three of his pursuers might be dead, but there was still one left, and too many unanswered questions to allow the luxury of vulnerability.

The bartender broke away from the clustered men, grabbed a bottle and two glasses and came around the bar to the table. Without a word he set them down, nodded at Joe and returned to the bar. Joe pulled the stopper and poured two healthy slugs into the glasses. Putting the bottle down, he raised his glass, motioned with it toward Calico in silent salute and took a drink.

Calico echoed the gesture, the sharpness of the whiskey spreading warmth through his mouth and throat. After everything he'd gone through, a little inner comfort was exactly what he needed.

"Okay," he said, setting his glass down. "Now, suppose ya tell me just what in hell's goin' on around here."

Joe stared at him for a moment, shrugged and took another drink.

"Yeah," he said, setting his glass carefully beside Calico's, "I guess you got a right. Don't know as I know exactly how t' start."

"The twins," Calico suggested.

"Yeah, the twins." Joe poured them both another drink. "Well, folks around here heard they was comin', and they're a mite nervous."

"About two seventeen-year-olds?" Calico was incredulous. "Why in hell would anybody be nervous about two seventeen-year-old kids?"

Joe took a long drink then stared directly into his eyes for several seconds, as though searching for something.

"Because they're afraid the kids'll be...well, too much like their aunt."

Calico had raised his glass halfway to his lips, and Joe's words froze it there for a long moment of silence. Then the glass resumed its movement, and he drained it in one gulp.

"I expect you're goin' t' explain what that's supposed t' mean," he said, his voice husky from the burning alcohol.

Joe poured him another drink then edged his chair closer to the table and leaned forward.

"Well, I might as well start at the beginnin'. Seven years ago," he began, "the Durants moved t' Bow Ridge from up north of Denver an' bought the Kincaid spread up near Cold Springs, 'bout ten miles north of here. It was pretty clear right from the start that it's Rebecca wears the pants in that family.

"I never seen a man fall all over his wife like Mike Durant does. Whatever she wants, she gets—a fancy piano from Denver, furniture brought in special all the way from Chicago. They even rebuilt the main house. She don't want for nothin'—which I, for one, don't find as strange as other folks, since Mike never made no bones about its bein' her money."

He paused long enough to take a drink, and Calico was aware the bar had become strangely quiet. Joe didn't seem to notice and, after putting his glass down, leaned forward, resting both arms on the table.

"But I'm gettin' ahead of myself. They seemed like nice enough folks but kept pretty much to themselves—he was always friendly enough when somebody'd drop by to introduce themselves, but Rebecca could be right on the verandah and would all but ignore whoever was there. Just sit there an' hardly say a word, like she couldn't be bothered.

"Some folks suspected she might have a drinkin' problem, but nobody ever smelled it around her, or saw her drink anythin' other than tea—an' she'd hardly touch that, even when it was in front o' her.

"She never comes into town. Mostly it's Mike that comes in alone or with one o' their hands, who they brung with 'em from their other place. Whenever he buys somethin', unless it's somethin' real basic for the ranch, it's always 'Rebecca wants this' an' 'Rebecca says to get that.' Sometimes he'll say 'Well, that's not what I woulda chose,' or 'I don't really know what we're gonna do with this, but Rebecca wants it, so...' Amazin' how a man can act so henpecked an' still have folks respect him.

"But Mike Durant's the kind of guy who can charm the birds out o' the trees." Joe took another drink. "'Course, so can some snakes."

Calico knew he looked puzzled, but Joe was staring into his drink and didn't notice, and he decided to let him finish his story without interruption.

"Some folks chalk it up to his bein' from the big city," Joe continued after a bit, "an' that people's different there. Thing is that, while Mike don't generally make it known, he ain't no city-bred gentleman. He was raised out here in the West somewheres by common folk, but he had his eye on bigger things, so he moved off to the city an' made somethin' of himself, includin' marryin' one Miss Rebecca Howard."

Finishing his drink, he poured himself another and motioned with the bottle to do the same for Calico, who shook his head, indicating his still half-filled glass.

"Mike sure ain't stupid, that's a fact. He had t' work real hard t' get where he is. Taught himself t' talk city English—he's 'bout the only one around here that does, but folks don't resent it 'cause it don't seem like he does it just t' make himself better'n the rest o' us."

Calico, while fascinated with the information, was increasingly annoyed by the stares of the men at the bar. They had been surreptitious at first then gawked more openly; and he didn't like it one bit.

Joe, though he had his back to the room, sensed Calico's shift in mood and gave a quick jerk of his head in the direction of the bar.

"Forget 'em," he said. "They don't see many strangers in here. 'Specially one who shoots people."

He grinned, and Calico made an effort to ignore the stares and concentrate on Joe as he continued his story.

"The thing that really bothered most folks was when they didn't join a church right off. We got three they could o' chose from—there's even a Catholic priest who comes by every month or so for services. Naturally, the local pastors all went for a visit an' t' invite 'em t' join. Rebecca wouldn't even see 'em—Mike said she was upstairs sick, but they could tell he was just makin' excuses for her. It was pretty poor manners, nonetheless, even for rich city folk.

"When he was walkin' the Reverend Johnson—he's the Baptist minister—back to his carriage, Mike come right out and apologized, sayin' that while he'd try to come to services himself from time to time, his wife wasn't much inta church-goin'.

"Well, you can imagine what that news did f'r the local gossips—nearly every one o' who's a Bible thumper on Sunday an' a hypocrite the other six days o' the week. As far as they're concerned, if you ain't a churchgoer you're in league with the devil. If they thought she was a little uppity before, they really sunk their teeth inta the idea o' her bein' a heathen."

Calico knew exactly what he was saying and nodded his understanding.

"Frankly," Joe went on, "I think all that religion stuff is a lot o' nonsense—no offense intended." He sighed. "An', o' course, I go t' church every Sunday, too, but just because Ma'd be hurt if I didn't, so I 'spose I'm as big a hypocrite as the rest of 'em.

"Anyways, people started steerin' clear o' the Durant place. Mike comes into town pretty regular, but nobody hardly ever sees her. Far as most folks is concerned, he's got himself a real cross to bear with his missus. He's never said nothin', but it's interestin' how what some folks *don't* say speaks louder than what they do.

"Even his ranch hands won't talk about her when they're in town. They hint plenty—enough to keep everybody gossipin'—but they don't come out an' say anythin' direct."

Calico's annoyance over being watched was back, and turning to outright anger. He drained his glass and slid it across the table. Joe refilled it and continued.

"About six years ago she went off to Chicago to visit her family—her ma'd died, as I recall. She wasn't gone more'n three days before Mike hightailed it to Chicago after her. Well, I guess you know what happened there."

Calico nodded. "The fire," he said.

Joe grunted in agreement. "The fire. Well, when Mike brought her back, she was practically more'n anybody could handle. Mike was real protective, wouldn't let nobody go near her, even for a visit—not that there was many who tried. Ma rode out there one day right after they got back. Rebecca wouldn't even see her. Mike tried makin' all sorts of excuses, though Ma did catch a glimpse of her peerin' out from behind some curtains in one of the windows upstairs.

"He puts on a pretty noble show of protectin' his wife—maybe a tad too noble for my taste. Nobody'd dare say so much as a word about his missus in front of him—and he's man enough t' make sure they'd be more'n a little sorry.

"Well, word started goin' around that her whole family was pretty strange—rumor is her ma died in a nuthouse—an' when folks heard she had a niece and nephew, they just assumed there's probably somethin' peculiar about them, too.

"When her ma died, Rebecca apparently inherited quite a sum o' money, not that she didn't have plenty t' start with. Right after they come back from Chicago, she started havin' Mike buy up some o' the ranches surroundin' their place until now she owns just about the whole valley, an' a good part of Bow Ridge itself—includin', incidentally, this here bar. Mike did all the buyin', him bein' the husband, but it's no secret around here who's behind it. And, o' course, when you own just about everythin', you own just about every*body*—an' nobody around here much likes bein' owned.

"So, when folks heard the kids was comin' here to join her they really got upset. They figure with her money an' their money they can buy out anybody they want. Hell, to hear some of 'em tell it, the three of 'em'll be runnin' around torchin' every house an' barn in the area. The latest gossip has the two kids burnin' down some hotel in Fort Collins the day they got off the train."

Calico held his tongue, wanting to be sure he'd heard Joe out completely before he said anything, but he wondered how word of the hotel fire could possibly have circulated in Bow Ridge even before he and the twins arrived. His gut told him it wasn't that hard to figure out.

"That it?" he asked after a few moments of silence.

Joe nodded. "Pretty much."

Calico looked once again at the bar to see several patrons still staring at him, and he decided he'd had enough of being the local freak show. He pushed away from the table and got to his feet, picking up his rifle from the empty chair beside him. The men at the bar turned away.

He strode over to about five feet behind the cluster and slowly, deliberately, cocked his rifle.

"Ya seen enough," he said calmly. "Now I think it's time y'all went home."

In a body, not even turning to face him, the men sidled out, some still carrying their glasses.

Calico, Joe and the barman were alone. The barman was backed up against the wall.

Calico turned toward him.

"Ain't ya got somethin' t' do out back?"

The man's frightened eyes moved from him to Joe and back. He gulped loudly and nodded, edging toward the back door. He paused, hand on the knob.

"Well, go do it!" Calico commanded, and the barkeep dived through the door and slammed it behind him.

Satisfied, Calico walked back to the table, propped his rifle carefully against the chair and sat down.

"I hope your bein' seen with me ain't gonna cause ya no problems, Joe," he said.

Joe was staring at him, and just waved his hand in dismissal. Then, slowly, his face broke into a broad grin, which Calico mirrored.

"Now that's the way to clear a bar," Joe said, refilling their glasses.

They toasted each other silently then sat without talking for several minutes, the only sound in the now-empty saloon the persistent buzzing of several flies.

"Well?" Joe asked, finally.

"Well...I guess it is my turn," Calico acknowledged. "I reckon you're as curious about all this as I am, an' ya do deserve t' hear my part o' the story."

Setting his glass to one side, he leaned back in his chair and began with the day Dan received the letter informing him of his brother's death. When he reached the end of his tale, in Bow Ridge and at the point where Joe entered the scene, he paused.

"So, let me ask ya—ya figger anybody 'round here might be so nervous 'bout the twins comin' they might want to make sure they never got here?"

Joe shook his head. "Frankly, nobody 'round here's got the power or the guts to do somethin' like that...'cept the Durants. An' I can't comprehend them tryin' t' kill their own kin."

Calico nodded. "Those men—the ones I killed today. I don't suppose ya know 'em."

Joe shook his head. "Nope. Never seen any of 'em before."

"Ya ever hear of a gunslinger named Jessie Riles?"

Joe's eyebrows rose. "You think Jessie Riles is in on this? Not that I'd be surprised if he was."

"Then ya do know him?"

"Sure do. He's supposed t' be the Durants' foreman, but word is he's just Rebecca Durant's hired gun. He's gone more'n he's around, and that suits everybody hereabouts just fine."

"An' he's been gone lately, I'll wager," Calico said.

Joe shrugged. "Hard to say—he comes an' goes, an' nobody in town hardly ever sees him. Just knowin' he might be around is enough."

"Why don't the sheriff arrest him? I hear he's wanted nearly everyplace in six states an' a couple o' territories."

Joe grinned. "The sheriff's sixty-two years old an' wants to live t' be sixty-three. This's a small town, an' mean as Jessie Riles may be, he's kept his nose clean around here. If somebody else wants him, they can come get him."

"Well, one thing's for damn sure," Calico said, rubbing his hand over his chin, "I ain't leavin' those twins with nobody till I know for sure what's goin' on, an' why. For two cents, I'd just take 'em back with me right now, but Josh's in no condition t' travel just yet. An' I won't rest easy till I find out why Uncle Dan was killed, an' why somebody wants the twins dead."

Joe started to pour another drink, but Calico put his hand over his glass.

"Obliged, Joe, but I ain't been t' drinkin' these past few weeks," he said, "an' I got a feelin' it ain't a good idea t' start feelin' too relaxed around here."

Joe gave him a quick smile and nod then poured a small shot into his own glass.

"So, what are you plannin' t' do?" he asked.

Calico rubbed the back of his neck. "Go up t' Cold Springs, I reckon. See just who's what…an' why. I'd be mighty obliged if you'd look after Sarah an' Josh while I'm gone. What I said 'bout not leavin' 'em with nobody, that didn't include you or your ma, if ya'll have 'em."

Joe drained his glass before answering then set it down carefully on the table and stared directly into Calico's eyes for a long moment.

"I was figurin' on ridin' up there with ya, if ya wouldn't mind the company," he said. "Ma'll be happy t' watch after the twins. She don't look it, but she's a tough old bird, an' there ain't nobody around here who's likely to try to put anythin' over on her," Anticipating Calico's hesitation, he added, "An' I don't think ya have t' worry about Jesse Riles. If it was him behind this, ya killed everybody he was with. Jesse ain't much of one t' do anything without backup."

Calico pursed his lips and returned Joe's stare.

"Well," he said, "I rightly should refuse your offer, since it's my problem—mine an' the twins—but I'd be pleased t' have ya come along, if ya've a mind to."

Joe snapped his head in a cursory nod of agreement, pushed back from the table and slapped his leg.

"Okay. Now that's settled, what say we get back t' the house? Ma'll be startin' supper."

They walked out into the hot, dusty late-afternoon, headed for the livery stable to pick up Calico's horse—he had already decided he might as well leave the other two there for now. The brightness of the lowering sun causing them to squint until their eyes became accustomed to the light. The street was nearly deserted, but Calico knew they were being watched by dozens of pairs of hidden eyes.

Supper consisted of roast chicken, boiled potatoes, string beans, fresh-baked bread and coffee with molasses. For dessert, there were two huge apple pies—Calico hadn't eaten so well since he left the ranch. Josh, despite his weakness and the pain of his wound, insisted on coming to the table over the objections of Sarah and Mrs. Potter and a raised-eyebrow look from Calico. Sarah offered to cut his meat for him, but he bluntly refused.

"Why don't you just use your fingers, son?" Mrs. Potter suggested with a smile. "We're not fancy here."

Josh, looking relieved, grinned back at her and picked up a drumstick.

By the time supper was over, however, he was visibly exhausted and was, despite his protestations, convinced to go back to bed. Calico wanted to spend more time with the young man than he thought was advisable under the circumstances, but he could manage to look in on him frequently. It was getting to the point where neither he nor Josh had to speak—there was a lot said, or so he could not help but think, in their exchange of looks.

Sarah and Mrs. Potter had become fast friends, and Sarah moved as naturally about the kitchen as if it were her own. Once again, he was struck by her emerging grace and beauty, and saw that Joe noticed it, too.

After supper, he and Joe spent a few minutes with Josh until they sensed he was ready to go to sleep. They said their goodnights and started back into the kitchen.

As they were closing the door, Josh called, "Calico?" and he went back into the room.

"Yeah, Josh?"

The young man motioned with his good hand for him to come closer.

"You know," he said softly, "this is the first time since Sarah and I got off the train that I've slept in a real bed without you in it."

Calico blushed and grinned at the same time. "Yeah, I know," he said.

"Couldn't we—" Josh began, but Calico, still grinning, cut him off with a shake of his head.

"No, we couldn't, an' you damned well know it. Now get to sleep."

Still grinning, he returned to the kitchen and sat at the table drinking coffee with Joe while Sarah and Mrs. Potter did the dishes. It was a hot, quiet summer night, filled with silences studded by the chirping of crickets and bathed in the yellowed lights of the oil lamps. It stirred in Calico memories of nights many, many years before, when he had been a very small boy seated at a long-forgotten kitchen table with his father, listening to the stillness.

When the dishes were done, Sarah and Mrs. Potter joined them at the table, talking of many things but carefully avoiding any mention of the trials of the twins' journey—or of the Durants. Calico sensed Sarah's awareness of the game, and saw in her willingness to play along further evidence of her growing maturity.

In the parlor, a clock began to chime the hour, and he and Joe simultaneously pulled their pocket watches from their vests to check the time.

"Nine o'clock!" Joe said, shaking his head. He looked from Calico to Sarah, snapped the watch closed and replaced it, as Calico had done with his. "I reckon you're both pretty tired."

Sarah responded with a gentle smile and nodded.

"A little," she said. Her eyes reflected the same warmth Calico had noticed every time she looked at Joe, and he smiled. He glanced at Mrs. Potter and saw her looking thoughtfully from Sarah to her son. Then she looked at Calico and shared his smile.

"Well, then," Joe announced, unaware of the silent communication going on around him, "I'll make up the sofa for you, Miss Howard, an' if you don't mind, Calico, you an' me can bed down in the barn."

"Fine by me," Calico said. He patted his stomach and shook his head then turned to Mrs. Potter. "Ma'am, I don't know when I've had a finer meal."

"Would you like another piece of pie before you go to bed?" she asked, pleased.

He raised his hands and shook his head.

"No, thank you, ma'am. One more bite an' I'd burst. All I know's ya got yourself three travelers very much in your debt."

The older woman, flushed with pleasure, gave a series of flickering little smiles then rose from her chair and hurried into her bedroom for blankets for Sarah.

"Never you mind about making up the sofa," she said to Joe. "You never could make a proper bed. You two just go on."

Calico, Joe and Sarah looked in on Josh and found him sleeping soundly. Joe closed the door quietly.

"He'll be just fine," he said to Sarah then moved to the counter to pick up and light a lantern. "You 'bout ready, Calico?" he asked, heading for the back door.

"Yep." Calico reached out and took both of Sarah's hands in his. "Ya get some sleep now, y' hear?"

She nodded and smiled.

"Goodnight, Calico," she said, but her eyes were on Joe.

Joe must have felt them, for he turned at the door, his face haloed by the lantern light. When their eyes met, he gave her a slow-spreading smile.

"'Night...Sarah," he said.

"Goodnight...Joe," she replied, then flushed and turned quickly to join Mrs. Potter, who had just emerged from her room, arms laden with bedding.

Shaking his head and chuckling, Calico followed Joe out into the night.

CHAPTER 16

SOMETIME TOWARD MORNING, CALICO THOUGHT HE HEARD HORSES; BUT THEY SEEMED far off, and he was too tired to bring himself fully awake. Next thing, he was vaguely aware it was daybreak. Joe's deep, steady breathing set a soothing rhythm that tempted him to let go of consciousness and re-submerge in the warm, lazy depths of sleep. He stretched and began to turn over, facing the door.

Abruptly, he was wide-awake, muscles tense. Standing in the open doorway were three men, watching him. He bolted upright, left hand automatically feeling for his rifle, which lay between him and Joe.

The tallest of the three raised his hand, palm out, and stepped forward.

"Mr. Ramsay?" he asked in a soft, cultured voice. "I'm Mike Durant."

Calico felt rather than saw Joe come awake and rise up on one elbow.

"Mike!" Joe's voice was thick with sleep. "What the hell you doin' here at this time o' the mornin'?"

Mike Durant advanced until he stood at their feet. His two companions remained motionless in the doorway.

"Sam Anderson sent the Calhoun boy out to the ranch with the news."

Unnerved as he was by the unannounced arrival, Calico was impressed by the steady, warm tone of the man's voice. There was just enough light in the barn for him to make out Durant's face, and it, too, was impressive—handsome, but not ruggedly so. More like what he imagined a riverboat gambler's face must be like.

Calico guessed his age to be about forty, his face beginning to be creased by what on other people would probably be called wrinkles, but on him were likely referred to as "character lines." Graying temples only added to the overall effect of efficient self-assurance.

Joe, yawning and rubbing his face vigorously with the palms of his hands, struggled to his feet, slapping idly at bits of hay clinging to his clothing. Calico also got up to accept Durant's extended hand. The grip was firm, but not powerful.

"How long you been here?" Joe asked.

"We rode in almost as soon as we heard," Mike replied. "Got to town about three o'clock this morning, I imagine. Caught a little sleep down the road."

"I reckon you could use some coffee."

"Your mother's fixing some already. We stopped at the house first, and she told us you were out here." He turned to Calico. "Mr. Ramsay, you and I need to have a little talk."

Joe took the hint.

"I'd best get in the house t' see if Ma needs some help." He left, nodding to the two men in the doorway. In unison, they returned the greeting, still saying nothing.

"Well, now, Mr. Durant," Calico said when Joe was gone, "I do think you're right about us havin' t' talk, an' since ya rode so hard t' get here, I expect now might be as good a time as any."

Durant motioned to his men, and they moved away toward the house. Walking past Calico, he pulled a bale of hay out onto the floor and sat down. Calico followed him and leaned against a stall, where he could keep his eyes on both him and the doorway.

Durant looked at the straw-strewn floor and spread his hands.

"I really don't know how—or where—to begin. I owe you a great debt of gratitude for having safely brought Joshua and Sarah to us, and I'm deeply sorry for the inconveniences you have suffered—inconveniences for which I must take full responsibility.

"I am a man who treasures his privacy, and that of his family, and I feel strongly that family problems—I'm sure you will agree with me—are of no concern to anyone outside the family."

Calico started to say something, but Durant stopped him with a gesture.

"However, you have earned the right to certain information that may clarify the situation in which you now find yourself. I understand you are a man of honor and discretion, and I know that what I am about to tell you will go no farther."

Calico, not knowing how to respond, merely shrugged.

"My wife..." Durant said after a long sigh, "My wife, you see, is not...is not well, and I fear that in her...illness...she may have inadvertently been the source of a great many of your recent difficulties."

"You're saying it's your wife been tryin' t' kill us?" he asked levelly. "I'd be mighty curious t' know why she'd want t' do that."

Durant looked up and met his eyes. He took a slow, deep breath.

"You must understand, Mr. Ramsay, that I love my wife. She is the dearest, most precious thing in the world to me, and I would die before letting any harm come to her. But I have known for many years, since shortly after we were married, that there was a strain of...illness...in her family. Her own mother died in an institution. I had hoped that, by taking her away from Chicago, I might spare her the pressures that could bring on what I refused to see as the inevitable.

"Rebecca is an amazing woman in many ways. She comes, as I'm sure you know, from a very wealthy family, and she has always had her own money. The combination of having an extremely strong will and the financial wherewithal to implement her independence have, as you might imagine, created some very interesting challenges in our marriage.

"All was well until her mother passed away. Though she could not make it back in time for the funeral, Rebecca insisted upon leaving for Chicago immediately upon hearing of her death. I was unable to leave the ranch at the time, and although I didn't want her to go alone she is, as I've said, a very strong-willed woman. As soon as I could get away, I followed her to Chicago. You already know what happened there."

He paused and stared intently into Calico's eyes. Calico returned the stare then nodded.

"What you do not know," Durant continued, "what nobody knows, other than myself, is that the fire was...not accidental.

"There had been a scene earlier that evening between Rebecca and her sister—a fight, really. I had never known until that evening the depth of animosity that existed between them. Rebecca had always been jealous of her older sister, and intensely resented the fact that her sister had two children while she herself was unable to bear one.

"We retired for the night, and I awoke a short time later to find my wife gone from our bed. I went downstairs into the parlor to find Rebecca walking around the edge of the room with a glowing poker from the fireplace in her hand, touching it to the curtains, the furniture..."

His face was tight with anguish, and Calico listened in fascination.

"I rushed up to her, and we struggled. She hit me—accidentally, I'm sure—with the end of the iron and knocked me temporarily senseless. When I regained consciousness, the room was enveloped in flame. Rebecca was in the hallway, as casual as though she were out for a Sunday stroll, setting fire to everything she could.

"It was too late to give warning to anyone else in the house—I assumed they had already been aroused by the smoke and flames and made their escape. I knocked the poker from her hand and dragged her outside. She didn't appear to know what had happened.

"The twins emerged from a bedroom above the porte-cochere and were saved; their parents perished in the fire." He heaved a heavy sigh. "From that day to this, she has no recollection of how the fire actually started, but has been obsessed with the idea that someone is out to do her harm.

"It was I who, after hearing of the death of her father, encouraged her to bring the twins to live with us. It never occurred to me, I swear to you, that she would apparently believe the twins were coming to avenge their parents' death."

There was a long pause, and Calico sensed Joe's presence. He had no idea how long he had been there, or how much he had heard. Durant's back was to the door, and Calico made no acknowledgment Joe was there.

Once again Durant took a deep breath before continuing.

"I've told you this, Calico…may I call you Calico?"

He nodded.

"…because you deserve to know. I shall expect your word as a gentleman that what I have told you will go no farther, and that the twins will never hear of it. I assume I have your word."

"You do," Calico said. "But now let me ask you a few questions. First off, what do you know about those bushwhackers who tried to kill us?"

Durant sighed deeply yet again then wiped a hand slowly over his face, closing his eyes and opening them slowly, looking directly at him.

"You mean our former foreman, Jessie Riles. I assure you, I have no idea who the other men were nor what Mr. Riles's involvement with them might have been. All I can tell you was that he was extremely devoted to my wife, who must have seen some good qualities in him and insisted we hire him when we had our ranch near Denver. Mr. Riles never forgot her kindness to him, and I'm sure that, somehow, he thought he was protecting Rebecca by attempting to do harm to those she considered were out to harm her.

"Jessie Riles has had what I have always considered to be an undeserved reputation for lawlessness, but..." He sighed again. "At any rate, he is no longer in our employ. He was fired several weeks ago, and I have not seen him since."

He looked at Calico as if seeking some sort of reaction. There was none, but Calico wondered how Durant knew Jessie Riles was involved at all. He also wondered if Durant seriously believed he was stupid enough to swallow the guff he was being fed.

The only time he remembered ever having heard any man speak the way Mike Durant did was once when he and Dan had been in Grady when a medicine show came through. The pitchman had sounded very much the same way.

After a moment of awkward silence, Durant continued.

"As I say, I had, of course, been aware of his reputation for many years, but I never had any firsthand evidence that it had any validity. He would disappear from the ranch for several weeks at a time, but we overlooked it because he is an excellent ranch foreman. He has never caused any trouble on the ranch itself, and the men respect him.

"My wife, I suspect, rather romanticized his alleged reputation, as women have a tendency to do, and looked upon Mr. Riles as something of a protector. But due to her increasing reliance upon his being at hand, his habit of disappearing for long periods of time could no longer be tolerated. I had spoken to him about this on numerous occasions, but to no avail. When he returned from the last episode a month or so ago, we let him go.

"While I deeply regret that he may have taken part in the attempts upon your life, I can assure you there is absolutely no connection between his actions, however reprehensible, and either my wife or myself."

Calico did not believe it for a moment but gave no indication. He simply stared at the older man for a moment then said, "What do ya plan t' do about the twins, considerin' your wife's...condition?"

"Why, I'll take them home with me, at least until other arrangements can be made. I understand they will be turning eighteen very soon, and can then make their own decisions as to their futures."

"Yeah, it's their futures I'm thinkin' about—ya say your wife already almost killed 'em in Chicago. Bein' around her too close don't seem like too good an idea t' me."

Durant smiled and waved away the objections.

"There is no need to worry, Mr.—Calico. As I've told you, she remembers nothing of the events in Chicago, and I'm sure her actions then were not a deliberate attempt to harm the children. I've arranged for a doctor to come from Denver to care for Rebecca until she has completely recovered. The twins will be in absolutely no danger, and their presence may, indeed, be just what she needs to help her recover."

Calico kept his face impassive. He had the discomforting impression that he and Mike Durant were engaged in a cardless game of poker, and he resisted the temptation to look past the man's shoulder to meet Joe's eyes where he stood at the door.

Joe made a deliberate noise.

"Coffee's ready," he said.

Calico and Durant followed him from the barn to the kitchen. Durant's two ranch hands sat on the steps of the kitchen porch drinking coffee. They nodded as the others passed.

When they entered the kitchen, Mrs. Potter poured steaming cups of coffee for them then excused herself to see if Sarah was dressed. A few minutes later, Sarah came in, her face beaming.

"Uncle Mike!" she said as he rose from the table to greet her.

He held out his arms, and she ran to him, hugging him tightly. After a moment, he held her at arm's length and shook his head.

"I don't believe it," he said incredulously. "Why, you're a young woman...and a beautiful one, at that. You look very much like your mother."

Sarah flushed and glanced at Joe, who was watching her with a small smile. Turning again to Durant, she said, "Have you seen Josh?"

Calico, aware that Durant had not asked to see the boy, again studied his face for a reaction. Again, there was none.

"Why, no, Sarah, I haven't. I didn't want to wake him—I understand he's still a little weak. I can't tell you how shocked I was to hear he'd been injured, and I thank God it was not more serious."

"But he'll be so happy to see you," Sarah said, taking his hand and leading him to Josh's bedroom. She opened the door and looked in then entered, taking him with her.

Calico and Joe remained at the table, now and then exchanging a look. They could hear Josh's voice, and the creak of the bedsprings as Durant sat down beside him, then the low murmur of all three voices, which Calico made no effort to hear.

"More coffee, Calico?" Joe asked, moving to the stove.

"Yeah," he replied, draining his cup. "Somethin' tells me I'm goin' t' need it."

After a huge breakfast prepared by Mrs. Potter, during which the conversation was, by unspoken agreement, limited to small talk, Durant turned to Josh, who once again, over the objections of Sarah and Mrs. Potter, had insisted on getting up and joining them at the table, and said, "Do you think you'll be up to traveling, Josh?"

Josh looked at Calico then back.

"You mean today?"

Durant nodded. "No point in putting it off. I can get a wagon, and that way we won't have to impose on the Potters' gracious hospitality any further. Once we get to the ranch, you can just relax and concentrate on recovering."

Mrs. Potter seemed about to say something, but a sharp look from her son changed her mind.

Josh and Sarah looked at each other for a long moment then turned to Calico.

"You'll come with us, won't you, Calico?" Josh asked, his eyes intense.

Calico glanced at Durant, and for the first time thought he saw a flicker of fire in the man's eyes—but only for an instant.

"I'm sure Calico is anxious to get back to his own ranch, Josh," he said casually.

Noting the concern on the faces of the twins, Calico stared at each of them then slowly swept his eyes to meet their uncle's.

"Not that big a hurry," he said.

Again there was the flicker of fire.

"Well, of course, you'll be more than welcome..."

"Thank you, then, I think I will. Just t' see they get settled in proper."

It was Joe's turn to speak up.

"Well, you're welcome t' use our wagon, an' I'd be pleased t' ride out with ya."

"That's very generous of you, Joe," Durant said, and Calico thought he detected a note of frustration in his voice, "but it won't be necessary. One of my boys can drive the wagon, and—"

"I think it would be very nice if Mr. Potter would ride along with us," Sarah interjected then blushed.

Josh stared at her, wide-eyed, then slowly turned to look first at Joe then at Calico and burst into a wide grin.

"Me, too," he said.

Durant smiled—a bit artificially, to Calico's thinking. "Well, then, I guess that's settled. I'll go tell my boys they can head back for the ranch and we'll be along shortly."

Mrs. Potter rose from the table and moved to the stove.

"Let me see if they'd like a little more coffee before they go," she said, using her apron as a potholder to lift the coffeepot from the stove.

Mike Durant also got up, excused himself to Sarah and followed Mrs. Potter from the house.

Calico and Joe once again exchanged a long look, which was not lost on Josh.

"Joe," Calico said, "me an' the twins gotta have a little talk. You mind keepin' an eye out for a minute?"

"Happy to, Calico," he said, and went outside to engage Durant in conversation.

Sarah and Josh shared a puzzled look as Calico motioned them to lean a bit closer.

"Now, we ain't got much time, so I'm gonna have t' talk fast an' ask ya both t' just bear with me, okay?"

They nodded in unison.

"First off, I'd like t' know how your grandma Overholt died."

Josh and Sarah looked at each other; Josh answered.

"She died in a sanitarium," he said. "She had tuberculosis."

And a sanitarium ain't quite the same as an asylum, Calico thought. Durant's clever, all right. He didn't outright lie, but he might as well of.

"Why do you ask?" Sarah wanted to know.

"No time t' go inta it right now," he said. "It ain't all that important, anyway. What is important's that you two know I ain't gonna leave ya no matter what till we find out 'zactly what's goin' on. We all know whatever's been happenin' is tied in t' that ranch. I've got half a mind t' take ya both back home with me…"

Immediately anticipating Josh's response, he looked directly at the young man and gave him a raised-eyebrow signal of caution. If Sarah noticed, she made no indication of it, and he continued talking.

"But I think it's pretty clear that probably wouldn't be the end of it."

Voices announced the approach of Joe and Durant.

"Point is," Calico said, lowering his voice, "there's no gettin' around the fact that you two's still in danger, same's ya been since ya got off the train. I'm real proud o' how well both o' ya's handled yourselves, an' I know ya c'n handle whatever's comin' up." There were footsteps on the porch stairs. He looked hard at Sarah and Josh in turn, and added, "An' I'm still gonna be close by t' make sure nothin' happens t' ya. Understand?"

The door opened, and Durant and Joe entered.

They left shortly before eleven, Josh's arm in a sling made by Mrs. Potter, who also wrapped a change of bandages in a kerchief and placed it carefully into a huge picnic basket packed with enough food to feed a small army. Sarah drove the wagon, with Josh sitting beside her and Joe, Calico and Durant riding behind. The day was bright and clear, the brilliant blue sky dotted with fleecy clouds. Josh and Sarah were uncharacteristically silent, while Joe, Calico and Durant spoke only intermittently.

The countryside was less arid now, with expanses of grassland sprinkled with shade trees and grazing cattle. It reminded Calico of Dan's ranch, which was now his, though that was still hard for him to comprehend.

The sun was low in the sky when they turned onto a tree-lined side road, and a few minutes later Durant rode up beside the wagon and said, "There it is, Josh, Sarah—your new home."

Through the trees, Calico could see a stately white two-story frame house with a high-peaked roof, gingerbread trim and tall, narrow windows. There was a small orchard to the right, and a stone outcropping with an abandoned outbuilding atop it on the left. Some distance behind the house were the barns, sheds, bunkhouse and corrals. He was favorably impressed by the obvious organization and efficiency of the ranch, evidenced by the condition, number and layout of the buildings, corrals, and livestock pens. There was certainly nothing like it anywhere near Grady.

They pulled up in front of the house, and a burly young man came down from the porch to take the horses. Josh was helped down from the wagon, and the five of them entered the house.

Again, Calico was impressed. The house was comfortably and expensively furnished, perhaps more befitting a wealthy city home than an isolated Colorado ranch. It was undoubtedly a reflection of Rebecca Durant's Chicago upbringing.

A stooped Chinese man came in from the kitchen, and Durant instructed him to make coffee for his guests. After the man left, Durant turned to the group and, with a sweeping gesture of one hand, invited them all to sit.

"If you'll excuse me, I'll go tell Rebecca you're here. I'll be but a minute or two."

He went out into the narrow hall and disappeared up a flight of stairs.

Calico, Josh, Sarah and Joe sat in a somewhat awkward silence, the only sound the ticking of a large grandfather clock. Josh, though obviously tired from the trip, looked with his usual open fascination around the room but always his attention always came back to Calico, who allowed himself a few long exchanges.

Sarah, hands folded on her lap, stared at the floor, occasionally glancing up at Joe, who sat directly opposite her. Whenever their eyes met, she would blush and drop her attention once more to the floor.

A few minutes later, the Chinese houseboy returned carrying a tray with coffee and sandwiches, which he passed around without a word. Thanks to the bounty of Mrs. Potter's food basket, which they had sampled along the way, only Josh accepted a sandwich. The man set the tray down on a table next to him and left the room as silently as he had come.

Josh disposed of his sandwich in short order and reached for another, making Calico wonder again where he possibly found the room for all he ate.

Footsteps on the stairs turned all eyes expectantly to the hall as Rebecca Durant entered, supported by her husband's arm around her shoulders. On the surface, it appeared to be an affectionate and casual gesture, but it didn't escape Calico that Durant was holding her perhaps a bit too firmly, though whether in support or warning he could not tell. But perhaps he was overreacting out of his so-far unsupported distrust of Mike Durant.

Everyone rose, Calico and Joe a bit awkwardly, not quite knowing what to do with their half-finished coffee.

Rebecca was, Calico noted instantly, a truly beautiful woman, and there was a striking family resemblance between her and the twins. She wore a frilled white blouse and a floor-length brown skirt. Her hair was neatly done, with just a few loose wisps here and there.

But her face was pale and drawn, her eyes confused and, he realized, frightened.

"Say hello to Sarah and Joshua, darling," Durant said, as though talking to a small child.

Sarah, unsure whether to hug her aunt and receiving no invitation or indication from Rebecca to do so, curtsied. When Rebecca extended her hand, Josh moved forward to take it. She scanned his face, either looking for something or trying to convey some message. She said nothing, and Calico was aware of the strangeness and awkwardness of the entire situation.

"And this is Mr. Ramsay," Durant continued, as though nothing were out of the ordinary, "the gentleman who brought the children from Fort Collins. And you remember Joe Potter, of course."

Calico and Joe nodded their greetings, which were returned by a brief struggle of Rebecca's lips that resulted in the frail ghost of a smile.

"Thank you, Mr. Ramsay," she said, and extended her hand.

When Calico took it, he was amazed by the strength of her grip. Then, she swayed, and Durant caught her by both shoulders.

"Rebecca, are you all right?" he asked and guided her to a chair.

"My pills," she said as he lowered her to the divan. "I didn't take my pills. Please get them."

"I'll have Sung get them, dearest," he said, bending over her. Then he lifted his head and called in the direction of the kitchen: "Sung! Sung, come in here."

There was no response.

"Go ahead, Mike," Joe volunteered. "We'll look after Rebecca."

Calico noticed a look of exasperation and—what? Anger?—flash across Durant's face.

"Very well. Excuse me." He rushed from the room and bounded up the stairs three at a time.

The minute he was gone, Rebecca straightened and motioned Calico closer then closer still, until her lips were only inches from his ear.

"Get them away from me," she whispered, her gaze moving from Josh to Sarah. "Now!"

CHAPTER 17

HAVING GIVEN REBECCA HER PILLS AND LED HER BACK UPSTAIRS, DURANT REJOINED Joe, Sarah, Josh and a stunned Calico.

"I'm terribly sorry," he said. "Rebecca has been so looking forward to your arrival, and I'm afraid the excitement was just too much for her. I'm sure she'll be in better spirits tomorrow." Without waiting for a response, he moved from the hall doorway toward the kitchen. "If you'll excuse me one more time, I'll just be sure Sung has prepared Sarah's and Joshua's rooms. Then I'll have the cook begin dinner."

No one said much in his absence, and Josh's weakness and fatigue caused him to nod off in his chair. Upon Durant's return Calico suggested that perhaps Josh could benefit from lying down for a while, and followed as he helped him upstairs to his room.

As he and Durant prepared to leave the room, Josh called, "Calico, could you stay for a minute?"

"Sure, Josh," he said, delighted at the chance to be alone with him. "Excuse us, Mike?"

He sensed Durant was not overly happy leaving them alone together but saw no alternative save to nod and leave.

"Close the door, please," Josh asked, and Calico did, first checking that Durant was actually going down the stairs. Moving to the side of the bed, he sat on the edge of the mattress.

"What is it, Josh?" he asked, laying a hand casually on the young man's leg.

"You meant what you said about not leaving, didn't you?"

"You know I did."

"I feel strange here. Sarah does, too. Can't the three of us just leave together?"

"I can't think o' anythin' I'd like better. But like I told ya back at the Potters', we really ain't got much choice but t' see this thing through to the end, hard as it may be. And if Durant or Rebecca wanted to stop you from goin' off with me, they got the legal right t' do it. You're their kin, not mine."

"I'll be of age in two more days," Josh pointed out. "Then I can do anything I want and they can't stop me. I–I want to be with you, Calico. I thought we…" He reached for Calico's hand and clasped it tightly.

"You thought what, Josh?" Calico asked, returning the tight grip.

Josh chewed on his lower lip a moment then said, "Don't you know?" he asked. "Don't you know how I feel?"

"I know how ya feel. I'm feelin' pretty much the same. But right now we got t' concentrate on what's goin' on outside o' us rather than what's goin' on inside."

A knock on the doorf made him drop Josh's hand and stand up.

"Come on in," he said.

It was Sarah, who informed them she had the room next to Josh. Looking from one to the other, she smiled.

"I just wanted to see if you needed anything," she said. "I guess you don't."

Calico felt himself blushing. "Well," he said, "I'd better be gettin' back downstairs."

Without another word he edged past her and went out into the hall, heading toward the stairs.

Durant showed him around the ranch; and although Joe had been there several times, he accompanied them, not saying much. Lengthening shadows announced the coming of twilight, and Durant suggested both men could spend the night in the bunkhouse. His continued concern for the twins and his newly expressed feelings toward Josh offset by the practicalities of the situation, Calico accepted the offer.

Dinner was much more formal than either he or, he suspected, Joe was accustomed to. Sarah and Josh, who had insisted he felt much stronger after a brief sleep, obviously felt right at home amid the fine china and bewildering array of silverware. Rebecca remained in her room, her dinner taken to her by Sung.

Conversation during dinner was subdued and somewhat strained, the twins—and Calico, for that matter—not sure exactly how to react to the situation. It was particularly hard for the twins, who he suspected found themselves in a world both familiar and increasingly strange, and not a little frightening.

After dinner, the houseboy came into the parlor to say that one of the ranch hands was at the back door and had to see Durant on a matter of ranch business. Durant, visibly irritated by the intrusion, excused himself to see what the problem was. There was no longer any question he did not want to leave his guests alone together any more than he had to.

In his brief absence, Calico volunteered to take Josh back to his room to change the dressing on his wound. Sarah, who would normally have insisted on doing it herself, agreed without hesitation, clearly delighted at the prospect of being alone with Joe. Calico went to the wagon to retrieve the extra set of bandages from Mrs. Potter's picnic basket.

Once inside Josh's room, he laid the bandages on the bed and helped him remove his sling and shirt. Any other time, the prospect of being this close, the chance to touch him, to feel the warmth of his skin, would have given him—and, he no longer doubted, Josh—a great deal of pleasure. But what he had said earlier was all too true—pleasure was a distraction they could not afford.

"There's a world o' talkin' we gotta do, Josh," he said as he wet a washcloth with water from the ceramic pitcher on the nightstand, "but now ain't the time. What I want ya t' do right now is what I tell ya, okay?"

Josh winced as the old bandage came off then nodded.

"Ya leave that lamp near the window lit low," Calico went on, concentrating on applying the new bandage. "If ya need anythin', or if anythin' unusual happens..." He hastily raised his hand to forestall Josh's anticipated reaction. "...not that anythin' will, mind ya. But just if it does, ya turn the lamp off. When Sarah comes in t' say g'nite, ya tell her to do the same, hear?"

Josh nodded again, though it was obvious he was full of questions.

Calico finished the re-bandaging and helped him remove the rest of his clothes, allowing himself the pleasure of doing it despite his own earlier injunction.

"We'll talk tomorrow," he said. "I better get back downstairs."

"Okay," Josh replied, eyes never leaving his.

He drew the covers up over Josh's chest and realized he was reaching out to run his fingers through the younger man's soft curly hair. Josh reached up with his good hand and grasped the arm to pull him closer, but Calico drew away.

"We better not," he said. "Plenty o' time for that later."

Josh gave a long sigh of frustration.

"Okay...I guess," he muttered.

Calico went to the door, turned and gave him a big smile and a wink.

"Sleep well, Josh."

"Oh, sure," Josh replied sarcastically as Calico closed the door behind him.

As he left Josh's room, he noticed the quick but silent closing of the door at the end of the hall—the door to the Durants' room. He wondered if perhaps Rebecca had been thinking of talking with him again, and he once more wondered exactly what she had meant by telling him to take the twins away. Was it a threat...or a warning?

He briefly considered going to the door and trying to talk to her then rejected the idea, since he had no way of truly knowing if it had been Rebecca or her husband who had closed it.

Returning to the living room, he found Durant sitting with Joe and Sarah, who shortly excused herself to go upstairs to get ready for bed. When she'd gone, the three men had a glass of brandy; but the conversation, as if by mutual agreement, avoided anything more substantial than the problems of ranching.

Shortly before nine, Durant offered to accompany them to the bunkhouse, but they declined, saying they could find the way easily enough.

Once outside, Calico said, "If ya don't mind, Joe, I think I'll just bunk out here near the wagon."

Joe turned back toward the house, looking up to where two of the upstairs windows were lit softly by kerosene lamps.

"Yeah," he said. "It's a nice night. I think I'll do the same, if you don't mind."

They took the bedding put into the wagon in case Josh might want to lie down during the trip and spread it on the ground within sight of the house.

"You want the first watch, or should I take it?" Joe asked.

Calico grinned. "Was I that obvious?"

"No, I'm that smart."

Calico sat down and leaned against a wagon wheel.

"You get some sleep," he said. "I'll wake ya after a bit."

Joe nodded, removed his boots and pulled a blanket over him. In a moment, he was asleep.

Joe awoke him at dawn; already, the ranch was beginning its day. The hands were up, two or three saddling their horses while another tried to separate one horse from several in the corral. A dog ran past chasing a squirrel, scattering the chickens wandering around the yard, clucking noisily.

They folded up the bedding and put it back in the wagon then sat on the tailgate until Durant came out. He didn't seem surprised to see them, and Calico suspected he knew where they'd slept—and why.

"Breakfast is about ready," he said. "Come on in."

Seated at the dining room table, they ate steak, eggs, hash browns, biscuits and gravy and coffee. Neither Sarah nor Josh was up yet, nor was Calico surprised by Rebecca's absence.

He was not as hungry as usual, and was aware his lack of appetite was directly related to the fact he had no logical excuse for remaining at the ranch a day longer. Yet he still was not comfortable with the twins being out of his sight, or where he could not at least readily speak to them.

Durant seemed to sense his mood, and went out of his way to reassure him, without saying so directly, that the twins'—and his—troubles were behind them. He spoke glowingly of the doctor who had agreed to come from Denver for an extended stay, who was confident of Rebecca's complete recovery, and who would remain until she was fully well. He repeated his opinion that the twins' presence would be of great assistance in her recovery.

"Mike, everything you've said makes a lot o' sense," Calico said in a tone of counterfeit agreement, "but with Jessie Riles still on the loose—"

A raised hand cut him off. "I understand your concern, of course. But Jessie would be a fool to stay around here after what has happened—and I know him well enough to know he is not a fool. I plan personally to arrange with the sheriff to form a posse to search the entire county, and my men have all been told to report immediately to me should he be seen."

Calico nodded. "That's all well and good, Mike," he persisted, "but after all that's happened in the past few weeks, I just wouldn't feel right unless I had a chance to talk to your wife about a few things that's been botherin' me."

Durant set his cup down carefully and pushed his plate off to one side.

"I really don't think that would be wise, Calico, considering the fragile state of Rebecca's physical and emotional health at this moment."

Joe's attention moved back and forth between them as they spoke, but his face remained impassive.

"Oh, I don't plan t' ask her about whether she might know anythin' about Jessie Riles tryin' t' kill us, or about the fire in Chicago or anythin' like that.

But these two youngsters have come t' mean a lot t' me, an' I just have t' be sure in my mind that...well, ya'll have t' excuse me f'r sayin' so, Mike, but I have t' be sure they're goin' t' be safe here."

Motioning to the cook for more coffee, Durant waited until the man had left the room before looking at Calico.

"While I can appreciate your concern, Calico," he said calmly, "and while I do not want to seem in any way unappreciative of your efforts, I must point out that the twins are in our custody now, and we will take full responsibility for their safety.

"As for your speaking with my wife, I'm afraid that's simply out of the question. My primary concern, as you can understand, is for her wellbeing. The doctor should be arriving on the stagecoach from Denver tomorrow, and until then I want her to remain calm. The past—regrettable as some of it may have been—is past, and I suggest we all leave it there."

Their eyes were locked, and neither had wavered the entire time he was speaking.

"And while I do not want to appear inhospitable," Durant continued, "I'm sure you're anxious to be getting back to your own affairs—I understand Mr. Overholt left his ranch to you."

Calico wondered how he could have obtained that bit of information but said nothing.

"The twins have been through a great ordeal, and it is time they, too, began putting the past behind them. Your duty to them has been done, and I know they will be forever grateful to you for it."

Calico ran his hand over the stubble of his beard, and nodded.

"Yeah, you're right. My job here's done. I should be gettin' on. I would like to say goodbye t' the kids, though."

Durant pushed back from the table, his face bearing a broad smile.

"Well, of course. Of course. There is no hurry—they should be down shortly."

As if on cue, Sarah entered, followed by a sleepy-eyed Josh, his arm in the sling. The moment he saw Calico, his face burst into a wide grin, which he hastily suppressed.

"'Mornin', Sarah, Josh," Calico said.

"Good morning, Calico," Sarah said, adding, "Uncle Mike...Mr. Potter."

She smiled brightly at all three, but her eyes lingered on Joe. Josh said nothing, but Calico felt the young man studying him.

"Sit down, please," Durant said, rising to pull out a chair for Sarah. "You must both be starved. Excuse me a moment while I go find the cook."

He left through the door leading to the kitchen.

The moment he was gone, both twins started to speak; but Calico, noticing the Chinese houseboy just beyond the doorway in the living room, gave them a sharp look and a shake of his head. After making sure Sung was not watching, he silently mouthed the word *Later.*

Durant returned, followed by the cook carrying the twins' breakfasts.

"Well, kids," Calico said, "I'll be leavin' today. Got t' get back to the ranch. Fall's comin' on, an' there's lots t' be done."

Josh studied his face carefully for a moment, then said, "But, Calico, it's our birthday tomorrow—*tomorrow*!" he pleaded. "Can't you stay until then?"

Sarah glanced at her brother. "Yes, Calico, please stay."

Joe, not fully sure of what was going on, volunteered, "Ya'd be more'n welcome t' stay with us for a few days, if ya'd like."

To Calico's surprise, Durant added, "Why, that might be a fine idea, Joe. If you'd really like to stay around for the twins' birthday, Calico, I'm sure Rebecca would be as happy as I to have you."

The likely reason behind his unexpected acquiescence suddenly struck Calico—if he were to agree to stay with the Potters, he would be seen...ten miles from the ranch. And with Jesse Riles still on the loose, his presence in the Potter house could well put both Joe and Mrs. Potter in danger.

"Well, I thank y'all, I really do," he said. "An' much as I'd like to be here for your birthday, I really got t' be goin' on home. Just one day'll get me a long ways towards Grady."

Although not even Josh appeared to be very hungry, he and Joe had another cup of coffee, waiting until the twins were through eating. When the houseboy had taken their plates away, he drained his coffee cup and pushed away from the table.

"You kids want to come out with me while I saddle up?"

As everyone rose, he extended his hand to Durant.

"Thanks f'r your hospitality," he said, shaking the man's hand and noting it was damp. "Ya take good care o' these young'uns, now, hear?"

Durant smiled and nodded. Then Calico, Joe and the twins went outside to find that one of the hands had already hitched the team.

As they reached the bottom of the stairs, Josh demanded, "Why were you always calling us 'kids' in there? You know we're not kids anymore."

As they moved on to the stable so he could saddle Dusty and bring Joe's horse out to tie it to the back of the wagon, Calico grinned.

"Sure I know it," he said, "but your uncle Mike apparently don't, an' I didn't want t' give him any reason t' think otherwise."

A ranch hand emerged from the stable leading both horses; Calico's saddle was propped against the stable door. Waiting until the man had gone back inside and was out of easy earshot, and while Joe led his horse to the wagon, Calico motioned the twins closer as he swung the saddle onto Dusty's back, careful not to look directly at either one.

"Now, listen close. I'm goin' t' have t' ride back through town with Joe so's people there can see me leavin'," he explained as he fastened the girth. "Then I'll have t' ride on out past town for a good enough distance so's anybody watchin'll be convinced I'm gone."

He made a production out of checking the straps, adjusting the bridle and nuzzling Dusty's head. Meanwhile, he continued in the same low voice. "Soon's I can, I'll circle back here t' the ranch. It'll take most o' the day, probably, so you're gonna be on your own for awhile. I don't expect nobody'll try anythin' today, anyways. Whoever's behind all this'll want t' be sure I'm long gone first.

"I gotta find a way t' get in an' talk to your aunt Rebecca in private, an' I figure that tomorrow might be a good time, 'specially if Durant rides inta town t' pick up the doctor off the stage."

Taking the reins, he led Dusty, the twins on his heels, toward Joe and the wagon.

"Stay as visible as ya can tomorrow without bein' obvious about it, an' whatever ya do, don't look f'r me. I'll be somewheres where I can keep an eye on ya." Without turning or making any gesture, he said, "Josh, don't look at it, but did ya notice that old buildin' up on the hill t' our right?"

Heeding the caution, Josh answered, "Yes."

"Well, that looks like a good spot t' see everythin' from. Don't make a fuss outta lookin' at it, but kinda keep a sideways eye on it. If I'm there an' need ya, I'll signal."

They'd reached the wagon, and he turned as Durant appeared on the front porch.

"We better make this a fairly convincin' g'bye," he said.

Sarah threw her arms around him and pressed her head into his chest. He returned the hug then held her at arm's length.

"Ya take care o' yourself, missy," he said, loudly enough so Durant could hear.

The man smiled at them like a politician running for office.

Calico gave Josh a very quick "watch it" glance and extended his hand. Josh took it and shook it strongly.

"An' *you* take good care o' your sister, or ya'll have t' answer t' me, ya understand?"

Josh nodded then, despite Calico's warning, moved his injured arm to one side and threw his good one around Calico in an awkward but surprisingly tight hug.

"Hey, we're just kids, remember?" he whispered as he nearly squeezed the breath out of the delighted but embarrassed larger man.

Without another word, Calico mounted and nodded to Joe, who was already seated in the wagon. With a wave to Durant and another to the twins, he waited until Joe had turned the wagon around and then rode beside it out of the yard.

As they passed the house, he glanced up to see Rebecca watching from her second-story window. As their eyes met, she shook her head slowly back and forth. Then, she turned and disappeared from sight.

CHAPTER 18

THEY WERE ABOUT A MILE FROM THE RANCH, RIDING AT A FASTER-THAN-NORMAL PACE but slowly enough not to arouse suspicion in anyone who might be watching, before Joe broke into Calico's reverie.

"He'll be okay," he said.

"Who?" Calico asked, embarrassed as he sensed what Joe was going to say.

"Josh, o' course," Joe said with a grin. "I know it ain't none of my business, but I do know there's somethin' special goin' on between you two."

Calico glanced at him from the corner of his eye then focused on the road in front of them.

"I'm not sure I know what you're talkin' about," he said, though he knew perfectly well.

"Look, if I'm touchin' some nerve, I'll back off. Like I say, it ain't none of my business, but I seen how you two look at each other." He raised his hand to forestall Calico's rebuttal. "Not that anybody else'd notice, I'm sure. Oh, Sarah's aware of it, I'd wager—she's a pretty bright young lady, besides bein' beautiful t' boot. An' I get the idea those two don't have many secrets from each other. I just wanted you t' know that if you feel like talkin', I ain't no judge and I ain't no jury, but I'll be glad t' listen."

"How'd you come by bein' so open-minded?" Calico couldn't resist asking.

Joe kept his eyes on the trail. "I had a chance to spend some time with the Lakota. People who call the Indians 'savages' ain't got a clue what they're talkin' about. They're a lot more civilized about some things than most of these local bible-thumpin' judgment-passers.

"The Lakota call people who are different the way I think you and Josh are different 'winkte,' which means 'two-spirit people.' They know they're just part o' life, like everything an' everyone else. Livin' with them for a while opened up a whole new way of lookin' at the world, as far as I was concerned.

"I'm pretty sure you ain't had much of a chance to talk about it with other people, so like I said, you want to talk, I'll listen."

Calico sighed. "I could use a talk, I guess."

There was no question in his mind he could trust Joe, or that Joe was acting out of friendship. So, after another moment of silence, in which he rode with pursed lips, trying to find the right words, he took a deep breath and began.

"I guess I been pretty lucky all my life," he said. "I always knowed who I was an' what I wanted, an' it's never been a problem. Never even had t' think about it much—it's just part o' me. I just always stuck pretty close t' myself, an' hoped that some day I'd come across somebody else in the same boat.

"Then along comes Josh an' Sarah, an' suddenly for the first time in my life I feel like I…well, like I belong with somebody. But, hell, Joe, Josh may be nearly eighteen, but in a lot o' ways he's still a kid—I'm nine years older'n him."

For the first time since he'd begun talking, he looked directly at Joe, whose eyes were on him.

"An' I'm ten years older than Sarah," Joe said, "but that don't stop me from wantin' to get to know her a whole lot better. My ma was sixteen when she had me. Hell, you know that a girl around these parts who ain't married by the time she's nineteen's practically an old maid. And you an' me was men by the time we was younger'n Josh.

"Granted, he's got a lot o' growin' up t' do, bein' raised pampered like he was, but he strikes me as a pretty sincere an' level-headed young fella. I don't think this whole thing's just a game for him. You say you knew what you wanted when you were a lot younger than he is—what makes you think he don't know for himself?"

Calico nodded. "Yeah, you're right," he said, "but I figure he—hell, I figure we both…need a bit o' time before jumpin' inta somethin'."

Joe grinned. "So take the time. Ya sure got a lot of it ahead o' ya."

Calico nodded again. "Yeah, well, first we gotta get this current mess straightened out."

The two men traveled in silence for a few minutes before Joe spoke again.

"Like I said at the ranch, you're welcome t' stay with Ma and me for as long as ya want," he said.

Calico smiled and shook his head. "Much obliged, Joe, but I don't think that'd be a good idea for you or your ma. I want everybody t' think I'm gone f'r good."

"So, what's your plan?" Joe asked, and Calico outlined basically what he had told the twins.

"Main thing's that I get a chance t' talk t' Rebecca. One way or the other, she's the key t' all this, an' I gotta get some answers."

"Gettin' t' talk with Rebecca might not be easy," Joe said. "Mike goes inta town often enough, but he never leaves her alone—at least one o' the hands is always around, an' either Sung or the cook's always in the house."

Calico shrugged. "Well, I'm goin' t' have t' find a way."

"'Course," Joe added, "it's pretty sure Mike'll be goin' in t'morrow t' pick up the doc. Fancy city doctor like that, I imagine the whole town'll turn out. Heck, the whole town turns out *whenever* the stage comes in." He grinned. "You an' the twins an' a fancy Denver doctor an' the stagecoach all in one week—folks in Bow Ridge'll be talkin' about it for years."

They rode a while again in silence until Joe said, "You want me t' go back t' the ranch with you?"

Calico shook his head. "Thanks, Joe, but no. If folks think I've left town an' then you're not around, it might look peculiar." He grinned. "'Course, they might think you an' me run off together—that'd sure get their minds off o' the stagecoach."

It was the first time in his life that he had ever so openly revealed himself, except to Josh.

They laughed, glad for a release of the tension that had been with them ever since Durant showed up in the Potters' barn.

"No," Calico said as the reality of the situation descended on them once again, "you done plenty for me already, an' if I need ya, I'll be sure t' call on ya."

"You do that."

They reached Bow Ridge shortly before noon, and Calico stopped at the Potters only long enough to thank Mrs. Potter for her hospitality and say goodbye. Joe rode with him to the general store while he picked up enough supplies to last a traveler to Clantonville and paid Arabella Boggs for the broken door of her father's store, then went to see Ezekiel Pitt.

"Well," said Pitt, unfolding a large sheet of paper taken from his shirt pocket, "the window'll run you ten dollars—I had to replace ever' single pane. The stool that was threw through it was layin' out there in the street and was ruint. That's two dollars. I'm goin' t' have t' repaint the entire front of the store so's it'll match the new paint on the window frame. That'll be about fifteen dollars. And somebody knocked over a very expensive mannequin and broke it. That'll be nine dollars and thirty-two cents, plus shippin' from Denver—add another two dollars. An' then…"

Calico held up his hand.

"Hold on right there, mister," he said. "I'll be more'n happy t' pay for the window, and even for the stool, which I see right there behind you an' it don't look ruined t' me. But I ain't made o' money, and I ain't gonna rebuild your entire store. I'm gonna give ya twelve dollars, which I figure is more'n fair. You agree, or ya wanna talk about it some more?"

Pitt's eyes moved from Calico's tight-jawed face to Joe, who was leaning against the frame of the open door and who merely raised an eyebrow and grinned, and then to the rifle in Calico's right hand. He gulped audibly then snorted in disgust.

"All right. All right. I don't want no more trouble than you already caused around here. Just gimme the money and get out o' my store."

Calico took the money out of his vest pocket, laid it on the counter and followed Joe out into the street. He felt as though every eye in town was on him as they shook hands and he thanked him for all his help.

Then, having secured all his purchases in his saddlebags, he mounted and rode down the dusty street out into the countryside toward Clantonville.

Cresting the hill on the far side of town, Calico passed down the other side out of sight of the farmhouse he recalled as being the first one they'd come to when approaching Bow Ridge from Clantonville. He rode to the top of the next hill and looked back to be sure he wasn't being followed. Satisfied he was alone, he turned off the trail and made a wide circle to the right around Bow Ridge and headed back toward Cold Springs Ranch.

He stopped at a stream a few miles from the ranch to fill his canteens and water his horse. Spotting a small but thick grove of trees around a rock outcrop, he led Dusty into the grove, and once sure neither he nor the horse could be seen, he sat down with his back against a large boulder to wait until dark, when he'd be less likely to encounter wandering ranch hands.

He planned to take a short nap, but his mind was far too active for that; and most of his thoughts centered on Josh. What, he wondered, was he really getting himself into? More importantly, what was he getting Josh into. Could the young man really adapt to this culture? Could he really survive the rigors of ranch life—a rich city boy?

The dam of self-control he had built up over the years to hold back his emotions and longings had already sprung several leaks. What, he asked himself, would he do if he gave himself totally over to another human being, as he felt he was doing now? And what if then, for whatever reason, Josh were to decide after a time to return to the city, to leave him? Could he survive such a loss?

But, as always happened when he was overcome with doubts or fears, Calico made himself take a mental step backwards. Of course, he'd survive. He always had, and he always would. If things didn't work out with Josh, he'd be devastated; but he'd lost his parents, he'd lost Uncle Dan. And if he had to lose Josh eventually...

By sheer will, he reined his speculation in. Why should he let what might or might not happen at some time in the future destroy his chances for happiness in the here and now? That was no way to live. As he so often said, and firmly believed, what happened would happen, and would be dealt with as it came along.

He knew life would not be easy for the two of them, given all the hatred and bigotry and intolerance in the world, but he was confident that as long as they had each other, everything would work itself out.

As the shadows from the rocks and surrounding trees began to stretch out across the open ground, Calico decided it was time to move on, closer to the ranch. He took his time, keenly alert to his surroundings, as dusk slowly deepened into night. He rode to within sight of the distant lights of the ranch house. Then, careful not to be seen, he circled behind the outcropping and led Dusty up a winding cowpath to the crumbling building—an old toolshed, he decided—at the top of the hill overlooking the ranch. As he expected, the spot gave an excellent view of the house, and there was ample room inside the structure for Dusty.

He observed the house closely, able to see occasional movement inside through the windows but unable to discern individuals. At one point, Josh and Sarah came out onto the porch and sat on the front steps for a few minutes.

One by one, the lights went out, and he bedded down for the night.

He woke before the first rooster's crowing in the morning and watched the slow rousing of the ranch. There was no activity from the house until about half an hour after sunrise, when Durant emerged from the back door and went toward the bunkhouse. Shortly after, Calico was relieved to see Josh come around the far corner of the house, appearing to be on what was likely supposed to be a casual stroll around the grounds. He went from building to building—exploring or inspecting, Calico guessed—and he was pleased by how calmly he went about it.

Durant reappeared from the bunkhouse, accompanied by two hands. They went to the stables and, after fifteen minutes or so, emerged with Durant driving a carriage and the two hands riding behind. Durant pulled up beside the front porch, dismounted and entered the house.

Josh strolled out of one of the barns and sauntered toward the outcropping. At the same time, Durant came out of the house and got back into the carriage. He called out to Josh, who responded with a cursory wave, and the three men moved off toward the main gate and down the trail toward Bow Ridge.

Calico, meanwhile, had noted three small groups of hands ride off in various directions on their daily chores. Now there was only Josh to be seen. He'd taken a seat on a tree stump just to the left of the foot of the outcrop and was scratching idly at the ground with a stick. He was certain Josh was aware of his presence, and that his apparently aimless wanderings were not a matter of satisfying his curiosity but deliberately intended to establish a logical reason for his eventually heading up to the abandoned shed.

He watched him get up, toss the stick away and wander toward one side of the outcropping, out of his line of sight. Some five minutes later, he heard footsteps approaching the barn and saw Josh's curly hair as he rounded the edge of the open door. He motioned him in, putting a finger to his lips to forestall his speaking too loudly.

Without a word, Josh came over to him, and once again threw his good arm around him and hugged him tightly, laying his head on Calico's shoulder. Calico slowly wrapped his arms around the young man, careful not to press too tightly against the injured arm.

After a moment, Josh backed away just far enough to look him in the eye.

"I'm eighteen now," he announced.

"I know," Calico said. "Happy birthday, Josh."

Then he leaned his head forward to kiss him long and hard, as he knew now he'd wanted to do since he first set eyes on him at the train station.

In that single action, Calico Ramsey felt truly free for the first time in his life.

Reluctantly, he broke away from the embrace, returning to reality. He rubbed his chin with one hand and tried to find something to say.

"Sarah change your bandage last night?" he asked.

Then he saw Josh's look of incredulity and started to laugh—catching himself from making it too loud—and Josh joined him.

"Yeah," Josh said with a grin, "but I like it a lot better when you do it."

"Not much t' like about gettin' a bandage changed," Calico retorted, totally back to reality to the point where he could again be slightly embarrassed by any form of flattery.

He took Josh's hand and led him to a couple of bales of hay set against the wall. He sat down on one, and Josh plopped down beside him, raising a small cloud of dust.

"How *is* your shoulder?" he asked, placing a hand casually on Josh's thigh.

"Fine."

Calico felt another flush of warmth when Josh's good hand moved naturally to cover his.

Flapping his elbow rapidly to demonstrate the flexibility of his injured shoulder—although doing so caused him to wince slightly in spite of his bravado—Josh added, "I'm going to stop wearing this sling tomorrow."

"Well, don't be in too much of a hurry for that," Calico cautioned, although with a grin. Then he forced himself to concentrate on the more pressing situation at hand. "Tell me, how many more people are around the ranch?"

Josh thought a moment.

"Most of the hands are gone, so there's just Sarah, Sung the houseboy and Cree, the cook, in the house. Oh, yes, and Aunt Rebecca, of course, but she's in her room and we haven't seen her since you left."

"No hands still around that you seen?"

He shook his head. "Not that I saw. I checked in all the buildings, and the ones I did find I later saw going off somewhere."

"You're a pretty smart feller, you know that?" Calico said, not even trying to conceal his admiration.

Josh beamed and gave his hand a quick, hard squeeze. Calico felt he could easily walk through Josh's bright blue eyes and into his mind, heart and soul. But when he felt Josh moving his hand slowly upward along his leg, he firmly moved it back down again.

"Oh, no, ya don't!" he said with mock seriousness. "Time for that—lots o' that—later. Right now we got t' figure out a way to get me inta the house t' talk to your aunt Rebecca, which is goin' t' be a problem with so many people around."

He was silent for several minutes thinking, yet always conscious of Josh's hand under his.

"Okay," he said finally, "here's what I want ya t' do. Ya go talk to Sarah, private. Tell her I'm here, but don't let her come up here. I want you two t' go f'r a walk way out in the pasture, then ya come runnin' back and tell Sung an' the cook an' anybody else ya might see that Sarah fell down an' got hurt. Have 'em come with ya t' carry her back t' the house. When they're outta the way, I'll go in an' see your aunt. Ya understand?"

Josh nodded eagerly, once again caught up by a spirit of adventure and possible danger.

"Okay, now," Calico said, standing and helping him to his feet, "git on down there. An' when they go with ya t' get Sarah, take your time gettin' back. I'll see ya later."

Josh left the barn, and a few minutes later he saw him sauntering back to the house. Not long after he entered, he and Sarah came out and strolled off through the orchard toward the open pasture beyond. At one point, Sarah turned and looked up toward Calico's hiding place, but Josh yanked her arm and pulled her forward.

It was ten minutes later when Josh ran back. When he reached the orchard, he started yelling. By the time he reached the house, Sung and the cook came out to see what the commotion was all about—or so Calico determined from the tone of the voices that carried to him. He could see Josh all but jumping up and down, urging the two men to follow him.

Sung came into view almost immediately and started off in the direction from which Josh had come, but Cree appeared only momentarily then hesitated, looking back to the house then turning back. Calico could hear Josh pleading, and with clear reluctance the cook reappeared and followed him into the orchard.

He looked around carefully for any other signs of activity around the house or outbuildings and, seeing none, left the barn, rifle in hand, and hurried down the path and around the outcropping to the house. He entered quietly and moved to the stairway. Mounting the stairs two at a time, he went to the closed door at the end of the hall and knocked.

There was no response.

Opening the door, he found Rebecca lying on the bed, asleep. He approached and leaned his rifle against the footboard.

"Miz Durant," he said softly, not wanting to frighten her. "Miz Durant, wake up. It's me, Calico Ramsay."

Rebecca stirred, her eyes opened, and she slowly rose, propping herself up on one elbow. She shook her head as if to clear it.

"Mr. Ramsay?" she said groggily.

"Yes, ma'am. I'm sorry to come in on ya like this, but we have t' talk."

She wiped her free hand across both cheeks, her eyes closed. When she reopened them, their expression had changed from confusion to fright.

"You must leave," she commanded. "Now, before you're seen. And take the twins with you."

Calico stood by the side of the bed, hoping his confusion did not show on his face. Again, was she warning him…or threatening him?

Apparently, she recognized his confusion. She studied his face intently.

"You're in great danger," she warned.

"Yes, ma'am, I know. My question is, from who? You or your husband?"

Rebecca shook her head and lowered herself back onto the pillows.

"Certainly not from me."

He was trying to think of what to say next when she opened her eyes wide and gasped. Calico turned to follow her gaze and found a man standing in the open doorway—a tall man dressed in black, hat pulled low over his eyes. At the same moment, he heard the click of a rifle being cocked behind him—from the direction of a door near the bed he had assumed to be a closet but which apparently opened into an adjoining bedroom.

He knew who it was before he turned around.

CHAPTER 19

MIKE DURANT STOOD IN THE OTHER DOORWAY, RIFLE POINTED DIRECTLY AT HIM.

"Mr. Ramsay," he said, as though he were addressing a dignitary at a church social, "I don't believe you've met a great admirer of yours. May I introduce Mr. Jessie Riles?"

The tall man grinned—an evil, canine grin—and his eyes glittered beneath his dark brows. His hand hovered just above his holster, while his gaze slithered across the room to rest on Rebecca, who shuddered and looked away.

There was the sound of several pairs of feet coming up the stairs, and Jessie moved aside without looking to allow the entrance of Josh and Sarah, followed by the cook, into the room. Durant nodded to Cree, who nodded in return and left. Josh looked sullen, Sarah defiant—until she recognized Jessie Riles.

"That's right, Sarah," Durant said, "you and Mr. Riles are old friends, as I recall."

Calico turned to face him.

"Mike, what in hell's goin' on here?" he asked. "I thought ya was goin' t' Bow Ridge t' pick up that doctor ya been talkin' about."

Durant smiled—more of a smirk, Calico decided.

"Stupidity is not one of my faults, Calico. Did you think for one moment you'd convinced anyone you were willing to leave well enough alone? The doctor was...detained—I should be receiving a telegraph message to that effect within the next day or so. I sent the wagon ahead to meet the stage, so no one would think it odd if no one showed up to meet the good doctor. You'd told me you wanted a private chat with my dear wife, and the least I could do was to provide you with the opportunity for one."

"Well, ya could o' done that when I asked ya the other day."

"I suppose I could have, but I rather enjoy games. And Mr. Riles was not available at that particular moment."

"Why? What d' ya expect t' gain from all this?"

Durant gave a dry chuckle.

"Are you really that dense, Calico? I'd be disappointed if you were. Do wealth and power mean nothing to you?" He paused and pursed his lips. "No, I don't really think they do, do they?"

"I tried to warn you, Mr. Ramsay," Rebecca murmured, her voice tired.

"I'm sure you did, my dear," Durant said. "But I must bear partial responsibility—I didn't realize until after it had been sent that the wording of your—our—letter to Mr. Overholt might very well antagonize him and ensure that he would not willingly send the twins to us. Fortunately, one of Mr. Riles's associates was able to resolve that little matter."

Calico felt a stab of pain through his chest at the memory of Dan's murder, and the anger building in him began to cross into fury. His pain was intensified when he realized that Dan's last words had not been an instruction for him to take the twins to Rebecca but a warning for him not to.

"So, now what happens?" he asked, though he was sure he knew.

"Tragic," Durant said. "Tragic. I tried to stop it, God knows. Cree and Sung have already been dispatched to round up the others, who unfortunately are off at the very edges of the property, repairing fences. I was terribly afraid of what my dear, sick wife would do.

"While you and I, Calico, were outside—I, who had summoned you back to plead with you to take the twins with you for their safety—Rebecca somehow found my hunting rifle—this one, by coincidence—and shot the twins as an act of revenge against her hated sister. Tragic. Of course, you and I rushed into the house immediately upon hearing the shots. You, brave man that you were, tried to wrestle the gun away from my dear wife, but it went off. I, fearing for my life, fled from the house and galloped to Bow Ridge for help.

"In my absence, my darling helpmeet, her mind completely gone, set fire to our home, reliving that blazing night in Chicago, about which everyone within a radius of fifty miles has heard in some detail."

"A great story," Calico said, ice in his veins. "But what about Smiley here. How do you account for his body?"

He glanced at Jessie Riles and saw a look of contempt flash across the outlaw's sinister face.

"There'll be no body. Mr. Riles will be long gone by the time help arrives...belatedly," Durant said. "I will leave the details—including the setting of the fire—to him. He dearly loves fires, as I believe you have already discovered."

"You probably ain't so bad at it yourself," Calico said, surprised by the calmness of his own voice. "It was you set the Chicago fire, wasn't it?"

Durant feigned shock. "You offend me, sir! I am not a common murderer. Fortunately, Mr. Riles is. He accompanied me to Chicago, where my charming sister- and brother-in-law were once again trying to convince Rebecca to leave me. For some reason I can't possibly fathom, they didn't particularly like me.

"My unexpected arrival led, of course, inevitably to quite a row, and the only solution to the problem seemed to be to put an end to the source. Mr. Riles was the instrument to that end. After the household had retired for the evening, I let him into the house, where he first dispatched my dear brother- and sister-in-law, and—"

Josh lunged for him, but Jessie Riles caught the boy easily with one hand, deliberately grabbing him by his injured shoulder and causing him to turn pale and nearly pass out from the pain, though he did not utter a sound. Sarah went to her brother's side and held him from falling, glaring at Riles with eyes that burned with loathing.

Ignoring the interruption, Durant smiled at Rebecca.

"I'm sorry if all this comes as a shock to you, my dear," he said gently, reaching out to stroke her hair.

She shuddered as she drew away from his touch.

"Cut the talk and let me get busy," Riles said, his voice as cruel as his face.

"Just one more thing before ya start, Riles," Calico said, desperate for some way out of the danger. "I don't think Mike here told the story quite right. He's spent a lot of years buildin' his story about poor, crazy Rebecca. But you're part o' the story, too, don't forget—the gunslinger she hired with her own money. Now, no matter how good his story is, people are goin' t' be a mite suspicious o' what he jus' told us here.

"Supposin' the story he really tells is how it was you an' Rebecca that did the killin'? After all, he's made a point all this time o' lettin' people know she's the one with all the money, the one that paid ya, that needed to have ya around. An' supposin' when the help comes ridin' up there's the body o' one Jessie Riles out there in the yard somewheres? Mike's off the hook, clean as a whistle. That part wasn't in the story he says he's gonna tell, was it?"

Durant aimed his rifle directly at Calico's chest with slow deliberation, and his finger began to tighten on the trigger.

Riles stopped him with a motion of his hand. Calico showed no reaction, just continued talking, looking directly at the outlaw now.

"With you dead there won't be no loose ends a'tall. I'm sure you and him have a real nice financial arrangement set up. But as important as money seems t' be to Mike, why should he give you any o' it? Not only'll he save himself a heap o' money but he'll be wealthy an' powerful, an' a hero t' boot."

To his considerable surprise, both Durant and Jessie Riles broke out laughing.

"Very good, Calico," Durant said as Calico turned back to face him. "You have a vivid imagination, and I'm sure your little attempt to turn Jessie against me might have worked under different circumstances."

Calico knit his brows, trying to understand what Durant was getting at. His confusion must have shown on his face, for Durant grinned broadly and lowered his rifle.

Though he stood exactly between Jessie and Durant with his back to Riles, Calico could see in the dresser mirror the outlaw had silently drawn his gun from its holster. He saw, too, that Josh leaned in pain against the dresser, his free arm resting among an assortment of Rebecca's toiletries.

"Jessie, you see," Durant continued, "is more than an excellent ranch foreman and an efficient...ah...handler of problems. He is also my cousin. We grew up together, and we long ago realized that our unique talents—mine intellectual, his more...direct—complemented each other very well. What neither of us might be able to attain individually we've always managed to attain jointly, and that is not about to change now.

"Together, we have done quite well for ourselves. Neither of us would willingly jeopardize so successful an arrangement. I have plans far beyond this ranch, and Jessie is vital to my achieving them."

Not allowing himself to look directly at his rifle, which was still propped against the foot of the bed, Calico shifted his weight in preparation to make a casual sidestep toward it.

Durant instantly raised a finger in caution. "Ah-ah-ah."

Calico shrugged. "So why kill Uncle Dan?" he asked.

Durant issued a dramatic sigh. "I'm afraid that was largely Jessie's doing, though it turned out well despite the considerable problems it created. With Mr. Overholt out of the way, a last potential claimant to the twins'—and Rebecca's—combined fortunes was eliminated. Greed, I'm afraid, runs in our family.

"Until this entire business with the twins came up, neither Jessie nor I was even aware that Rebecca had an uncle. The opportunity to acquire not only the twins' assets but that of your 'Uncle Dan,' for which papers are already in preparation by my Denver and Chicago lawyers, presented a temptation just too strong for Jessie to resist, despite my own misgivings."

He nodded toward Jessie and gave a smile that struck Calico as far more bitter than congenial.

"With your uncle Dan out of the way, not only would the twins have automatically come to us without incident but Rebecca would have inherited his property as sole surviving relative. But..." Another long sigh. "...we had not anticipated your existence. Jessie, therefore, took it upon himself to wrap everything up at once by eliminating you and the twins before you reached Cold Springs, where their demise might cause a stir. Unfortunately, brains were never his strong suit."

Calico, watching in the mirror, saw Jessie tense just slightly at the slur, although not enough that Durant noticed.

"An' Rebecca?" he asked, trying to keep Durant talking while he sought some course of action. "She'll die in the fire, I suppose?"

Durant shook his head with an expression of feigned shock and disbelief.

"Kill Rebecca? Never! Odd as it may seem to you, I truly do love her. No, killing her won't be necessary. I've rather grown into the role of brave, long-suffering husband. With a dead wife, I would not have that protective coloration, as it were. I fear no one will believe anything she might say after all this, and certainly no court—not around here, at any rate—would convict her of a crime, considering her fragile mental state."

He smiled once again at his wife, who had moved as far away from him on the bed as she could get.

"Eventually," he said, "we may even begin to reduce the amount of her...medication."

Calico had seen Jessie Riles's eyes narrow as Durant spoke.

"That the way you see it, Jessie?" he asked.

"Not exactly."

Calico glanced at Durant and saw his eyes open wider.

"Now, Jessie," he said, "you know we'd decided there's no need for any harm to befall Rebecca."

"*You* decided."

Calico sensed an opening, and he took it.

"Why, sure, Jessie. You do all the dirty work, as usual, an' Mike an' Rebecca live happily ever after with everythin' ya helped him t' get over the years."

Jessie's jaw muscles tightened, and his eyes narrowed to slits. Calico pressed on.

"Ya'll be on the run—not that ya ain't used t' that, but ya won't have no place t' come back to. Did ya think o' that?"

"That's enough, Calico," Durant said evenly, but he wasn't about to let up.

"Maybe Mike'll send ya some money every now an' then, you an' him bein' so close, but—"

"I said that's *enough*!"

Durant raised and cocked his rifle, pointing it once again directly at Calico's chest. Calico's blood froze as he saw Durant's finger begin to tighten on the trigger, and he sensed that this time the man meant business. He heard Sarah gasp.

At that moment, Josh swept his arm across the top of the dresser as hard as he could, sending bottles, combs and brushes flying. With all his strength, Calico dived toward the foot of the bed and his rifle just as Durant pulled the trigger. The blast caught Jessie, who had still been directly behind him, in the center of his chest and sent him toppling backward into the hallway.

Still in motion, Calico grabbed his rifle, cocked it and aimed almost by instinct. He heard the shot and saw Durant lurch backward into the wall, a surprised look on his face. He stood a moment staring at Calico then slowly slid down the wall and onto the floor.

It was over.

CHAPTER 20

THE STAGE STOOD VACANT IN THE CENTER OF BOW RIDGE'S LONG, DIRTY MAIN STREET. Calico, Josh, Joe, Sarah and Rebecca were on the wooden sidewalk in the warm afternoon sun.

Sarah set down her small satchel and turned to her brother.

"You're sure, Josh?" she asked yet again.

Their eyes met and held for a long time, love and understanding flowing almost visibly between them.

"I'm sure, Sarah," he said with a smile.

Her eyes and smile moved from Josh to Calico.

"Come on, you two," Joe said. "It ain't the end o' the world. Chicago ain't all that far off nowadays. An' Rebecca's still got the ranch—she'll be wantin' t' come back often t' make sure I'm runnin' it proper. A girl as pretty as you, Sarah, you deserve a chance in the city. An' you're eighteen now—you got a lot of socializin' t' do. Josh, he belongs out here."

He shot a quick glance at Calico and winked, and Calico felt himself blushing. Then, Sarah and Joe exchanged smiles that told him she might, indeed, return someday.

She turned back to him, her eyes questioning.

"Yeah, Sarah," he said, anticipating her question. "I'll take good care o' him, though he'll probably be the death o' me yet."

The stage driver came out of a nearby saloon with a sack of mail and mounted to his seat.

"You folks for Fort Collins?" he asked.

Rebecca nodded, and Joe and Calico lifted the women's bags onto the coach, where the driver secured them with rope. That done, they stepped back, leaving Rebecca, Sarah and Josh alone for their goodbyes.

Calico wasn't quite sure how to feel. There was gladness and sorrow and the excitement that always comes with a the start of a new chapter in the book of life and, overpowering it all, the sense that yet another adventure—one he'd wanted all his life—was about to begin.

He looked at Rebecca. She was still pale, but in the short week since the shooting, and now free of the enforced medication she had endured for so long, she was showing signs of blooming once again into a beautiful woman. She would be happier in Chicago, he knew, just as he knew Sarah would be better off with her aunt than on some Western prairie—at least for now. He hoped that in the future, they might return, and perhaps Sarah might even get together with Joe, who Rebecca had asked to manage the ranch in her absence,

But that would be a decision Sarah would have to make for herself. Right now, it would be a shame to waste her blooming beauty on the gophers and cattle.

In the short time he had known her, Sarah had made the definite transition from girl to woman, just as Josh had crossed from youth to manhood. Well, he thought with a sigh, that's what life's all about, ain't it?

"Loadin' up," the driver said, and Calico and Joe hurried to rejoin the others. There were hugs all around, and cheek-kisses from the women, and then they boarded the stage. Sarah reached out the window and took both of Joe's hands in silent thanks, and perhaps something more. Then she turned to Calico.

"I'm going to miss you, Calico," she said, her eyes brimming, the tears sparkling in the afternoon sun.

He felt his nose running, and he brusquely wiped it with an index finger.

"Yeah," he said, rather surprised that he couldn't see too well.

With a crack of the whip, the stage jounced off, rounded the corner and began its long journey to Fort Collins and the train that would carry Sarah and Rebecca to Chicago and a renewed life.

When the stage was out of sight, he turned and extended his hand to Joe. They shook warmly, and long.

"See ya, Joe," he said.

Joe merely smiled and nodded.

Josh extended his hand, and Joe took it. Both smiled, but neither said a word.

Calico and Josh swung into their saddles, exchanged a final wave with Joe then wheeled Dusty and Belle around and rode down the long street toward home.

END

ABOUT THE AUTHOR

DORIEN GREY STARTED OUT AS A PEN NAME, NOTHING MORE, FOR A lifelong book and magazine editor who wanted to write his own novels as a bridge between the gay and straight communities. However, because he was living in a remote and time-warped area of the upper Midwest where gays still feel it necessary to keep a very low profile, he did not feel comfortable using his own name—a sad commentary on our society, he admits.

But as his first book, a detective novel, led to the second and then the third, he found Dorien slowly became much more than a pseudonym, evolving into an alter ego.

"It's reached the point," he says, "where all I have to do is sit down at the computer and let Dorien tell the story."

As for the Dorien's "real person," he's had a not-uninteresting life. Two years into college, he left to join the Naval Aviation Cadet program—he washed out and spent the rest of his brief military career on an aircraft carrier in the Mediterranean. The journal he kept of his time in the military, in the form of letters home, honed his writing skills and provided him with a wealth of experiences to draw from in his future writing.

Returning to college after service, he graduated with a BA in English and embarked on a series of jobs that led him into the editing field. While working for a Los Angeles publishing house, he was instrumental in establishing a division exclusively for the publication of gay paperbacks and magazines, of which he became editor. He moved on to edit a leading LA-based international gay men's magazine.

Tiring of earthquakes, brush fires, mudslides and riots, he returned to the Midwest, where Dorien emerged, full-blown, like Athena from the head of Zeus.

He—and Dorien, of course—recently moved to Chicago, and now devote their energies to writing. After having completed ten books in the popular Dick Hardesty Mystery series, and now Calico, a Western historical romantic suspense, they are currently working on a new mystery with a new protagonist, which may have the potential to become a series.

"Too early to tell," Dorien says. "But stay tuned."

But for a greater insight into the real person behind Dorien Grey, the curious are invited to read *The Poems of Dorien Grey*, an ebook available from GLB Publishers.

ABOUT THE ARTIST

MARTINE JARDIN HAS BEEN AN ARTIST SINCE SHE WAS VERY SMALL. Her mother guarantees she was born holding a pencil, which for a while, as a toddler, she nicknamed "Zessie"

She won several art competitions with her drawings as a child, ventured into charcoal, watercolors and oils later in life and about 12 years ago started creating digital art.

Since then, she's created hundreds of book covers for Zumaya Publications and eXtasy Books, among others. She welcomes visitors to her website: www.martinejardin.com

Printed in the United States
108913LV00008B/17/A

9 781934 135334